MICKEY CHAMBERS SHAKES IT UP

Also by Charish Reid

Carina Press

Hearts on Hold
The Write Escape

For additional books by Charish Reid,
visit her website, charishreid.com.

MICKEY CHAMBERS SHAKES IT UP

CHARISH REID

CANARY STREET PRESS

ISBN-13: 978-1-335-45355-6

Mickey Chambers Shakes It Up

For questions and comments about the quality of this book, please contact us at CustomerService@Harlequin.com.

Canary Street Press
22 Adelaide St. West, 41st Floor
Toronto, Ontario M5H 4E3, Canada
CanaryStPress.com

Printed in U.S.A.

Led Zeppelin was right about roads—
there's always time to change the one you're on.

MICKEY CHAMBERS SHAKES IT UP

1

Plink, plink, plink…

Mickey Chambers's heart stuttered as she held her breath. Each prescription pill she dropped into different days of the week was an ominous warning of finite resources. When she got to Saturday and found a nearly empty bottle of her thyroid medication, she had to do quick math in her head. To refill her prescriptions, she'd have to visit Dr. Curtis and get bloodwork done.

Another expense…

She'd been counting pills for most of her adult life. But at thirty-three, it was getting hard to pay for them. At her kitchen counter, Mickey carefully spilled the remainder of her medication onto a place mat and slowly separated them. Two weeks.

She quickly started on the mood stabilizer next, counting with the same slowness, and making note of how few were left in the bottle. Three weeks. Any gaps in medication could be bad news for her hormone levels, knocking her flat on her ass.

This was going to be a hellish summer if Mickey couldn't fund the medication for her hyperthyroidism. Her teaching load had always been somewhat precarious, but this was the first time she worried. Hargrove University's English Department had always made room for her, but they had also hired more adjuncts like her. Other part-time instructors who needed to grab up as many classes to cover their bills.

She gathered her medications and placed them back on the top of her refrigerator before checking her cell phone again. She was expecting a call from the department chair today with confirmation of her summer schedule. So far, Mickey only had one online class.

Because she'd taught a few distance-learning courses before, Mickey had a slew of class plans ready to be taught online. She'd need to update a few PowerPoint presentations from last year, but she counted on her Food Studies and Culture course to be easy to navigate. Now, if Lara could just give her a heads-up on a Comp 101 or an American Lit, she'd have extra syllabi for those as well.

But alas, no missed calls.

Mickey sighed as she tucked her phone in her skirt pocket. No point in waiting around her apartment when she needed to be at her parents' home for Saturday dinner. This was the first dinner she'd shown up to since a hectic finals week and logging grades, so she missed them. She grabbed her purse and locked up before running into the Columbus, Georgia, heat. Even in late May, she felt the blast of the outdoor furnace that frizzed her curls and made her under-boobs sweat. She blew out another frustrated sigh. The heat was an annoyance for any average Georgian, but for someone with her condition, these summers were hell.

When she got on Forest Street, she tapped out a quick message to her mother, letting Rita Chambers know she was on the way. Mickey made a quick loop around Lakebottom Park, admiring the people who could stand jogging in the bright sun and catching a glimpse of her favorite brick red house on the corner of Cherokee Avenue.

She loved how it stood out from the surrounding houses with its delicate white trim and shutters and large wraparound porch. A couple years back, two rocking chairs used to sit near the door, now only one remained. The owner also seemed to neglect the spread of kudzu vine clawing its way up the west side of the house. Mickey noticed the changes and it made her sad.

Her mind quickly went back to the road toward her parents' home. Through the shaded boulevard of dogwood trees, Hargrove students were already walking to the downtown area, ready to tear it up. She drove past them carefully, trying her best not to hit the pregame wobblers.

When she reached her parents' house, she parked her car in the driveway behind her brother's Beemer and walked past the pecan saplings piled up in the yard. Mickey's father must have been amid a landscaping project. Her mother would object to Virgil Sr. lifting more than necessary, but she'd let her parents argue about that.

She checked her phone once more and found no new messages.

Mickey closed her eyes, trained a smile on her face and readied herself for dinner with her family. As she stepped through the threshold of her childhood home, she called out, "I'm here, let the festivities begin!"

Her little brother, Junior, was the first to reply. "Girl, ain't nobody waiting on you."

Mickey laughed as she hung her purse in the yellow foyer her father had painted earlier in the year. Judging by the smells coming from the kitchen, she wouldn't have waited on her either. She found her family eating dinner in the bright and airy living room, using the collapsible TV trays while her mother's lovely dining room remained untouched.

"Baby, fix a plate and join us." Her mother pointed her fork toward the kitchen.

"Thanks, Mama."

"Michelle, when's the last time you had that car looked at?" her father asked apropos of nothing.

Mickey bit back her grin. "Last time I was here."

Virgil Sr. shook his head as he scraped at his plate. "Lemme change that oil before you leave. How them tires lookin'?"

It didn't matter how she answered, her father would just examine the entire Honda Civic before she left the house. Even after a week of working for Columbus Public Works, he still needed to come home and tinker around with something. "I'll let you have a look," Mickey said on her way to the kitchen.

If it was hot outside, Rita's kitchen was an inferno. Her mother's cast-iron skillet had put in the work that day, producing fried chicken, fried pork chops and corn bread. Side dishes covered the counter like a small buffet line, with a roll of aluminum foil and Styrofoam plates sitting on the end, serving as to-go plates for Mickey and Junior.

A bottle of Ardbeg scotch sat near the refrigerator with a yellow sticky note pressed to the glass. If there was one thing she could count on her brother for, it was a free bottle of booze. No doubt, an end-of-the-semester gift. She smiled as she picked it up and inspected the label. She and Junior tried to get together as often as possible to try different spirits and share their opinions, but lately they'd grown too busy. He with his start-up in Atlanta and her constantly grading papers. As expensive as it was, his little reminder of simpler times touched her.

While she fixed her plate, Mickey listened to her parents

give a familiar rundown of the Columbus, Georgia, happenings for Junior, who now lived in Atlanta.

"You remember Celestine on the West Side," Rita said. "Henry Richard's sister."

"Uhh..."

"Taught at the dance school back in the nineties. Volunteered at the soup kitchen?"

"Mama, I can't remember," Junior said.

"Well, she passed a couple weeks back," their mother went on. "I went to the visitation and saw her granddaughter, Layla. I didn't know it, but she took over the dance school recently. You remember Layla? Real pretty girl..."

"Maybe?"

"Henry still working at Wilson's Paper?" their father interjected.

"Sure is," Rita said. "Coming up on twenty years. Oughta be retiring soon."

When Mickey returned to the living room, she sat next to her brother on the sibling-designated couch, facing her parents, who sat in their own cushy recliners. On the television, an action movie played with the volume set low.

"Anyway," Rita said, "you oughta let me introduce you to Layla. She's such a professional little lady teaching those kids, and I heard she was single..."

Junior made a noncommittal noise before stuffing his mouth with fried pork chop.

Rita switched gears and turned her focus on her other child. "Michelle, my *favorite* teacher! Are you feeling good? Have you taken your medications?"

"This morning, Mama," Mickey said, trying to keep her smile up. Every time her mother laid eyes on her, she asked the same questions.

"Do you have enough for the month?"

Mickey nodded, trying not to worry about the number of pills she counted out earlier. "I get my refills on time."

"Is that Obamacare still working for you?" her father asked. "'Cause Roy said he's paying an arm and leg over these prescriptions."

Mickey eked out a strained smile. "It's fine, Daddy. The ACA plan I'm on is okay."

"Are you teaching this summer?" Junior asked, steering the conversation away from Mickey's health.

She gave him a grateful look. Since she was first diagnosed with hyperthyroidism, her parents had dropped everything in their lives to make sure she was well taken care of. Now, at the age of thirty-three, they hadn't quite stopped. "I am," she said, quickly changing gears. "I'm still at Hargrove, in the English Department."

"They had a hell of a busted pipe by that athletic center," her father said. "I told Roy, they gonna have to dig up some of that parking lot that goes to Seaver Avenue."

Her mother ignored her husband, who routinely rambled about construction. "Are you going to be busy this summer? How many classes will you have? Will you have to be on your feet in the classroom, or can you teach from home?"

Mickey followed her brother's example and shoveled mashed potatoes in her mouth to avoid her mother's interrogation. She hoped it would give her time to figure out a good enough lie about her unstable employment. She nodded. "Mmm-hmm."

Her parents understood that she taught at a university. They bragged on her to everyone they knew, from the cashier at Winn Dixie to Monique at the salon. What they didn't quite grasp was what nontenured track looked like at a place like Hargrove University.

While associate professors could use their summers for scholarship and traveling to conferences, adjuncts scrambled to find all the classes they could to make ends meet. Mickey loved teaching and her students…but she had the sneaking suspicion that her love for the job was being used against her by the university machine. She wasn't making nearly enough money for the work she kept doing—the grim evidence hit her every time she paid her bills.

She swallowed the lump of mashed potatoes. "I'll be fine," she lied. As soon as her phone vibrated in her pocket, Mickey would know for certain. "Sorry, I gotta take this."

She quickly excused herself from the living room and took her call in the kitchen.

Her boss started off on the wrong foot immediately. "Hey, Michelle…" she said in a contrite voice.

Mickey's heart dropped. "Hey, Lara."

"I'm sorry," Lara said. "I had hopes for English 200, but there weren't enough students for the Registrar's Office to sign off on it. And then I only had 101 left, and I know you just taught it…"

"No, no, I get it," Mickey said. "Matt needs a class too."

"I tried to split the leftover classes as fair as I could," Lara said. Her boss sounded so close to tears that Mickey had no choice but to let her off the hook. The availability of classes wasn't necessarily her fault. She couldn't help the fact that the administration had tightened up on summer course offerings.

"So, I've got the Comp 102," she said with an upbeat voice.

"You do! Luckily, it's the condensed early summer version, just four weeks. And you'd really be doing us a favor." Doing them a favor made Mickey sound heroic instead of an under-paid professional who didn't receive health-care benefits.

"Of course, no worries. Listen, Lara, I gotta let you go," Mickey said.

"I get it," Lara said. "Michelle, I'm so sorry. You'll be okay?"

Even though she didn't feel like coddling Lara's feelings, she still lied. "I'll be fine."

"Okay. We'll talk later?"

"Of course," Mickey said brightly.

By the time she hung up, her mind was already on the next problem. What did the money situation look like for the next two and a half months? A quick calculation of savings told her she could handle rent—that always came first. Then came medication. Her savings account would take a hit, but it could cover those necessary pills. She had a roof over her head, but food and utilities were a different story.

"Was that work?"

She jumped at the sound of Junior's voice behind her. Mickey could lie to her boss and her parents, but her brother would always be a tough sell. He may be five years younger than she, but he'd had to grow up fast when she was at her sickest. "It was," she sighed.

"Are you going to need help this summer?" he asked.

He didn't mean any harm, but it stung to be so far behind her brother, who graduated school on time, who found a career at an appropriate time. Meanwhile, Mickey's constant absences due to illness meant flunking out of high school. She didn't catch up to her peers until a proper treatment plan was put in place. Getting her GED, earning a bachelor's and finally a master's degree, in literature, gained her employment… just not a steady career in her thirties. "Please don't tell Mom and Dad," she whispered, glancing toward the living room. "They still see me as a sick teenager—reminding me to take my meds, offering me money they don't have."

"You need to come work with me and James," her brother suggested as he rubbed his beard. His dark brown eyes focused on the stove behind him and narrowed. She could tell his computer-programmer mind whirred with a plan. "If you lived in Atlanta, I could help you get set up with a little apartment nearby. We could finally start the whiskey podcast…"

"You know I'd love to do the podcast," Mickey said with a chuckle. "But I don't want to move to Atlanta and I don't want to work for my little brother doing—what are you doing?"

Junior rolled his eyes. "Coding the MedPlus app. We're still trying to find a decent marketing manager… You could be it?"

Mickey grabbed her brother by the hand and dragged him to the kitchen patio door. "Let's talk about this outside," she sighed, hoping her parents weren't listening. In the backyard, she finally felt relief from the stifling heat of the house.

"How long are you going to keep working for that school?" Junior asked, facing the setting sun. The vibrant red shone on his deep brown skin as he squinted his dark eyes against the light. He took his coloring and height from their father, while Mickey's pecan-brown skin and short, chubby stature mimicked their mother.

She didn't know the answer to that. "I don't know. I guess I'll teach until I find something else I'm good at." Sometimes she woke up in a cold sweat, wondering why she'd chosen literature and composition as areas to study. The job market was rough for even those who had doctorates. What had felt like a comfortable job was quickly becoming an albatross around her neck. Any time she tried to think about another vocation, her heart pounded and her brain froze. "I know I'm really good at organizing and planning, but those skills feel too vague to become a…*career*."

"Well, you're good with people—always friendly and helpful. I wish I knew how you stay so damn cheerful," he said with a chuckle. "A bunch of spoiled-ass freshmen in English class would drive me up a fuckin' wall."

"Oh, it's not them," Mickey sighed. "When I step foot in the classroom, they respect me, they listen. Hell, they don't even realize I'm a part-time lecturer. My students think I'm a scholar like everyone else."

She certainly didn't feel that way when she left the classroom. Since she didn't attend department meetings, many of the tenure-track professors barely knew her name.

"Can I be honest with you?"

Her brother nodded.

Mickey blew out a sigh. "Teaching was accidental. After the bachelor's degree, I didn't know what to do with literature studies, so I continued and got a master's degree. The first job I got was teaching English and I just stuck with it. I like doing it, but without a doctorate degree, being an adjunct is a permanent internship. It's an aspiration job that will never become a career for me." She took a deep breath before continuing. "It's a hamster wheel masquerading as a noble pursuit."

Quiet blanketed the back patio as Mickey fought to keep her shit together. That was the first time she'd spoken the truth to another person.

"Got it. So, you're spinning your wheels at Hargrove," Junior said in a serious voice.

Mickey kept her eyes on the horizon ahead of them. Anything to avoid her brother's piercing stare. "I'll need to make some real changes come fall."

"For real though, if things don't work out in Columbus, you can stay with me. I know MedPlus is still young, but James has a couple investors lined up. You're a writer. I could get you in on the ground floor."

Mickey nodded. "I hear you, and I'll keep it in my back pocket."

While Junior's job offer was a lovely gesture, she was reluctant to accept it. Her family had done too much as it was to help her. Her parents had given up their time, getting the runaround from health professionals. And then their money to send her to doctors and specialists. Junior even helped her with her college applications and her move to Athens for her master's program. Living with her brother, while working for him, seemed like taking a step backward.

The patio door slid open. Their father stuck his head out and looked between the two of them. "It's too hot out here for Michelle to be standing around," he said with a frown. "Y'all come in here and get a cold drink."

Mickey shot her brother a look that said, *See?*

Junior smirked as he shook his head. "Coming, Pop." As she followed her brother back inside the house, she hoped that she could continue pretending things were fine. She adjusted her face, forcing the smile that people were accustomed to, and tried to forget about the ever-present money worries. *Positive attitude, Mickey.* She wouldn't get anywhere feeling sorry for herself.

2

"For fuck's sake," Diego Acosta growled under his breath. "Did Ramón change the Jumpin' Jack Flash IPA yet?"

His bar partner, Jeanie Harris, reached under the counter for a fresh rag to clean the latest spill caused by the gaggle of young women sitting at the bar. "Yep," she said, smiling at the girls as she tucked a loose loc back into the large twist on her head. "That's why we're nearly out of glasses."

"Fuck."

"Yep!" Jeanie repeated. The cheer in her voice was for the patrons' sakes. Diego couldn't give two fucks if she smiled or not. He found plastered grins a giant waste of time during a full-on melee.

And that was the current status of his bar. A goddamn melee.

College kids were everywhere. Their spring semester was officially over, and these stressed-out hooligans were ready to tear shit up. Starting with his bar, The Saloon. While he kept his eye on the group of rowdy boys near the entrance, he and Jeanie were the only bartenders serving the group of young women who insisted on getting his attention.

Yeah, he could hear their raunchy comments, and he wasn't in the least bit interested. He was more concerned with the amount of sugary drinks they consumed. They took forever to make, and he only had two hands. His only server, Irene Cho, ran around, tending to every single table all by herself because their new-*newest* girl had called in sick.

And to top it off, the goddamn Jumpin' Jack Flash IPA sputtered and fizzed like a dying tap that Ramón still needed to change. If one more college kid asked him for Jumpin' Jack Flash IPA he'd lose his ever-loving shit on them. A painful sensation was bubbling just below the space between his eyes, warning him of an impending sinus headache.

Irene hurried to the end of the bar and slapped her tray down. "I need twelve Slammers," she panted, blowing a limp lock of black hair out of her flushed face.

"Are you kidding me?" Diego blew up.

"Twelve," she repeated in a dry voice. His reaction didn't faze her. Irene also worked as a costume designer for the local theater and was used to meltdowns more dramatic than his.

"Fuck."

"I'll help," Jeanie said, tucking her towel in the waistband of her apron. She reached behind him and started placing shot glasses on Irene's tray. Diego stuffed his frustrations down and began collecting beer glasses until he came up three short.

"Ramón!" he shouted, as though his barback could hear him. The Saloon was too damn loud for anyone to hear themselves think. "Don't Stop Believin'" was playing for the third time that night, and if he heard it again, he'd have a fucking stroke. "RAMÓN!"

Ramón Silva came bustling out of the back with a steaming crate of freshly cleaned glasses. "Got it, got it," he said as sweat poured down his face. He slammed the crate down and immediately began stacking glasses. "The IPA should be ready."

"Thanks," Diego muttered as he grabbed his remaining three glasses and began filling them with Guinness. "Someone said there was a spill near the bathroom. I don't know if it's a drink or something else."

Ramón heaved a sigh and swept a beefy arm across his forehead. Diego didn't have time to pity his brother-in-law since they were currently experiencing the third circle of hell: gluttony. But he hoped to God the fifty-four-year-old could keep up the grueling pace for one more hour. They were so close to shutting down without incident that every drink poured felt like a minor victory. He just needed to focus on making these twelve abominations…

While Jeanie prepped his shots, Diego pulled his half-pints. Another girlish giggle erupted from the group of young women at the bar as they talked behind their hands. "He's not married…" one of them said. "He's kinda old though," said another. Diego swallowed a groan and cursed the day he took off his wedding ring.

Jeanie said flirting helped with business, that it was good for tips. But he wasn't interested in entertaining women who came to his bar for a good time. Especially those who were young enough to be his daughter. *Christ.*

"Set 'em up!" he called out as he moved around his bar partner. He set down his beers two at a time.

"Knock 'em down," Jeanie replied. "You got this, Irene?"

Irene shot a glare.

"I'm fuckin' with you," Jeanie laughed.

"We're firing Newest Girl, right?" Irene said, cracking her gum from the side of her mouth.

"We are," Diego said, setting down the last of the glasses. The Newest Girl called earlier in the evening with a raspy cough that sounded rehearsed, and she was about as good of an actress as she was a server. Jeanie should have fired her over the phone. The bar betting pool had the Newest Girl clocked for three weeks and she couldn't even handle that. That's why he never took down the "Help Wanted" sign from the window.

They watched as Irene, a rather small woman with a big mouth, flipped one of her pigtails over her shoulder before hoisting twenty-four glasses of the most offensive drink to her chin. Diego shouldn't have doubted Irene's ability, but they're batting too close to a perfect game. They were going to slip up somewhere. But she transported her tray of Slammers to her table without fail. Diego almost took a breath of relief.

That was until he saw four inebriated boys teetering over the jukebox. He swore to God if one of them spent money on Journey, he'd take a fucking bat to the machine and call it a night. When the Beastie Boys' "Fight for Your Right" came on, he gritted his teeth.

"Excuse meeeee," said a singsong voice.

A young woman attempted to engage with him. She smiled at him with glassy eyes and a flushed face. "Are you okay?" he asked, genuinely concerned for her well-being.

She giggled, setting off a chain reaction of group giggles. "I'm sooo good," she slurred.

Diego didn't believe that for a minute. She and her girlfriends had been nursing Vodka Red Bulls for most of the night, and the results looked iffy. Jeanie had been serving them with a smile, but Diego couldn't bring himself to pretend. "Water?" he asked.

"I want Sex on the Beach," she said in a loud voice.

"I'm cutting you off," he said.

The girl's red face fell in disappointment and then quickly screwed into something angry. "I want another drink," she shouted, slapping her credit card on the bar.

Clinks of glasses caught his attention.

The twelve Irish Slammer bros were dropping shots into

their beers and chugging. Irene was already on to the next table, working on the next order. He didn't have time to react to the angry girl at the bar or the chugging dude bros, because the unmistakable scrape of wood against the floor captured his attention.

Right to party, my ass…

He glanced at the clock that hung above the Corona poster and growled. "Fuck."

Of course, they wouldn't make it to the end without a fight. Two young men, near their small stage area, sprang from their chairs and began a familiar dance.

"Wassup, bro?"

"'Sup, bro."

"I'm right here, bro."

"You wanna go?"

"Come at me!"

Diego and Jeanie exchanged looks. She looked just as defeated as he did. *Fuck*, she mouthed, echoing his sentiment.

He glanced at the entrance for their bouncer, Stevie, who was nowhere to be found. Diego craned his neck, searching for the man who was supposed to enforce the law at his bar. He had a feeling Stevie was somewhere off to the side of the building, hugged up with a girl he'd met earlier in the evening. Which meant two things—one: there were a plethora of college-aged students who may not have been ID checked, and two: Diego needed to break up this fight himself.

"Goddammit," he muttered, slapping his towel onto the bar.

"Excuuuse meee," said the red-faced girl, who was getting redder by the minute.

The gang of boys around the jukebox were still fucking around with their next selection.

Ramón approached him as he rounded the edge of the bar.

"Hey, Diego, I gotta clean the women's restroom. Jesucristo, the mess…"

As he stalked toward the two young men who were still sizing each other up, he realized what was wrong with The Saloon. His night crew simply wasn't enough. The daytime crew, which was just one bartender named Todd James, never saw this kind of mayhem. If The Saloon had a chance of staying afloat, Diego would have to hire more people immediately.

"Come on, bro, let's go."

Two Hargrove University students faced off in the dullest trash talk in the history of bar fights as Diego approached them. "Break it up, fellas," he said in a loud voice.

In his mind, he thought he would step between them like Michael Jackson in the "Beat It" video and somehow make a difference. Instead, Diego chose the perfect time to step into the cross fire of someone's sloppy right hook. The impact of a meaty fist connected with the left side of his face, knocking him back two steps. His hands flew to his face to shield himself from the next strike while he bulldozed into the general direction of the attacker. Pain bloomed in his jaw as he fell upon one boy.

On the floor, adrenaline took over. Diego took the offender by the collar of his Hargrove hoodie and dragged him up. The kid had a wild look in his eye that Diego completely ignored. "Hey, man, I'm sorry," the boy sputtered as Diego pulled him toward the exit.

"I'm cutting you off," he growled.

When they reached the cool night air, Diego released the lanky kid, pushing him to the sidewalk just as a patrol car rolled past. He raised his arms to flag them down. "Over here," he shouted.

The car stopped right in front of The Saloon. Sheriff's Deputy Rivera rolled down his window and peered at the drunk student lying on the sidewalk. "You good, Acosta?"

"Fuck no!" Diego shouted. "This kid decked me in the face."

Rivera turned on his lights and took his sweet time getting out of his patrol car. "Hold on," he called.

While he was outside, Diego scanned the side of the building for his bouncer, Stevie. Again, nowhere to be found. Before the aging deputy could amble to the sidewalk, Diego marched back inside to grab the other kid by the scruff of his neck.

"You can't touch me," he squeaked.

"The hell I can't," Diego growled. He tossed the second offender on the street, next to his drunk partner in crime.

"Which one assaulted you?" Officer Rivera asked, flipping his citation pad.

Diego looked between the two groaning boys, and immediately had trouble figuring out which floppy-haired Hargrove hoodie was which. As he tried to remember, their friends exited the bar in a rush.

"Please don't arrest them!" one shouted. "I'm the DD, I can take them home."

Rivera raised a brow. "How 'bout it, Acosta? You pressin' charges?"

"Jesus..." he said, heaving a sigh. "No, just get 'em outta here."

The group's DD hauled his friends off the ground and shoved them in the general direction of the Riverwalk. As the two men watched the group make a hasty getaway, Diego rubbed the side of his face and muttered a low curse.

Rivera tucked his ticket book back in his belt and let out a whistle. "It's hoppin' at The Saloon tonight."

"And I'm missing a bouncer."

The deputy peered around Diego into the chaos of the bar. "I'm lookin' at a lot of young people in there," he drawled.

Diego went still. "Yeah?"

"You say you're missing a bouncer?" Rivera asked, his eyes narrowing. "I'm not gonna find any minors in there, am I?"

Now *that* Diego couldn't be certain of. Irene checked when she could, but the first line of defense was really Stevie…who could not be found at that moment. He was also uncertain of Rivera's desire to step inside The Saloon and check every single college student.

"Imma take your hesitance as a warning," the older officer said as he crossed his arms over his chest. "I'll let you clear 'em out tonight, but you're gonna have to get a new bouncer, son."

"You want me to close up now?" Diego asked, incredulous. "Don't you have other bars to check on, Hector?"

He shrugged his shoulders. "None so dysfunctional as The Saloon."

"Fuck."

Diego turned on his heel and stepped back into his bar. Jeanie's worried eyes followed him as he headed straight for the jukebox and yanked the plug. Silence quickly settled over the room as he continued to the bar and issued his partner a command. "Ring the bell."

"We're closing?" Jeanie asked.

"I guess so," he said.

As Jeanie rang the brass bell that hung behind the bar, Diego flicked the houselights on and off. A groan rose from the crowd as patrons turned their attention to him. "Settle up and get out," he called.

"How are you making a last call at midnight?" some kid from the back of the bar shouted.

"I didn't say shit about last call," Diego said as he continued to flicker the lights. "I said settle up and get the fuck out."

"Diego..." Jeanie started.

"Irene, collect these tabs!"

Somewhere in the mass exodus of young folks leaving The Saloon, Stevie reappeared to help herd drunk kids to the street. While Diego balanced the cash register, The Saloon employees conducted the usual closing tasks in utter silence. All of them were hesitant to interact with the pulsing rage emanating from Diego's direction. All of them except for Stevie, who was oblivious to the quiet storm.

"Hey, man, I'm sorry about tonight," he said from the other side of the bar. "I got caught up with Patrice outside."

Diego said nothing as he counted ten-dollar bills.

"Is he okay?" Stevie murmured to Irene.

"You don't know how to interpret uncomfortable silence, do you?" she asked.

"Diego, I said I was sorry, man," Stevie tried again.

Diego held his tongue because he'd say something caustic to his late wife's fuckup of a cousin. Because he was still *technically* family, he had hoped Ramón would step in and talk some sense into the kid.

"Cállate, primo," Ramón said in a low voice. "You fucked up tonight."

"But I'm sayin—"

"Wipe the tables," Jeanie said, cutting him off.

They fell back into another uncomfortable silence and Diego continued to count. He stopped only for the buzzing in his back pocket. A phone alert reminded him of another stressor on his horizon.

CALENDAR: HARGROVE ENGL 102

"Uh... Jeanie, could you take over the drawer? I left off with the tens. I'll be in the office."

He escaped into the back office, closed the door behind him and sagged against it.

Diego had made promises that he needed to cash in.

Five years ago, when his wife, Lucía, died, Diego told himself he'd finally return to college to finish his bachelor's degree. Before breast cancer claimed her, Lucía had convinced him that she had full control over the bar, that they were finally making enough money for him to go back to school. She told him he needed to treat himself to the education he'd missed to care for his mother, who fell ill when he was only a freshman in college. The fact that he never went back, even after his mother passed, had always bothered Lucía.

But after burying his wife, he couldn't think about school. The Saloon needed his attention. Only last year, when Ramón brought the idea up while they closed the bar together, did he start to imagine the possibilities. He quickly ran into problems when he began the admissions process. When Diego dug out his old transcripts and presented them to Hargrove University, the Registrar's Office informed him that many of his credits were too old. Just like he was.

And now he was starting over. At forty-two…

Diego slid against the door and down to the floor, burying his head in his hands as he went. Why had he thought he could do two things at once? He couldn't run The Saloon like Lucía could. She had charm and laughter, a real desire to get to know all her patrons. Diego took care of the books and the back of the house. Together, they kept the bar in the black, but without her…he couldn't keep enough employees on hand for these wild nights. All he had left was her family, Ramón and Stevie, and his "damn-near family," Jeanie and Irene.

The knock behind him pulled Diego from his thoughts. He groaned and pulled himself from the floor to open the door.

Ramón leaned against the frame and peered at him with narrowed eyes. "You okay?"

Diego sighed. "I don't know how long I can keep this up," he admitted. "Tonight was a fuckin' mess."

"What do you wanna do?" Ramón asked.

Diego looked down at his phone, at the calendar alert, and pursed his lips. One thing at a time. "We have to open up tomorrow and spend the day looking at new workers or something. We need another barback to help you in the kitchen and the basement, we need another server, and we definitely need another bouncer."

"Stevie's just a—"

"I'm not gonna fire the boy...yet," Diego interrupted. "But he's gotta get his shit together."

Ramón nodded. "So, we'll just comb the applications and call folks tomorrow?"

"Tonight," Diego said. "We don't have time to wait. I'm gonna send out emails and hope that people come in for interviews."

Ramón didn't look convinced. "If you say so." His eyes flitted to Diego's phone. "What's going on there?"

"College shit," he breathed. "I have an English class coming up. That online thing... I don't know, I guess I'll figure it out."

"Hey, hey," Ramón said in a hushed voice. He moved past the threshold and gripped Diego by the arms. "You got this, hermano, you got us."

Diego heard the warmth of his brother-in-law's voice and wanted to sag his tired weight against it. He had to believe he could hold on for a little while longer. Hopefully, the cavalry would show up during tomorrow's interviews. Otherwise, he might lose control of Lucía's and his dream. The Saloon was *their* baby, and his employees were his main priority. Outside of school, he couldn't afford any other distractions. "Okay," he said. "Alright."

3

Mickey was on a mission.

She had planned to post up at Fountain City Beans and browse through job ads until she found something to stick her CV to. But on her walk to the café, Mickey had to pass her favorite independent bookstore, Dust Jackets, an old building whose brick facade was nearly covered in green kudzu vines. When she was a kid, and before getting sick, Mickey frequently rode her bike to downtown Columbus to buy a book with allowance money and eat ice cream next to the town square fountain. Until the bigger bookstore chains came to town, Dust Jackets was the only place she could find her favorite romance novels.

This month, the owner was showcasing graphic novels. She paused to take note of the titles, wondering if they were books she'd need to include in future classes. *No, stop it*. Finding a decent paying job was more important than creating new and interesting lesson plans. If she decided to continue teaching, Mickey had a plethora of creative syllabi in her files. She didn't need to give Hargrove any more labor than was necessary.

Keep to your mission, Mickey.

She forgot about the books and pushed herself toward Fountain City Beans. She walked briskly, but Mickey's eyes landed on The Saloon's window. A help-wanted sign sat in the corner of the bay window. She did a double take before stopping. *The Saloon?* She'd gone there a couple times with her best friend, Cleo, but found the atmosphere a little dull. From what she remembered, the bar had a skeleton crew, and it took forever to get served.

She paused like she had at Dust Jackets and thought about walking inside. As she peered through the darkened windows, it didn't appear that they were open for business, but there *were* people inside. Should she? Mickey hesitated because she had no idea what she would apply for. But she paused long enough to think about the possibilities… She knew a lot about alcohol from sampling spirits with her brother, and she had experience in the food industry.

She had worked in a coffee shop in Athens while finishing up her master's degree. A bit different, but she still served people. Standing behind the counter and pouring shots of espresso was more or less the same as mixing drinks, right? Plus, the tips could be helpful during a dry summer.

"You goin' in?" asked a voice behind her.

Mickey jumped and turned to find a purple-haired Amazon behind her. The white woman wore a black motorcycle jacket and distressed jeans with rips stretching across her skinny thighs. She flipped her purple hair over to reveal a shaved temple. Mickey tried not to stare in wonderment, but the woman looked like a badass superhero. "I don't know," she said.

"You got an interview?" the woman asked. Her maroon-painted lips pursed as she looked Mickey up and down.

Mickey forgot her original purpose for being downtown and nodded at the woman. "Sure."

"Cool." The woman stepped past Mickey and disappeared into The Saloon. Mickey hitched her laptop bag on her shoulder and considered, for a moment, how silly it was to follow this woman...

But she followed, nonetheless.

Most of the chairs sat on tables, except for a couple where a Black woman in thick ropes of locs sifted through papers. A young Black man sat before her, rubbing his hands on his thighs as he waited for the woman to speak. Mickey spotted the purple-haired Amazon sitting at the bar and sat beside her. She rested her laptop bag on the bar and leaned close to the woman. "What are you applying for?" she whispered.

"Whatever they got," replied the woman, her gaze sliding over to Mickey. "You?"

"Whatever," Mickey repeated with a nonchalant shrug. She absolutely did not have a plan.

The purple-haired woman seemed satisfied with her answer because she gave a nod and lounged comfortably against the bar. They sat quietly, waiting for the woman with the locs to finish up with the young man. He looked young enough to be one of her students, but Mickey didn't recognize him as a Hargrove kid.

Anxiety shot through her as she thought about working at a place where her students frequented. Could she serve an English student a beer? Fuck it. If by some miracle she landed this job, she'd do it. At the end of the day, making money was more important than worrying about her students' judgment.

"If you're hired, when's the earliest you can start?" asked the woman. She sat back in her chair and folded her arms over her chest.

The young man cleared his throat and answered quickly, "As soon as you need me, ma'am."

She gave an efficient nod and referred to her stack of papers. "Sounds good. And I can reach you at this number?" she asked, pointing to a piece of paper. The young man leaned forward and nodded.

"Yes, ma'am."

"Okay, then. Thank you for coming in, Jerry," she said, standing. She held out her hand to him. "You can expect a call this evening if we decide to go with you."

He stood and clasped her hand, shaking it a bit too frantically. "Yes, ma'am."

Jerry grabbed the backpack that sat at his feet and exited the bar.

The Black woman looked between Purple Hair and Mickey, while adjusting her black-rimmed glasses. "Olivia Yoder?"

"Ollie," Purple Hair said, raising her hand and standing.

She left Mickey at the bar and sauntered over to where the interviewer sat. Mickey tried to busy herself while the two started on their interview, fiddling on her phone as she turned away.

Because she didn't know what she was doing in a bar, she thought it best to search job ads while Ollie was busy. She started with the usual recruiting sites, placing potential positions in her bookmarks folders.

"You want a drink while you wait?" asked a man's voice in front of her.

Mickey looked up from her phone and was instantly awestruck.

The man at the bar was positively beautiful… Tall and broad with a toasted almond tan. His dark brown eyes skewered Mickey to her bar stool as he rubbed the inside of a beer glass. He wore a gray T-shirt that drew tighter around his chest as he scrubbed. Dark hair peppered his forearms, flexing over powerful muscles with every twist and swipe.

"I'll have a Gin and Tonic," Mickey answered without thinking.

The man with the dark brown eyes quirked a heavy brow. "Yeah?" he asked, pausing his glass rub.

"Yes, please."

He placed the glass on the bar and regarded her with a quiet stare. "You interviewing?"

She nodded as she quickly appraised him. Salt-and-pepper hair, more salt on the buzzed sides and back, while the top flopped over his forehead in jet-black. He was taller than Ollie and herself, and definitely built with powerful upper-torso muscles. The bar prevented her from seeing the rest of his body, but she had a feeling he had powerful thighs as well.

He grunted as he pulled a rocks glass from the cabinet behind him. "Well gin alright?"

"Oof," she grimaced. "No, thank you. I'll have a Hendrick's if you got it."

The eyebrow shot up again, creasing the few forehead wrinkles he had.

"It's so much better," she went on. "It's got the loveliest hints of rose and cucumber, and tastes really fresh. It's not at all heavy on the pine smell like your well gins. It's far better than Beefeater."

"The well gin isn't Beefeater," he said in a gruff voice.

Her eyes widened. "You mean you give customers something worse than Beefeater?"

The man tilted his head to the side. Mickey could tell when she was being studied, and this guy was staring at her like she might issue him a quiz after their interaction. His hand tightened around the rocks glass as he struggled to think of a response. Instead of using his words, he turned around and retrieved a bottle of Hendrick's from a shelf.

She watched him splash a bit of gin and then reach for a

nozzle from beneath the bar. “Wait,” she said, flinging her hand out.

He paused.

“Is that tonic?”

The eyebrows were back to work. “Well, that’s one half of a Gin and Tonic, right?”

Mickey flashed him a grin. “You’re right,” she said with a chuckle. “But I think I’d actually like to go with soda water instead. Hendrick’s is so good I don’t want to overpower it with the quinine.”

She could tell he was fighting the urge to roll his eyes. “And would you still like a lime? Or is that too traditional for you?”

“I’ll have a little lime,” she said with a smile.

He paused again to quietly regard her but grunted before squeezing the nozzle of club soda into her drink. He then plopped a slice of lime in the glass before setting it before her. “Your gin and soda,” he muttered.

“Oh, thank you,” she said, reaching for her purse. “I don’t think I’ve ever had a drink in the afternoon like this. But when you asked, I thought, why the hell not, right?”

“I’ve never seen anyone order an *alcoholic* beverage right before a job interview.”

She laughed. “I’m sure you’ve seen more interesting things than this. How much do I owe you?”

He appeared to be thinking it over, glancing from her face to her drink before answering. “It’s on the house,” he finally said.

Mickey frowned at her drink. “Are you sure?” she asked. “Because Hendrick’s is a little pricey.”

He shrugged. “Why not?”

She glanced over her shoulder at the interview still in progress. “Are you sure you won’t get in trouble with your boss?” she asked, hitching a thumb at the two women.

The man's gaze flitted to the interviewer, and for the first time, Mickey thought she spotted mirth in his eyes. Not a lot, but enough to break up the intensity in his piercing dark stare. "I think it oughta be alright this time. What if you don't get the job? You don't want to be saddled with a nine-dollar tab."

She hadn't thought about it like that.

"Thank you," she said with another smile. "That's really nice of you."

The man grunted again as she took her first sip.

Mickey's eyes fluttered shut as she gave a delighted sigh and licked her lips. "Good lord, you make an excellent gin and soda, sir," she murmured. When she opened her eyes, she found him staring at her again, but this time his tanned skin flushed in embarrassment.

"Thanks," he said, grabbing the closest rag.

"What's your name?" she asked. If someone was generous enough to give her a free shot of Hendrick's, she should know their name. "I'm Mickey Chambers." She stuck out her hand and held it over the bar.

He looked at her hand with another raised brow before reluctantly taking it. His warm calloused hand gripped hers and gave it a decent shake. "Diego Acosta," he said.

When Mickey was ready to pull away, Diego held on for a split second longer than she expected. When he noticed, he quickly released her and went back to his glass cleaning. "It's nice to meet you, Diego," she said, still feeling the warmth of his skin pressed against hers. The heat traveled up her arm, spilling into her chest. No, it wasn't the gin… It was him.

"Next!" announced the woman behind her.

Mickey jumped in her seat. "Be right there," she said. Turning back to Diego, she gave him a thumbs-up and knocked back the rest of her gin. "Wish me luck, Diego," she whispered.

Purple Hair came up to her and clapped her on the back. "I'm the new barback," she said with a surprised smile. "Good luck."

"Hey, that's great," Mickey said, putting her empty glass on the rubber mat before her. She didn't know the woman from Eve, but she was still excited for her good fortune. "Congratulations!"

She glanced over to Diego, who watched them with a curious expression. He shook his head and went back to cleaning the same glass. What a handsome grump... Mickey disregarded his gruff attitude and girded her loins for the next step in a weird day. She had bigger things to worry about, like how to get through a random bar interview.

Diego wasn't sure what he'd just experienced.

As this Mickey woman hopped off her bar stool and snatched up her satchel, she flashed him another beautiful grin with two perfect dimples at her cheeks.

Beautiful grin?

He shook his head and put away the glass he'd been rubbing so hard. It had been dry nearly fifteen minutes ago, but he needed something to keep his hands busy while Mickey talked incessantly. Her expensive gin and soda, with a twist of orgasmic moan, was more than enough excitement for one day.

Her soft hands were enough excitement, too.

"Hi, I'm Mickey Chambers and I don't have an application," she said as soon as she sat before Jeanie. "But I can email you a CV right now, if you'd like."

Jeanie sneaked a quick peek at Diego, who still lingered over the bar. He shrugged. "I'm Jeanie Harris. Can you tell me about your previous bar experience?"

"I don't have any," she said, not skipping a beat. "But I've worked at a coffee shop during morning rush, so I'm quick on my toes. And I know my alcohol. Not in a problematic way, though! Just that I know my brands and my palate is great. My little brother sometimes surprises me with a new bottle of something, and we drink it together. We were thinking of doing a podcast, but he's really busy with his start-up thing in Atlanta."

Jeanie seemed to be at a loss for words but nodded along anyway.

Diego gave her another once-over as she sat erect in her chair, being cheerful as fuck. She wore a floral sundress and platform sandals; her hair was full of humid Georgia air, but she had arranged the curls prettily around her face. Mickey was short like his wife, Lucía, but curvier, and softer in some areas that dared to be squeezed. Generous hips and big thighs gave her dress a lovely flair, stopping just short of dimpled knees and shapely calves. *Jesus Christ, what are you thinking, man?*

He wasn't interested in squeezing anything.

He needed to dry another glass as he stood there listening to her word vomit. What else was she going to say? Diego found himself stuck in place, wanting to listen to more of this interesting woman.

"Okay..." Jeanie said. "Did you do any waitressing at the coffee shop?"

"I basically made drinks behind the bar, so...no, I guess not."

Diego didn't like how she lost her confidence at the end of her sentence. Her voice dipped into something low and self-conscious.

"But I'm a quick learner," she said, regaining her footing. "I can pick up anything with a little instruction and practice. Plus, you might not want a server to bring bad habits with them. I'm starting off fresh, which might be better."

Jeanie appeared to be conflicted about Mickey's answers.

She gave Diego another glance before looking through her stack of applications. He let her conduct today's interviews, because it was better for applicants to see a friendly face rather than his mean mug. But he understood what made Jeanie nervous; there weren't enough server applications. People mostly came in for the position of bouncer, barback or bartender. But nary a server.

"Just so you know, we've got a Riverwalk Blues Festival coming to town in two weeks," Jeanie warned. "It gets crazy in here. People get impatient for their drinks. Sometimes fights break out. We're looking for new bouncers, but you should know…it can get a little wild." She looked her up and down, floral sundress and all, before adding, "It takes a strong personality to deal with drunks."

Mickey didn't seem fazed. "I know how to handle big crowds and riffraff. I've worked the counter during Bulldogs games and homecomings, plus I run a tight ship at my current job. My students know not to try me."

"You're a teacher?" Jeanie asked.

"I am," Michelle said with a bubbly chuckle that made Diego grip the bar. "I teach dozens of college freshmen every semester, and whipping people into shape is part of the job."

Jeanie nodded. "Okay…" Diego could practically see the wheels turning in his partner's head. How long would it take to train her? Would she stay longer than three weeks? How much time and money could they afford to invest in a complete novice? When Jeanie looked at him again, Diego offered her a *why not?* shrug. "When could you start?"

Michelle tried to contain her excitement. "I could start anytime! I'm only teaching an online class at Hargrove, so I'm free until I have to grade assignments."

Diego went cold. *An online class? At Hargrove University?*

Jeanie offered a smile and clasped her hands together.

"Okay, Mickey," she said. "Let's have you fill out some paperwork. We'll have you come in on Wednesday as the new server."

"Really?" The woman acted like she was the winner of Publishers Clearing House. "Oh, my god, thank you, Jeanie. I—this is—omigod! Okay, okay, I can totally start Wednesday. Do I need an apron or something? Or one of those notepads for orders?"

Jeanie gave a genuine laugh as she waved a dismissive hand. "We'll give you an apron, but if you need a notepad, you'll have to pick that up yourself."

"I can do that," Michelle said. "I'll go to the store once I leave here."

"Fine. Show up Wednesday at six p.m., so you can shadow our other server, Irene. She'll show you the ropes."

Diego had had enough eavesdropping in the shadows. He cleared his throat as a signal for Jeanie's attention. "I'm sorry, did you say you're a professor at Hargrove University?" he asked in a voice louder than he'd intended.

Both women looked at him. "Well," Mickey replied. "I'm an adjunct instructor, but yeah, I teach English at Hargrove. I've got an online class scheduled for the summer—" she turned back to Jeanie "—but I swear it won't take up too much time. I've already used the syllabus last year, so I'll basically be grading occasionally. On my own time, of course."

Diego's heart kicked into a full gallop as he stared at the woman. Her smooth brown skin, those full lips and bright brown eyes brimming with excitement threatened to knock him on his ass. He'd seen cute women in the last five years, but Mickey Chambers wasn't like anything he'd experienced before. Her easygoing smile and delightful chuckle were alarmingly comfortable to be around. She was a bright neon sign that said "DISTRACTION," something he didn't want to deal with.

He didn't need that in his bar. "What class are you teaching?" his voice croaked.

She cocked her head with a confused smile that creased both dimples in her cheeks. "I'm teaching English 102."

Fuck.

He breathed through his nose as he took inventory of the facts. He'd given Jeanie silent permission to hire *his* professor. None of this was good. Especially the part where he stared at *his* professor's shapely calves. How old was this woman? She couldn't have been over twenty-five. And here he was, a forty-two-year-old man, offering free drinks to *his* young professor. Was that considered a bribe?

"So, I guess we'll be working together," she said, making his realizations even more painful. "How exciting!"

He nodded slowly, but Diego felt many things… Excitement wasn't one of them.

4

"Get in, loser, we're going to The Saloon," Mickey shouted through the passenger window.

Her best friend, Cleo Green, tiptoed down her driveway in ambitiously high heels. "Hold your horses," she said, hitching the gold chain of her purse on her shoulder. As she climbed inside Mickey's Honda Civic, she shifted her black bodycon dress down her thighs.

"I don't want to be late on the first day," Mickey said, turning her music down. "That's a very cute dress by the way."

Cleo rolled her eyes as she slammed the door. "You can borrow it after I wear it to Mayor Keaton's fundraiser dinner. Also, what do you know about working at a bar…let alone one called The Saloon?"

"Not everything," Mickey said, pulling away from the curb and driving toward the local Publix. "But it's a new thing to learn, right?"

Though her friend held her tongue, Cleo was a pessimist who always reminded Mickey of the eventual fallout of everything. Being the campaign manager for a mayor who was currently running for reelection would make anyone hypervigilant about bad news or scandal, but Cleo had always been a glass-half-empty kind of girl. Even when they were childhood friends, Cleo reminded her to be careful, stay alert and not take unnecessary risks.

"Pretty hot out today, huh?" Mickey asked, changing the subject.

"Unbearably hot," Cleo sighed.

"I'm wearing biking shorts under my dress," she joked. "I can't stand the thigh-rub."

"I told you to get that anti-chafing cream," she admonished. "You don't want to start a fire down there."

Mickey chuckled to herself. "I'll pick some up tomorrow."

"It does wonders, you know," her friend said, rubbing her own legs together.

Around her mid-twenties, after Mickey had found the right treatment, she reached a normal, higher weight, like her mother's. And since Cleo had the budget for cuter fat girl clothes, Mickey could borrow quite a few fun things from her friend. Tonight's sundress, a flouncy yellow number with a stylish boatneck, had hung in Cleo's closet last summer.

"How's the campaign going?" Mickey asked.

Her friend shook her head. "I swear, that man is trying to run me ragged. One minute, he tells me he's got nothing planned for Thursday, the next, I suddenly need to write up a statement on National Ice Cream Day." She heaved another sigh. "I think I have to plan a trip to Ira's Ice Cream."

If this was Cleo *running ragged*, there wasn't hope for the rest of the world. From her mink lashes to her wine-painted pedicure, her friend was quite put together. "But you like working for him, right? He's cool?" From the TV ads she kept seeing, Mayor Keaton fit the bill for most Columbus voters. A middle-aged white man and a University of Georgia graduate who still attended the same Baptist church from his childhood.

"Yeah, yeah, he's cool. He's just worried about reelection. He keeps threatening to hire a second campaign manager when he knows I have it handled." Cleo's phone buzzed in her purse. She let out another frustrated sigh. "He wants to know about hunting permits and deer season?"

"He's a Democrat, right?" Mickey asked.

"Yes, he's just running against a nut. Don't worry, I'm shutting that shit down. I'm not about to stomp all over the woods to watch this man pretend to know how to hold a gun." She tapped out a quick message before shoving her phone back into her purse. "Now, let's get back to the subject at hand. You're going to work in a bar where we vowed never to return."

Mickey nodded. "Yes, we said that. But that was before I found out my summer classes didn't measure up to my checking account."

Cleo's mouth was set in a thin line as she shot a glare. "You know damn well you could be on Keaton's staff. You already have the rhetoric background. Shit, you could be a speechwriter."

"He has a speechwriter."

"I need him to fire Billy, anyway." Cleo scowled. She flipped her Senegalese twists over her shoulder and checked her ruby-red lipstick in the mirror. "You would be much better at that job, and you know it."

"I don't know..." Mickey said. She didn't have a political science degree to make a career out of speech writing. "I think I just want to—"

"—try something new," Cleo finished. "You've always said that. When you finally got to go to college, it took you forever to pick a major."

"Indecision isn't a bad thing," Mickey argued. "I spent so much time being sick that I missed out on everything you got to do. I needed time to figure things out."

Cleo's expression softened. "I know… I'm sorry."

"Nothing to be sorry about. But I'm allowed to think about my future."

"Even at thirty-three?"

Mickey rolled her eyes. "Yes, even at thirty-three. I'm not on anyone's timeline but my own," she said with as much confidence as she could muster. "I'm good at teaching. Let me see what else I'm good at."

"Cocktail waitress?" Cleo asked.

"I might be good at that, too."

"Do you know who you're going to work with? If they're nice?"

"The woman who hired me was really nice and professional. I think she runs the place. I showed up with another woman who got hired on the spot. She seemed cool, too."

"Interesting…"

Mickey glanced at her friend. "It *is* interesting. I'm gonna learn a lot tonight."

Cleo grinned. "You're my constant student. Still learning even while you're teaching."

"About that…" They were getting close to the downtown strip, and she still had something she needed to say. "Last night, I set up the Blackboard site for my class and I discovered something interesting about the roster."

"Yeah?"

"Diego Acosta is in my class," Mickey said in a hushed voice. The discovery made her nervous because she'd never had a colleague who was also her student.

"Who's Diego Acosta?"

"He works at the bar," Mickey explained. "He's a little older than us. He's very handsome, and very…"

Cleo positioned herself in her seat to look her square in the face. "Very *what*?" she asked pointedly.

Mickey struggled to put her finger on it. As she parked, she remembered his stern attitude. Standing behind the bar, he'd stared at her with such an intensity that he was difficult to read. Was he angry? Was that just his face? "Very…grumpy?"

"Handsome and grumpy," Cleo said. "And a student."

"Right."

They sat in a parking spot near The Saloon and waited, Cleo thinking hard and Mickey wondering what Cleo was thinking. "How handsome?"

Mickey took the question seriously. "On a scale from one to ten, I'd put him at a nine. I feel like a smile would really help him. But even without the smile, very handsome."

"How grumpy?"

"He grunts a lot," Mickey said. "But he offered me a free drink before my interview. He didn't have to do that."

"Have you seen you?" Cleo asked with a grin. "I'd offer you the whole damn bottle."

"Oh, you always know what to say," she said with a chuckle. "Admittedly, I was *very* cute. I wore the floral Ann Taylor sundress."

Cleo did a small praise dance in the car, raising her hands to the ceiling. "Yaass, Jesus! The V-neck for the boobies!"

Mickey thought back to her dress and agreed her tits *did* look great. "But I don't think he was looking, anyway. Which is a good thing. No need to muddle things, right?"

"And how old is he?" Cleo asked.

"In his forties? It was hard to tell with the graying hair and the hard body." Mickey smirked. "I haven't had a nontrad student in a minute."

"You said they're usually better performers," Cleo said, unable to contain the mirth in her voice.

Mickey's gaze slid over to her friend. "I *did* say that, didn't I?"

"So what's your concern?"

Mickey wasn't quite sure. As attractive as Diego was, and however potent their brief spark felt, she couldn't act on something that could fuck up her chances of doing *both* jobs properly. She couldn't find anything—specifically—in the Hargrove Faculty Handbook about adjuncts fraternizing with their adult students, and Mickey had looked. She was concerned about her desire to look up that information in the first place. "Nothing," she said, waving it away.

"How long is the class?" Cleo asked.

"Five weeks. It's an early summer term, a bit shorter than the average summer class."

"Mmm-hmm."

"Indeed."

Mickey locked up her car and linked arms with Cleo on their walk to the bar. Two men stood at the entrance, one of them she recognized as the young man from the interview. The other tall, Latino man with a cute face and bored expression sat on a bar stool and watched them with curiosity.

"Good evening," Jerry said, a bit unsure of himself. He looked over his shoulder at the man sitting on the stool. "Do I ask them for an ID?"

"Ask everyone tonight. Rivera's on our asses," said the man.

Mickey tried to hide her grin as she thumbed through her purse. Cleo let out a loud laugh as she handed over her ID card. "You've made my night," she said. "And here I was feeling the sting of being over thirty."

Jerry flashed his light over the ID. "You don't look over thirty at all," he said in an earnest tone. His soft brown eyes looked her up and down before handing the ID back.

"Calm down, kiddo," Cleo said, tucking her card back in her purse.

"I'm new, too," Mickey said. "I saw you get interviewed."

He extended his hand after he checked her ID. "It's good to meet you. I'm Jerry."

"Mickey," she said brightly. "Good luck tonight."

"I'm Stevie," said the man on the stool. He jumped up and edged past Jerry to present himself to the two women. Mickey noticed he tried to get a jump on Cleo before Jerry upstaged him. Her friend gave a polite smile but said nothing.

"Are you ready to do this?" she asked Mickey, leading the way.

As ready as she'd ever be. She shook off the nerves and put on her high-watt smile. "I think so."

As the women entered the building, it relieved Mickey to find a quiet start to the night. Just a couple older gentlemen sitting at the bar and a small group of happy-hour men who still wore office attire at a table.

"Ooh, those guys look like donors for Keaton," Cleo said, scrunching her nose. "I think I'll just sit at the bar."

Mickey gave a nervous nod. "Sure."

Jeanie Harris, the woman who'd interviewed her, was at the far end of the bar, wiping down bottles of fruity mixers and liquor. When she looked up, a smile lit her face. "Good to see you, Mickey," she said.

"Good to be here," Mickey said, leaning against the bar.

"Newest Girl?" asked a husky female's voice from the kitchen. It took a minute, but a young Asian woman stepped around the corner. Her dark eyes looked Mickey up and down before a half grin touched her lips. "I'm Irene and I'll be training you."

Mickey returned her grin even though she didn't understand the joke. "Great, I'm Mickey."

Irene tied her apron around her small waist and chuckled. "Right."

"Don't mind her, Mick," Jeanie said, placing a clean bottle

under the bar. "Irene's just tired of training new girls. Our last one made it a week before I fired her."

Mickey straightened away from the bar. She didn't mind being an inside joke because it offered a new challenge that interested her. Irene doubted she could hang for longer than a week? Of all the random hobbies and skills she'd picked up over the years, proving people wrong was one of Mickey's favorites. "I'll try to last two weeks, then," she joked.

Irene didn't laugh, but she didn't frown, either. "We'll see, Newest Girl," she said, reaching behind the corner. When she revealed a black half apron that was identical to her own, Mickey tried to hide her excitement. It was silly to freak out over an apron, but with it, she would don a new identity: Cocktail Waitress Mickey. "This is for you."

"Thank you," she said. "I'll take good care of it."

Irene raised an eyebrow.

"Oh, before you get started," Jeanie said, reaching for another bottle, "Diego wanted to talk to you in his office."

Mickey frowned. "Why?"

Jeanie shrugged. "He asked me to grab you before you started working," she said. "I think he just wanted to go over some of the paperwork."

Why wouldn't Jeanie talk to her about these things? She walked toward the back of the bar, past the kitchen. Maybe Jeanie didn't have time to handle all the HR business of the bar and passed it off to her bartender, Diego.

Maybe a quick check-in with her student was a good idea. They could clear the air and discuss the fact that she was now his instructor. The thought made her walk with a straighter back. All she needed to do was assure him that, regardless of being coworkers, she'd still grade his work fairly. Simple as that.

Mickey gave three polite knocks on the office door's glass pane.

"Come in," said Diego's muffled voice.

The inside of the office was like a small warm rabbit's warren, filled to the brim with liquor boxes, books and dust. Mickey took one step inside and immediately began sneezing. "Excuse me," she said into the crook of her elbow. Sneeze. "Excuse me." Sneeze. "Excuse me!"

When she looked up, she found Diego perched on the corner of a massive desk, watching her with the same piercing dark stare from the other day. He extended a box of tissues toward her. "Bless you," he said.

"They come in threes, you know," Mickey said before sneezing again. She plucked two tissues from the box. "Excuse me. Or fours," she said behind the abrasive napkin.

"It gets a little dusty in here," he said without inflection. He straightened away from the desk and placed his hands on his hips. He wore a forest green T-shirt that stretched around his broad chest. Mickey sneaked a quick look below his waist and treated herself to the sight of long, sturdy legs wrapped in dark denim. "Look, I figured we could get this out of the way before you started working."

Mickey averted her gaze as she tucked the tissue into her apron. When her eyes settled on an exciting sight just over Diego's shoulder. "Oh, wow, is that Glenlivet 21?" she asked, moving toward the box behind him. It took a little squeezing past the other stacks of boxes and his body, but Mickey's hands landed on the open box with a hushed gasp. "Oh, my god, I've never seen a bottle close-up. How much does an entire box cost? You'll never go through all this with *your* clientele. I wonder why Jeanie would order so much?"

She hadn't realized that she was babbling until Diego cleared his throat. Mickey looked over her shoulder to see him standing directly behind her. With one muscular arm, he reached around her and closed the flaps of the box. "Jeanie didn't order that," he said in an irritated voice. "I did."

Mickey spun on the heels of her ballet flats and faced him. He was standing much closer than she had expected, smelling like warm aftershave and soap. She had to tilt her face upward to look him in the eye and felt her heart race from the stern line his lips formed. His gaze studied her with a mix of curiosity and annoyance. "I was just curious," she said in a smaller voice.

"I figured that much," he muttered, taking a step back.

Once she had room to breathe, disappointment washed over Mickey. She rather liked how small the office felt, how warm her skin got when he stood nearby. *No, this isn't right.* She frowned and shook her head. "I think we need to talk, Diego," she said in her teacher's voice.

"Excuse me?"

Mickey carefully edged past a stack of boxes, and his body, to get closer to the door. "I feel like we should work together with full disclosure before my shift starts. Now, I've never been in this situation before, and the rules aren't very clear, but I think it's best you know—"

"—that I'm in your class, Professor Chambers," Diego finished.

Mickey's mouth clamped shut. Okay, so he was fully aware of the situation… "Right. Well, you don't have to call me that, but yes, I'll be your instructor for the next month. I just wanted to assure you I will, in no way, take advantage of our power imbalance. Your grade is not in any danger while we work together."

When she stopped talking, Diego did a curious thing.

He smiled.

If it hadn't confused her so much, she would have welcomed the new handsome addition to Diego's features. The way his eyes crinkled at the corners and the fine lines around his mouth creased. When his smile turned into a dark chuckle, Mickey grew concerned. "What's so funny?"

He lowered himself onto the edge of the desk and continued the mirthless laugh. "You," he sighed, running his hand down his jaw. "You're worried about our *power imbalance*."

Mickey crossed her arms over her chest. "Well, I'm your instructor and I don't want to cause you any anxiety."

"And I'm your boss, Mickey," he said with a lopsided grin. "And I *certainly* don't want to fire you for being an incompetent server."

Mickey let out an audible gasp. "How are *you* my boss?"

He frowned. "I own The Saloon."

She searched her memory for any indication that he might be right. She'd naturally assumed since Jeanie interviewed people, that she was the boss. Plus, she carried herself in a no-nonsense manner that Mickey appreciated from ladies in leadership. "But…but you're…" she stammered before giving up "…my boss?" Mickey slapped her hand over her forehead and groaned. "Jesus Christ."

"That's what I wanted to talk to you about before you got distracted," he said, pushing away from the desk. Mickey silently watched him move around her to open the office door. "I'm just as interested in full disclosures as you are," he said, gesturing to their lack of privacy. "Starting with an open-door policy, if you don't mind."

Mickey's face burned with embarrassment. "Right."

"You can imagine how awkward this might be for me," he continued. "I've never employed one of my teachers."

"Right," she repeated. Irene's words echoed in her mind: *Newest Girl*… She now occupied a position that most servers quit after a couple weeks.

"But we can keep this tidy," Diego said.

Mickey took a deep breath before nodding. "We can," she said in a firm voice. "I'll do my best at this job, and you'll do your best with my assignments."

"And if we need to have a meeting about either, let's agree to some office hours," Diego said with a serious face. He pointed to the desk behind her. "We can meet here and talk shop."

She flashed him a bright smile. "That actually sounds good."

Diego's dark eyes narrowed slightly. "Right… Have you punched in yet?"

Mickey shook her head.

He glanced at his watch. "Then you're five minutes late."

Mickey watched him exit the office in stunned silence. *Seriously?* She raced after him, but his long stride carried him past the kitchen. To her right, she spotted the clock he referred to and found an empty card to scrawl her name on. She was already off to a rocky start. She was technically late to her first shift, and she hadn't known her boss was her student.

You wanted a new challenge, Mickey… Here you go.

5

Two bartenders.

Two men on the door.

Two barbacks.

And…one and a half servers.

Diego was cautiously optimistic about Wednesday night.

Mickey still shadowed Irene, but after two hours, she was bringing her serving tray to the bar for her own orders. He left that work to Jeanie. He focused on his end of the bar while trying to ignore his young professor, who wore a pretty yellow dress. It was difficult, considering the constant flash of sunshine swishing in the corner of his eye. It was also hard to ignore her laughter. He heard it every time she greeted a new patron.

At one point, he even caught Irene giving her an appraising nod. After training a dozen servers in the last five months, it took a lot to impress Irene. As if he'd summoned her with his thoughts, Irene slapped her tray on his end of the bar. "Three JJFs," she said, popping her gum.

Diego got three glasses ready. "How's Newest Girl doing

so far?" he asked in a low voice as he watched Mickey swan from one table to the next.

"Surprisingly well," Irene said honestly. "She's already trying the register by herself."

Diego grunted as he pulled the lever for one IPA. Mickey caught his attention again when she leaned over a four-top's table. She whipped a white towel from her apron and gave the surface a wipe down. He also noticed a guy from the four-top leaning back in his seat to get a better look at Mickey's ass. Diego's jaw clenched as if he hadn't already glimpsed at it twelve times himself.

"Boss."

He hadn't noticed the cold slosh of beer on his knuckles until it was too late. He quickly set down the glass and shook his hand out. "Shit," he muttered.

"Little distracted?" Irene asked with an impish smile. She cracked her gum as her eyes flitted to the mess he'd made.

Diego didn't answer as he continued to pull pints. "What are your bets?"

Irene followed his gaze toward Mickey, who put a friendly hand on a patron's shoulder as she laughed at his joke. "She's charming as fuck," she admitted. "I'll give her three weeks before she gets tired."

That's all the time Diego needed. In a month's time, he'd finish her class, and she'd get tired of carrying drinks and turning up chairs. This work was too hard for a professor with soft hands. Diego sent Irene on her way with a tap of his knuckles against the bar. He gave himself a moment to breathe as the bar was only half-busy. After all, he now had...*two* servers.

"Hey, Diego, I gotta take a phone call," Jeanie said, leaving her towel on the bar. Her panic-stricken expression made him alert.

"What's going on?"

She shook her head. "My mom's calling. She never calls this late." Jeanie ran off before saying more. The last time they'd talked about her mother, Jeanie had been worried about her dizzy spells. Diego bit the inside of his cheek as he waited on answers. He understood her panic all too well. After learning that his mother had pancreatic cancer, his world collapsed quickly. The time between "something feels off" to the actual diagnosis felt like a blink of an eye for him. The treatment and her decline before her eventual death felt even faster…

He forced the intrusive thought from his mind.

This wasn't about him.

By the time Jeanie reappeared, her normal reddish-brown complexion was ashen. "I have to go to the hospital," she said. "Mom called for an ambulance because of chest pains."

"You talked to her? She's conscious?"

"Yes," Jeanie said, fumbling with her apron and searching for her keys. Diego reached under the bar for the purse she hid. "It's something to do with her heart. They—they're talking about surgery…"

"Breathe, Jeanie," he said, pushing her purse into her arms.

Tears stood out on her eyelashes as she sucked in a deep breath. "I don't know—"

"If she's talking, that's good," Diego said, pushing his own panic down. "They might give her a stent or a pacemaker. They *will* help her."

She turned around to face the shelves of bottles. "Yeah?" she asked with a quivering lip.

Diego's stern expression settled over his face. "Yes, Wilma Harris will get better. Now, do you want Ramón to drive you?"

Jeanie stopped pacing long enough to look him in the eyes. "No," she said in a resolute tone. "No, I'm good."

“You sure?” he asked, grasping her by the shoulders. “We don’t need you driving like a bat out of hell, getting hurt.”

She nodded. “I know.”

“Breathe deep and drive carefully. Text me whatever you find out.”

When he released her, Jeanie hurried around the bar and out the door, just in time for Mickey to approach the bar. Worry knitted her brow as she looked from him to the door. “Is she okay?”

“Family emergency,” Diego said in a clipped tone. “You need something?”

Mickey hesitated. “My table wants a round of Macallan 12s. Double shots.”

Diego looked at the four-top of business bros, who were still checking her out. “You’ve got some fans, huh?”

The woman whom Jeanie had been taking care of snorted behind white wine. “Now I know how I recognized those guys,” she said to Mickey. “They’re members of the Randolph Country Club.”

Mickey grinned. “Ooh, okay…so my trainer, Irene, said a little harmless flirting is good for tips,” she said, lowering her voice to a whisper. “They oughta have deep pockets, right?”

The woman, who Diego assumed was Mickey’s friend, glanced over her shoulder at the table of men. “If they’re ordering Macallan, they gonna treat you right. Look at you workin’ it on the first day!”

“Girl, I’m trying,” she giggled. “Are you good on the wine?”

“I’ll take care of the bar patrons,” Diego interrupted.

The two women looked at him as if they’d forgotten he was there. Mickey’s friend twirled a thin braid between her red-tipped fingers and glanced him up and down. “I’m guessing you’re Diego?”

Before he answered, Mickey jumped in with introductions.

"Diego is my *boss* and he *owns* The Saloon," she said. "And this is my best friend, Cleo. She works with the mayor."

Cleo's eyes darted between him and her friend before they widened with understanding. Diego felt like he was on the receiving end of an inside joke and tried to ignore the heat rising up his neck. As if he hadn't heard that a little T & A loosened up men's wallets. But the way she leaned over the bar, invading his space with her light floral scent, made him remember how he was also staring at her T & A. He pulled back, ashamed of his voyeurism and a little shocked that *his professor* was working the room for tips.

"They said they wanted them neat," Mickey said, pulling him from his thoughts.

Diego grunted.

"Double shots," she reminded him.

"I heard you."

"How much is that going to be?" she asked, in awe of the amber liquid he poured. He assumed the wasteful flex impressed her.

"Just keep an eye on their tab, and if they give you shit, let Irene know."

"You think they're going to give me shit?"

"I'm just saying if they do," Diego said, pouring the fourth. "Can you carry that?"

Mickey gave a cocky scoff. "Ha!" As if to prove her point, she arranged the glasses on her tray before hoisting it above her head. "What do you think?"

Diego was not amused. There was about one hundred dollars on that tray and her twirl made him pretty fucking nervous. But she sauntered off with her tray held aloft, full hips swinging in a sensuous rhythm, back to the table without incident. His breath only returned to normal when she passed out the drinks and walked off. When she gave him a saucy wink, he gripped the edge of the bar and gritted his teeth.

There was something wrong with him.

He didn't know her well, but he knew for damn sure *who* she was. Professor Chambers was the online instructor who sent the class a morning email containing a syllabus and a cheerful note saying, We're going to have fun this summer! She looked young as fuck and her constant chipper jibber-jabber made her seem more like a kindergarten teacher. But his body refused to listen to reason. Watching her still made him hot under the collar and set his nerves on edge.

The clatter of Ramón's dish rack shook him out of his thoughts. "More glasses," he announced while he stacked. "Listen, hermano, that Ollie is a lifesaver. She's down in the basement right now getting you more bottles."

Diego grunted.

"Newest Girl is great, too," Ramón continued. "You have time to talk to her yet?"

"Mmm-hmm." No one was aware of their odd relationship yet. Probably for the best.

"Real curious about my job, wanted to know everything about the kitchen." He laughed. "I had to shoo her out when she offered to load the dish rack for me. I tell ya, Diego, this is feeling like Lucía's bar again."

A sharp stab of irritation hit him in the gut, but he remained quiet. *Lucía's bar...* Diego hadn't felt like he'd cared for the bar like she had. She'd had fun with it, while he was just the serious dude in the back office. Diego liked it that way. And he would have happily kept it that way were it not for Lucía's death. But now, he needed to loosen the reins and delegate responsibility. He also needed to protect his small clan. Fear made him tighten his control over every aspect of operations.

Except for hiring. The one time he left it up to Jeanie, he accidentally hired his professor.

"Hey," Ramón said, his hand on Diego's arm. "Jeanie's gonna be okay. Wilma's full of piss and vinegar."

Diego nodded. "I know."

"Then what's got you so tense?"

Just waiting for the hammer to fall.

When Mickey and Irene returned to the bar, Diego ignored Ramón to focus on their mixed expressions. Irene's gaze pointed to the door; her mouth turned downward with a scowl. Mickey's eyes widened with excitement. Diego followed their eyes and saw a sight that made his insides flip-flop: a bachelorette party.

"Fuck," he growled.

"Okay, okay, no need to panic," Irene said, clearly panicking. "Diego, you're going to be nice, right?"

Nice?

He tilted his head back and pinched the bridge of his nose. "Irene, don't start…"

"I mean it," she said in a stern voice. "Without Jeanie, you're a bit of a dick."

"She's right, hermano," Ramón said, staring at the women who were being carded by Stevie and Jerry. "Sé amable."

"I can help!" Mickey said.

Everyone's gaze shifted to her. Mickey bubbled with excitement as she bounced up and down. The shining brightness in her brown eyes almost made Diego believe the night *hadn't* gone to shit.

"Actually…" Irene began.

"No," Diego finished. "Absolutely not. I don't allow servers behind the bar."

"Yeah, this could work," Ramón agreed.

"I'll cash out her tables," Irene said. "If she just pulls pints, it will free you up to make drinks."

The tighter he tried to hold the reins, the harder his clan bucked. Rather than shout Irene down, which he couldn't do, he relented. "Fine."

"Yay!" Mickey screeched.

"Here, give me your tickets," Irene said. "I'll close them out and start over."

"What about my tips?" Mickey asked cautiously as she went through her apron pockets.

"You'll get your tips, sweetie," Irene said with a chuckle. "I'm changing my bet to five weeks."

And before he knew it, Diego was babysitting a newbie behind the bar while a herd of women surrounded them.

"Oh, no, someone needs to cash me out," Cleo said, pulling her purse onto her shoulder. "I can't do a bachelorette party tonight, too loud."

Diego empathized with her. "I'll take care of you," he said, grabbing her receipt from the back counter.

"You're leaving now?" Mickey asked.

"Girl, you're the only one who likes these kinds of parties," Cleo said with a grin. "I've already ordered my Uber."

"I'll call you tomorrow."

"Please do."

Diego moved toward the end of the bar with Cleo's receipt so that she wouldn't be swarmed by the bachelorette women. "You can sign here."

Cleo did quick math and gave him a sizable tip before scribbling her signature. As she placed his pen on the bar, she gave him a curious look. "Take care of my girl, Diego."

It wasn't a request. He could tell that much from the arch in her brow. He nodded as he grabbed her receipt. "She'll be fine."

She scoffed. "For three weeks?"

Diego's heart tripped over itself. He hadn't noticed her sitting at the bar while he and Irene talked about Mickey's performance. "It's a hard job," he explained.

"I just wouldn't underestimate her," Cleo said with a shrug. "Mick thrives on being hardheaded."

It was difficult to toss back a witty response when he was embarrassed about getting caught. Cleo strode from his bar before he could gather himself. But he couldn't care about someone else's feelings when he needed to focus on the evening's minor setback. His right-hand woman had been replaced with the Newest Girl, and a drunk horde had descended upon them…

"Congratulations!" Mickey screamed at the blonde woman wearing a sheer white veil.

"Thank yoooooou," said the woman, who was already a few drinks in.

"Ladies, we'll be with you in a minute, I just need to go over a couple things with my new girl."

"New girl!" the collective cried, as if it was something to celebrate.

"I know," Mickey said, excitedly. "It's my first night and I'm not even supposed to be behind the bar!"

The women cheered again at this news. "Okay, quick lesson," he said, moving her off to the side. "This right here is your new best friend." He grabbed a nearby jigger.

"Oh, what's this?" she asked, taking it from him.

"It's going to help you accurately measure a shot," he said. "If someone wants a shot of anything that goes in a rocks glass, you use this. Keep a close eye on it."

"Okay!"

He directed her attention to the space under the bar. "This is your soda gun. Every mixer you need is going to be in it. *T* is for tonic, *S* is for soda, et cetera." Diego didn't wait for her to ask questions before moving her to the next task. He picked up a beer glass and held it below a tap. "When you're pouring beer, tilt it away from you at a seventy-five-degree angle."

"Why?" she asked.

"You don't want too much head," he said.

The look on her face made him roll his eyes. Mickey bit on her bottom lip to stop herself from giggling. "No?"

He blew out a frustrated sigh. "How old are you?"

"Thirty-three, you?"

He didn't believe that for a second. "Old enough to know that's not funny."

Mickey trained her face. "You're right," she said, trying not to smile.

Maybe if he weren't so stressed out, her cute smirk would have been something to smile at. "You think you can handle that?"

"Handled!" she said, beaming at him.

Diego would have to trust her.

6

Being behind the bar felt a little familiar.

At the coffee shop in Athens, Mickey had had to work fast grinding beans, squirting syrups and pouring lattes. Her mind lit up like a pinball machine as she took the bachelorette party's orders, getting back in the swing of doing several things at once. However, catering to drunk women was slightly more challenging. Two of them wanted a Seven and Seven, which turned out to be easy to throw together. But the ones who wanted complicated cocktails and shots, she had to pass them to Diego. All of them were loud and slurring their words.

"Can I just have a Miller Light?" asked one of the more sullen bachelorette friends. Her mouth pursed with annoyance as she picked at the corner of a coaster. "I'm keeping an eye on them."

"Of course," Mickey said, flashing her a smile.

"What did I tell you about the head?" Diego asked, coming out of nowhere. His abruptness startled her, but not enough that she didn't chuckle into her fist. He rolled his eyes again, which would be the closest he'd get to acknowledging the joke. "That's too much foam."

Mickey held up the glass to her customer. "Is that too much head?" she asked, trying to keep a straight face.

The raven-haired woman with heavy black eyeliner looked from the glass to Mickey and smiled. "I've never complained about too much head, but…yes, that's too much foam."

The two women fell out in loud cackles at Diego's expense.

He ran his hand down the tight jaw that he kept clenching and stepped behind her. "I told you seventy-five degrees," he said, as his arms surrounded her body. One hand closed over hers, holding the lever, while his other covered the hand she used to hold the glass. "Tilt the glass."

Mickey's body froze in place as she allowed his hand to angle the glass away from them. The warmth of his body enveloped her back as they pulled the lever together. "Let it flow slowly at first until you get the hang of it," he said in a stern voice, his chin brushing her curls as he spoke.

Mickey's body was close to bursting into flames.

"I could have sworn I did that," she breathed, trying to keep her eyes on the glass and not the flexing muscles of his brown forearms.

"Nope," he replied. "You need a harder tilt. Let the liquid hit the walls of the glass, and when you're near the edge, pull it back before you top it off." He maneuvered both of their hands until they filled the glass.

"There," she said with a shaky breath. "That's it?"

"That's it," he replied.

Mickey tried to keep the tremble in her arm from sloshing the full beer as she handed it over to her customer. "How's that?"

"Much better," the woman said, taking a swig. Before she left the bar to join her friends, she gave Mickey a wink. "Good luck with your training."

Mickey's face went hot. "Thanks," she mumbled.

"Pour another one," Diego ordered, still standing behind her.

"For whom?" she asked, looking at him over her shoulder. "We handled everyone for now."

"It's for me," he said.

"Should you be drinking on the job?"

Quiet laughter shook Diego's shoulders. "Says the woman who ordered Hendrick's and soda before a job interview."

Mickey's lips quirked. "Okay, then," she said.

"Try it again."

She picked up a glass and gave it another go.

"Deeper," he said.

Mickey tilted.

"What are you afraid of?" he asked. "Push it, Mickey."

"It might help if you weren't literally breathing down my neck," she snapped, sloshing the beverage into the grates.

He stepped around to her side and leaned an elbow onto the bar. Maybe he wasn't at her throat any longer, but he was still very close. "That better?"

She glanced at him, noting the wicked glint in his eye. Was he trying to access some long-buried sense of humor? No, it wasn't better. Her handsome student was being far too handsome, and it threatened to rattle her out of her usual chipper mood. "Sure."

"So pour, Professor."

"You don't have to call me that," she said, shooting him a glare. "But perhaps we should talk about *your* teaching style."

"I don't teach with kid gloves."

"Kid gloves can help people feel comfortable enough to make mistakes," she said, trying to pull another pint. She tilted the glass as far as she could without spilling the contents.

"Like our first assignment?" Diego asked. "If I remember right, we're supposed to *have fun searching our memories for a personal food narrative.* I've never heard of food being the focus of an English class."

Mickey frowned. Was he criticizing her class plans? She worked hard on her Food Studies syllabus a few years back after students complained that the regular composition classes were too dull.

"Pull up," he said.

Mickey put her eyes back on her task. "How's that?"

Diego took the glass from her, grazing her fingertips along the way. He tipped his head to the side and appraised her pour quietly. She didn't know why, but his approval felt necessary. When she watched him take a sip, noticing how his Adam's apple bobbed in his throat, she licked her lips.

"Well?"

"It tastes like the piss beer," he said, smacking his lips before pouring the rest right into the grate. "Pour me a Guinness."

Mickey gasped. "That's a waste."

He shrugged. "It's not a Glenlivet 21 waste. Go ahead, Professor. Pour me another."

The cocky swagger on this one…

Still, the urge to "show him what for" was strong. Mickey felt like he was testing her, and she intended to prove him wrong. "Fine," she said, grabbing another glass.

"You sound a little huffy," Diego said, leaning forward to watch her technique.

"I'm not," she said, pulling the Guinness handle.

"You're not tilting far enough."

She wasn't. As soon as the liquid hit the bottom of the glass, it foamed hard. Mickey scoffed at her luck and dumped it in the grate so she could try again.

"Farther," Diego said.

Irritation furrowed her brow as she looked from his smirk to the foam. "That's what I'm doing," she snapped.

"I need three Irish Slammers," Irene called from the end of the bar.

"Oh, great," Diego said, clapping his hands. "Mickey's on it!"

Mickey's gaze flew up. "What goes in a Slammer?" she asked nervously. "And why are people still drinking those?"

"No clue. They're gross and awful to clean up," Irene said with a laugh.

"I'll get the shots ready while you fill three Guinnesses. Half-full cups, Professor."

Mickey began to sweat for the first time that evening. Before now, she hadn't felt the pressure, not even while juggling the few tables Irene gave her. Even while serving the women of the bachelorette party, she felt excited. Now, pouring three half-full beers under her boss's *close* supervision felt like work.

"Done," he said, gathering three small shot glasses filled to the brim with cream-colored liquor.

"How?" Mickey protested. "I'm still..."

As he waited, a few women from the bachelorette party came back to the bar, ready to order another round. "We want seven Lemon Drops!" someone cried.

"Coming up," Diego said. "How are you doing, Mickey?"

She ignored him and concentrated on filling her glasses. She placed her first Guinness on the tray next to his shots and started on the second. While Diego shook lemon juice and vodka next to her, he stared at her performance.

"Oh, no, that ain't gonna fly," he said, dumping the contents of her first glass. "Try again."

Mickey sucked her teeth and fought the urge to roll her eyes when he went back to violently shaking his mixer.

"And why the hell isn't the music on?" Diego shouted. "Ladies, what do you wanna listen to? Three free songs for the bride-to-be."

A series of squeals rose from the group as they ran to the jukebox. With her second Guinness complete, Mickey worked on the last one only to watch Diego pour out seven perfect Lemon Drop shots. He even found time to pour a cup of water for the DD.

"Still waiting on those Slammers," Irene called.

"I can't believe anyone would drink this shit," Mickey muttered under her breath.

"I got the shots," Diego said. "Just waiting on these beers."

"Maybe you want to do the last one?" Mickey asked, thrusting the glass toward his chest.

"I teach by throwing folks in the deep end," he said, nodding his head to the beer tap. "Keep going."

She buried her growl as her fingers tightened around the glass. "Fine."

Suddenly Rihanna's "Don't Stop the Music" blared over the speakers. "Oh, here they go. The party's just getting started."

Why did she have a feeling Diego was only creating chaos out of a stable situation to fuck with her? When she filled the last Guinness, she set it on the tray. "They're done," she called to Irene.

"And they're at varying volumes," Diego said, interrupting the server's grabbing hands. "Level 'em out, Mickey."

With her jaw set, she eyeballed the three glasses and poured them even. "They're done, Irene."

"They're done," he agreed. "Get these disgusting beverages to the three fools."

Irene swept them away before he could change his mind.

Mickey wheeled around to face Diego. "What was that all about?" she snapped.

He lifted a dark heavy brow and returned with that same cocky grin, revealing two rows of perfectly straight white teeth. Goddamn, he looked so hot when he smiled. "You sound irritated, Mickey," he said.

"I am," she said through gritted teeth.

"I wondered if that was even possible," he said, letting his gaze rove over her body, a slow stare that sent heat just below her belly. "You show up looking like sunshine and rainbows, flirting with the business boys. I thought you were Mary Poppins or something."

His admission confused her. "You have a problem with me being cheerful?"

"Nah, just don't want you to get the wrong idea about this job," he said, edging closer to her. "'Cause it's only gonna get worse."

"What makes you think I can't hack it?" she asked, trying not to tremble from his closeness.

"Irene is nice enough to give you three weeks, but I know better. Servers quit this job because people are terrible. And they get even worse after a few drinks. The only folks who have it shittier than us work at the local Waffle House because they get our drunks. The hours are long, the floor is hard, and spills are nasty."

"Well, I kinda figured that," she said, even though she grew nervous. Her feet *were* sore in her cute ballerina flats.

Diego picked up on her hesitation immediately. "And you got soft hands," he said.

Mickey frowned. "Soft hands?"

"Soft hands and a soft heart," Diego said, stepping beside her. "You're too damn nice to last for long." She watched him pull himself a pint of Guinness, angling the glass as far back as possible. Once it was half-full, he set it on the grate below the nozzle and turned to her. "No shame in quitting now, Mickey. You can keep the tips you earned."

Wow…

She folded her arms across her chest and stared at him, wondering if she could call her boss/student a dick to his face. After his Guinness settled, Diego filled it to the top and set it on the bar in front of her.

"Go ahead, have a drink on the house."

"A little severance pay?" she asked.

He shrugged. "Can't say The Saloon never gave you anything." The smile that played on his full lips confused her. Actually, it was the arousal that confused her. Anger kept her back ramrod straight, while the grin, muscles, and streaks of silver through his dark hair made her shockingly horny.

Mickey took up the glass and drank deeply. "Pretty good," she said. "But not tonight, Diego."

7

"Office hours," Mickey announced as she zipped her money bag shut.

Everyone in the bar looked up from their tasks, but Diego knew she was talking directly to him. He should have known that being hard on her would bite him in the ass later, but that's how he taught. The best education came from floundering in the deep end. The other, more insidious reason he tested her was because her chummy attitude made her distracting. Laughing with Mickey could make him relax. Relaxing might make him forgetful. And if he was forgetful, then the whole damn operation could fall apart.

"Sure," he said, closing the register.

Mickey got off her stool and walked to the back office without him. Diego didn't bother checking the others' expressions before following her. If he had, he'd probably see disappointment on Ramón's face. After just one shift, he already loved Mickey and was ready to go to bat for her. He'd get no sympathy from Irene, either; she had an instinct for spotting the folks who would stick around. For all he knew, Mickey was one of those folks.

Diego wanted her gone because she was the first woman, since Lucía, he'd looked at with intense interest. He wasn't sure how long was long enough, but for the last five years, his feelings lay dormant as he moved half-dead through a gray world. The feelings Mickey stirred up made him nervous. He shouldn't have had to think about this while at his own business.

When he met her in his office, she stood in the center of his mess of boxes with her arms crossed. She fixed her mouth in a fuck-you expression that immediately made him feel like shit.

"I'm not quitting," she said.

Diego took a deep breath, prepared to answer her.

"And tonight's chauvinistic display of alpha nonsense won't make me quit. I've been through too much to punk out like that," she said, taking a few steps forward. She stood toe to toe with him; her light floral scent threatened to knock him on his ass. He didn't want to step back because she'd know how intimidated she made him. "Whatever gripe you've got with me, it ends tonight," she said, poking him in the center of his chest with a hard finger.

So much for soft hands...

He stared down at her finger on his chest with raised brows. "I—"

"And just so you know, your behavior won't affect your grade, even though I know plenty of professors pettier than I am. I have integrity out the ass and I've dealt with boys way more petulant than you."

"Well, hold on—"

"And that's all I have to say on the matter," she said with another jab. Once she realized how close she was, and what she was doing to Diego, she looked down at her finger in surprise.

"Are you sure?" he asked.

Time slowed down to an aching pace as Mickey's eyes

reached his and she licked her lips. Seeing the flash of pink dart out to swipe across her plump bottom lip made him clench his fists at his sides. It took everything to bury the groan at the back of his throat. "Yes," she breathed.

"I was about to say sorry," he said, glancing at her finger once again. She hadn't moved it yet, and he wondered why. "I could have been…nicer."

"Telling me I have soft hands hurt my feelings," she said, finally letting her hand drop.

Diego couldn't stop himself, so he reached down, took her hand and held it. "You do have really soft hands, but they won't make you quit," he said.

Her eyes fell to their joined hands as he ran his calloused thumb over her knuckles. When she hesitantly brought her other hand up to touch his arm, Diego willed himself to remain still. He wasn't entirely sure what was going to happen, but he wanted to lean into it. He grew hyperaware of the shine of Mickey's black curls under the low lights of his office. How her eyes, now half-lidded and drowsy, stared at their joined hands. The elegant slope of her shoulder where brown skin met a yellow neckline.

It was difficult to tell which of those beautiful things Diego should focus on, so he settled on what was most immediate: the way her fingers gripped his forearm. "I'm not quitting," she murmured. Mickey proved it by raising herself up on her ridiculously flat shoes and pressing her lips against his. Desire overrode Diego's shock as he let her lean into his body. Desire forced him to interlock his fingers with hers and wrap his arm around her waist. Even as they were fucking up, desire made him hold the small of her back, pulling her deeper into his embrace.

While his brain shouted, *What the fuck are you doing?*, his body said, in a much darker, lower voice, *See where this goes…*

He moved at her pace and his lips matched her rhythm. She took the quickest lick of his bottom lip, and he returned the favor. When she took advantage of his open mouth, she kissed deeper. His tongue met hers in no time, sliding against and dancing with hers. Diego consciously stilled his hips in order not to mimic the same dance against her soft middle. Instead, he angled his face to meet her intensity, sweeping his tongue along her lip.

The deep moan Mickey released spurred him onward, taking a nip from her. When she clutched the back of his shoulder, he crushed into her further, unable to leave the sweet taste of her mouth. Every shift ended with a free drink for all employees and Mickey's choice was a Hendrick's and soda. Diego could taste cucumber and rose from her tongue.

His desire, once awoken, now drove him wild.

He walked her back to the edge of his desk, clearing away stacks of invoices behind her. With one leg wedged between her thighs, he leaned over her and drank the kiss she offered so recklessly. Her hands left his and settled on his chest, her fingers fisting his T-shirt and pulling him closer. A growl he hadn't heard in years climbed from his throat as she bit down on his lip. When Mickey licked the sting away, his arousal spiked.

And then they both seemed to think the same word: *reckless*.

As quickly as they began, they stopped. She pulled away first and stared at him with wide eyes. With their faces inches apart, they realized that they'd made a huge mistake. Her swollen lips and blushing cheeks were evidence of that. Diego stood over her, chest heaving, stopping his hand from tangling in her hair.

"Oh, god," Mickey said, staying perfectly still beneath him. "What have I done?"

"You kissed me," he said.

"I know that much," she hissed. "And I'm so sorry for that."

Diego wondered if this was the moment where he should back away. "Well, I kissed you back."

"What was I thinking?"

He honestly couldn't answer that question.

"You're my *student*," Mickey said.

Diego cocked his head to the side. "To be fair, you're my *employee*."

Mickey's blank expression would have made him laugh, were it not for the fact they'd royally fucked up their professional relationship on the first day. Earlier, he'd made a big show of explaining his open-door policy.

"Jesus, the door," he said, pulling away from her and closing them off from the rest of the bar. "I'm sorry I ever said anything about an open-door policy."

Mickey pushed herself away from the desk and wrapped her arms around her middle. "It was a good idea," she said. "But I'd rather not let people know I just kissed the boss."

They stood there, facing one another, trying to figure out what was next.

"Why did you do it?" Diego asked, hesitantly.

Her gaze flew to his face, wild-eyed and mortified. She opened her mouth and immediately closed it. After taking a deep breath, she tried again. "I'm not sure... Why did you return the kiss?"

Being put on the spot never worked well for Diego. He instinctively put his hands on his hips and scowled. "When a woman kisses you, you don't turn tail and run."

"You know that's not a good reason!" she said, releasing her arms and marching right up to him. "You could have pushed me away."

"Well, shit, woman, you seemed pretty insistent," he said defensively.

Mickey jabbed a finger at him again. "You're doing it again," she said in an angry voice.

Diego leaned into her finger. "Doing what?"

"Acting like a dick."

The way her brows furrowed in frustration aroused him all over again. "You sound a little huffy, Professor," he said, lowering his voice as he pushed his face to hers.

"And I thought I told you not to call me that." Mickey's pointed finger quickly became a fist, bunching his T-shirt and pulling him in for another kiss. A tiny growl escaped her lips as she grabbed the back of his neck. This time, Diego didn't hesitate to do what he'd had the urge to do moments before. He reached down, took her by the thighs and hauled her up to his waist. Mickey squealed in surprise as he lifted her into the air, but still wrapped her arms around his neck.

They'd simply picked up where they left off. Diego carried her back to his desk and continued kissing the fuck out of her, but this time, he let his hands roam without hesitation. One wound its way through her thick hair, curled with sweat and humidity. His other hand took her by her plump thigh and lifted it around his hips. As he ground himself into her softness, she moaned again. He thoroughly enjoyed that noise.

When she left his lips, Mickey trailed her kisses down his jaw to his neck. He lifted his chin to give her better access but missed her mouth. "Jesus," he moaned in pleasure. "Mickey..."

At the sound of her name, she froze in his arms.

Goddammit.

"What. Are. We. Doing?" she groaned in frustration.

He looked down at her crestfallen face. "I don't know," he said.

"I should go."

"Yeah?"

Mickey frowned. "Yes, of course. Because this might happen again."

Would that be the worst thing in the world? Diego shook his head out of the kissing fog. *Of course it would be. What are you expecting from her in your fucking office?* He separated himself from her, pulling down the hem of her dress as he went. "You're right," he sighed. Why was he so disappointed? "Right," he said, wiping his mouth.

"I finished counting my money," she said, patting down her hair. "I'm going to go home."

Diego stuffed his hands into his pockets, awkwardly adjusting his jeans. "You know your schedule for the rest of the week?" he asked in a gruff voice.

Mickey kept her eyes trained on the floor. "I copied it down earlier. I'll be in tomorrow night."

"Yep, sounds good. See you then."

"Yep," she said, moving around him. "Take her easy."

Diego raised a brow at the phrase, but let her pass without comment.

"Okay, drive safe," she said in a louder voice than what was necessary.

When she shut the door behind her, Diego collapsed against his desk with a shudder. "Fuck, fuck, fuck," he whispered. "What the fuck?" He slapped both of his cheeks and widened his eyes as if he were drunk. But he was stone-cold sober and fully aware of what had just happened in his office. He'd kissed the fuck out of *Professor* Mickey Chambers, ran his hand up her thigh and pressed his erection against her. Those were the facts.

He needed to talk to someone about this.

Oddly enough, the only person he could talk to was his wife, Lucía. He brought all his feelings to her and she sorted through them carefully until they could come up with solutions. And since her death, he'd kept quiet about every stab of anger and all anxiety and depression. Ramón told him to pray, Jeanie told him to find a therapist and Stevie indulged him with a shared drink every so often. He'd tried all of it, but not for too long. Managing the bar kept him sane, but he was wondering how long the work would help him. After all, he'd just lost control and kissed his professor. He was wound tight, alright.

Prayer. Therapy. Drinking.

If that's all he had in his arsenal, Diego needed to pick one and keep it moving. Because fucking Mickey Chambers, sure as shit, would not be an option.

8

Ninety-two dollars in tips.

Mickey counted the money twice just to make sure.

Holy shit! After sharing with two barbacks, she had nearly one hundred dollars? That wasn't bad at all. She pulled a notepad from her nightstand and began tallying figures. If she could consistently pull this off, she would be okay. The paychecks would be next to nothing, so tips would have to be the ticket. And this amount was just from a Wednesday night? Mickey grinned as she imagined how much money she'd make on the weekends.

She stacked the bills and put them in the notepad, stuffing everything in her nightstand drawer. Mickey rolled off her bed and padded into her kitchen, where her medication and grapefruit juice ritual awaited her. It was the same ritual she'd practiced since she was twenty-one. As she drank, her mind went back to the memory of last night.

She kissed her boss.

Not once, but twice…

Mickey couldn't think of anything more embarrassing. She'd behaved completely out of character last night and couldn't understand why. Usually, after being berated, Mickey was ready to square up. Instead, she rewarded Diego's smug behavior with a kiss. Not only that, but he kissed her back. He joined in on the madness. Were they both complicit in making two workplaces unprofessional? The horror of being unprofessional had burrowed into her brain as she drove home, when she went to bed and now while standing in her kitchen. She'd tried so hard to maintain a balance of caring but strict in her classroom. She strived to be there for her students, but maintaining her boundaries when she interacted with them.

Now, all of that had gone up in flames.

But it was difficult to put out the fire that she'd accidentally started with Diego. Even more challenging was having to push away the memory of last night. How his arms wrapped around her body, his hands stroking her with urgency and sliding up her thighs. Mickey's belly flipped, and desire pooled between her legs as she remembered how he lifted her from the ground. It caught her off guard because she couldn't remember the last time a man lifted her like it was nothing. Most men who dated her in the past didn't have qualms with her being a big girl, but none of them actually swept her off her feet, either. The thought made her sigh heavily in her kitchen.

Sure, Diego was hot as fuck with his smoldering brown eyes and sensual mouth stuck in a permanent scowl, but the question still remained: What could have possessed her to kiss a man who was a lousy teacher and an impatient jerk? Two obvious rules stared her in the face—one: you don't kiss your student, and two: you don't kiss your boss. How Mickey had fucked up both those things, and on the first day, was a mystery.

"Fuck," she muttered.

Okay, it's time to turn to work. She would grade the "Food Memory" journal entries that would prepare her students for their first personal narrative assignment. If she could get those out of the way, she'd be able to devote her attention to solving the Diego Acosta problem.

But she faced him rather quickly when she logged into her online class portal. His name was, of course, listed first in the student journal entries. She skipped him and saved his entry for last. Mickey read through, and graded, fifteen students before the portal made her round back to Diego's entry.

"Not right now," she muttered.

She would take a shower first.

Shower thinking proved useless because her mind immediately wandered back to Diego as the hot jets of water cascaded down her body. She imagined that the rivulets of water, tracing paths down the rolls of her belly, were actually Diego's fingers lightly massaging her skin. Her eyes sprang open once she pictured him on his knees before her. *Nope! We're not doing this today.* She finished up scrubbing her body as quickly as she could without lingering on any one part. Mickey was rather brisk with her lotion routine as well.

When she returned to her laptop, she had no choice but to grade Diego's work.

"Okay, Mr. Acosta... Let's see how much you hate my Food Studies course," she murmured as she pulled up his entry. But as she read his two-page response, much longer than the other students', a frown slowly creased her forehead.

...The steak was tough and dry, but I ate it because my mom tried her best. She was a terrible cook most of the time, but she always tried like hell to do something new. Unlike me, who has to be pushed. Mom was good at one thing, though: pasteles.

During most Christmases, she and my aunts got in the kitchen and made hundreds of pasteles. They were delicious, but they also offered an opportunity for me to see my family together. My earliest Christmas memory involves being in the kitchen with the women while the men played dominoes in my abuela's living room. Tía Elena argued for a new recipe, calling for roasted chicken instead of pork (she was going through a no-pork phase). Everyone ragged on her for it, but Abuela Chicki set aside a different pot for her and let her make a few dozen for her household. I got to help her, and that felt good.

I think my mom really valued those times, too. She was a single mother working hard in Chicago, and family made things better for us. I may not have grown up with a father, but I had plenty of tíos who had my back. I was in college for about a year when my mom got sick and I came home to care for her before finally dropping out. I didn't cook anything special, but when she had an appetite, she really liked my beef empanadas.

After she died, my family tried to surround me, but I don't think I let them in like I should have. Tía Rosa brought pasteles to the funeral, but when I ate one, it didn't taste right. I don't know… I moved to Georgia with my wife, Lucía. I got worse at keeping up with family after Lucía passed. I miss those times in the kitchen with the Acosta Clan, but I don't know how to come back to the fold. I feel like I've waited too long…

Mickey's fingers hovered over her keyboard, wondering what kinds of comments to give Diego, and came up empty. He'd basically emptied his heart onto the page and no comments would be useful. Most of her students were so bland with their journal entries that she could offer them an occasional *interesting!* This, however, needed a little more nuance.

"Okay," she said with a long breath. "These are the new facts—he dropped out of school to take care of his ailing mother. She died. And somewhere in the mix, he got married. His wife died, too."

Oh, god, what had she gotten mixed up in?

Diego, an older man with a painful past, who was full of grunts and growls, couldn't talk to her. He could kiss, but he couldn't talk. His communication lay in these journal entries.

Even as Mickey read the entry again, her heart sank further. Regardless of their heavy petting, Diego took her class seriously. He was still her student, and she was his professor.

Mickey shook out her hands and blew another heavy sigh. "Okay," she said, assuring herself to continue. "Make some comments."

She did her best, then she gave him the requisite ten points for his journal entry before closing the laptop. Mickey got up from her desk and threw herself on the bed. Christ... She had to see him again tonight, and she was no closer to figuring out how to approach him.

Her cell phone buzzed on her nightstand. She rolled over to grab it. Cleo.

"Hey, girl, what's up?"

"Just thought I'd call before your day got started," Cleo said in her efficient voice. She must have been on duty.

Mickey smiled. "Are you doing the ice cream thing today?"

"Yep, I'm at Ira's right now. We're just waiting on the news station and the *Ledger-Enquirer.* He's looking over flavors right now," Cleo said in a low voice. "What's a good flavor for a middle-aged mayoral candidate?"

"Butter Pecan," Mickey said immediately. "It's Southern, crosses the racial divide, and it's for old people. Gotta court the gray vote."

"That's why you need to work for him."

"I've got a job," Mickey reminded her friend.

"How did the first night go? Did you make good tips?"

"I did! And I—" Mickey stopped herself. Should she tell her bestie what really went down last night? "I've got a ways to go before I prove myself to my boss."

The pause on the other line made Mickey look at her phone's screen.

"Cleo? Did I lose you?"

"No, I'm still here," she said distractedly. "Hi? Yeah, we're going with two scoops of the Pecan Praline. Right, no, I don't want him to lick anything too complicated. Girl, don't pay that man any mind. You're going to crush the job. But you know..."

"Yes." Mickey waited for her friend's response.

"Just be careful with that..."

"Are you talking to me or Ira?"

"You," Cleo said. "If he's hot and grumpy *zaddy*-type, I need you to be cautious."

Mickey bit her lip and held her breath. Okay, then. Maybe she would keep last night's details to herself until she knew what was going on. "Sure."

"Good. I have to let you go, but before I do, I wanted to tell you how in your element you were last night. You looked cheerful as usual, which I don't get because waiting tables is awful, but you also looked good at it."

Mickey grinned. "Thanks, Cleo."

"Whatever job you do, you work your hardest, and I know your boss is going to catch on soon."

"I hope so," she said, blowing out a sigh. "Because this job is going to have to keep until the fall."

"No, Ira, I really cannot have you piling that cone any higher than that. Girl, I'm sorry..."

"You're fine," Mickey assured her friend. "I'll talk to you later, doll."

When she hung up, guilt gnawed at her belly. She'd have to return to work with a better plan. Diego Acosta was a complicated man. She'd need to handle him like any other student in her class: professional and distant, but ready to jump in when he might need her help.

Just remember his writing memory, Mickey.

Keep it in mind when you think you might want to kiss him again.

9

"Hey there!" a chipper voice called out.

When Diego stepped through the threshold of Fountain City Beans, he ignored the greeting from the young man behind the counter. He set his computer back at the nearest free table and made a beeline to the counter. "Large Americano," he said to the barista.

"Would you like to add a scone or a cupcake?" asked "Kevin," who offered a broad smile with the service.

"Nope," Diego replied as he slapped a five-dollar bill on the counter. "Keep the change," he said, walking back to his table.

The bell over the door jingled, pulling his attention just in time to see Mickey Chambers walk inside. He sucked in a deep breath as he watched her enter. Today, she wore a pair of denim cutoffs and a red-checkered top tied at her belly. She'd tied her thick curls back into a ponytail and wore a red kerchief. She looked like the cutest pinup girl in the entire state of Georgia. He stayed still in his chair, waiting for her to skip past him in favor of a table near the back. But there were no more free tables. He held his breath and tried to make himself invisible.

"Large Americano?" Kevin called.

Diego stifled a groan. He reluctantly left his table, making himself visible to Mickey. "Thanks," he muttered.

"Diego?"

When he turned to face her, he tried to purse his lips instead of struggling with a tense smile. Why wouldn't he want to smile at her? It couldn't hurt after the kiss they'd shared. No one had kissed him like that in a long time. No…she might misinterpret a smile. A smile could hint at the warm feeling that filled his belly when he looked at her for too long. Diego kept his face neutral. "Mickey."

Her eyes flitted to his drink. "Grabbing some coffee?"

He nodded and took a sip, immediately burning his tongue. Jesus… He trained his face into a placid expression despite the pain. "Yep," he rasped.

"I was hoping to get some work done here," she said, raising to her tiptoes to look at the packed space. Even with her platform sandals, she was still a short woman who could barely survey the building. "But I don't think there's any room…"

"You can sit with me," Diego said without thinking. As soon as the words flew out of his mouth, he bit his burned tongue and buried the whimper in his throat. "I mean, if you don't find an empty table."

Her dark sable eyes widened slightly as she hitched her laptop bag on her shoulder. "Oh," she breathed. "If you don't mind."

"I just offered, didn't I?" he said, clearing his throat. He went right back to the frown-and-pursed-lips combination he was so good at. "Do whatever you want," he added for good measure.

A sunny smile lit up her face. "Well, let me order something and I'll find you."

He took a deep breath through his nostrils and tried to

dismiss her smile. It didn't just light up her face; it illuminated the drab atmosphere of the coffee shop. Without confirmation, he stepped around her and went back to his table. While seated, he worked on looking busy and steadying the jiggle of his knee.

But Mickey's chatter lifted in the air, and the sounds found him. She laughed with Kevin about something as if they were old friends. Her light chuckles made him jealous. Surely, Kevin wasn't *that* interesting. To be fair, Diego didn't actually know. He rarely made small talk with anyone.

"And that's why you have to know your audience," she cried through her laughter. "God, you crack me up every time..."

"I'll bring out your latte, Mickey," Kevin said.

Diego kept his gaze focused on his screen, but he raised an eyebrow. *I'll bring out your latte?* He didn't get that offer. Was the kid getting fresh with her?

When she made her way to his table, she hung her bag on the chair and sat down. "What are you working on?" she asked, easing the anxiety Diego had had about who would speak first.

He looked up to see her beautiful smile, two dimples indenting her cheeks. His heart hammered in his chest. "I'm starting your next assignment."

"You're a busy bee," she said with a chuckle. "Don't let me interrupt you."

He grunted as he reached into his bag for his glasses case. Before he could get to work, he would need his glasses to see his too-close screen. As soon as he slipped them on his face, he heard a small gasp from the other side of the table. He glanced up to see Mickey biting her lush bottom lip. The small action made his heart gallop. "What?"

She shook her head. "Nothing. I just didn't know you wore glasses."

"You've only known me for two days," he said defensively.

"True," she said politely.

"I'm farsighted," he said.

"Okay."

"And sometimes I need them to read." He didn't know why he was explaining himself. They were glasses, so what? People wore glasses all the time. He wasn't a fan of them, but Lucía had made him get his eyes checked because he mixed up his gins and vodkas too often.

"They look nice," Mickey said, setting up her laptop. A small smile played on her lips, and it made his face warm.

He coughed and returned to his screen. "Thanks."

"Your almond-chocolate latte," Kevin said a moment later.

"Oooh, thank you so much!" she said with a smile. "Kevin, this is another one of my students, Diego Acosta."

Diego looked up in confusion.

"Aw, man, you're in Mickey's summer class?" Kevin said with an appraising nod. "I had her Comp 1 for the spring semester. I was going to try the summer class, but I need to work."

Diego looked at the boy who appeared to be no older than twenty and immediately felt embarrassed. "Yeah, well, I know what that's like."

"You're going to have a great time in Mickey's class. Our class learned about American anxiety through these *Twilight Zone* episodes," Kevin continued. "We got to watch them in class and then talk about them. I wrote my final paper on xenophobia."

"I'm doing a food studies theme for the summer students," Mickey said, blowing on her coffee.

"Really? Are you going to do it again in the fall?"

"It really depends on what the department has available for

me," she said with a shrug. He noticed that her smile dipped slightly as she glanced away.

"You're so lucky to have Mickey," Kevin told Diego. He didn't know how to take the comment. He mostly felt uneasy.

"Yeah," he said with a nod.

"Take it easy, Mickey," Kevin said, backing away. "And nice to meet you, Diego."

"Yeah," Diego repeated.

Back to the silence.

Somehow, even *that* made Diego anxious. The quiet set his nerves on edge. He suddenly wanted Mickey to talk to him. He wasn't sure if he could add anything meaningful to their conversation, but he needed her to fill the silence. Especially after last night's kiss. He was open to sweeping everything under the rug and listening to her prattle on about anything but how hot the moment felt.

"Kevin's a good kid," she said.

Diego let out a deep breath through his nose and waited for her to continue.

"And a brilliant student," Mickey added. "That class was so much fun."

"Anxiety?" he asked.

She shot him an impish grin. "*American* anxiety," she said with a giggle. "Oh, my god, how I scared them."

"You enjoy scaring your students," he said, but was secretly curious about her humor. He wanted to know more about what an actual classroom experience was like with Professor Chambers.

"Oh, pssh." She waved her hand in response. "You saw how young Kevin was. His generation understands anxiety, but they don't get it in the same way we do."

"We do?" he almost whispered. It was as if they shared a secret…of age and experience.

"All of my students are so young," she said. "They kind of have a flat historical landscape. To them, troubles with Russia and China are new. Obama should have solved racism and all that nonsense. So when I lay it out for them, they understand why they feel so nervous about the economy and frustrated with their parents."

"He said that you had them watch *The Twilight Zone*," he said. "What did that teach them?"

She leaned forward, excited to explain her course to him. He was excited to let her talk. "I assigned them the timeless episodes. I know most of them are about the Cold War, but they loved my favorite episode, 'The Monsters Are Due on Maple Street.' Have you seen it?"

Diego shook his head. "I don't remember."

"It stars the guy from *Gunsmoke*," she said.

Without thinking, Diego laughed. Not a full belly laugh, but a snort that even caught him off guard. "What do you know about *Gunsmoke*?"

She smiled with pride. "I watched a lot of television when I was a kid."

"I don't know how I feel about my professor being a TV addict," he said sarcastically.

"You'd be surprised at how much you can learn from TV," she said. "If I hadn't watched *The Twilight Zone*, I wouldn't have been able to make this class."

"Tell me about 'The Monsters on Maple Street,'" he said.

"Well, it's like Any Street, USA. Everyone knows everyone, and they're all friendly neighbors until—" Mickey leaned forward with large expressive eyes "—the power goes out and the whole street starts to question who belongs to Maple Street and who's the interloper."

Diego leaned forward, waiting for her to reveal the end. "So?"

"You should watch the episode," she said with a broad grin. "I don't want to spoil the ending."

"Okay, so they learn the Russians are hiding amongst them?"

Mickey chuckled. "Metaphorically, yes. But that's what our parents learned," she corrected. "*They're* learning that in any American crisis, fear can cloud good judgment, and in the end, we're more likely to take care of our own before seeing after our neighbor. Now, I could have let them watch *The Purge*, but I don't think they would get the same message."

"Maybe," he said, sitting back. "What kinds of journal entries did you assign?"

She laughed again. "Oh, my god, I really freaked them out with the Last Fifteen Minutes exercise."

"Do I want to ask?"

"I wanted them to write about what they'd do in their last fifteen minutes on Earth."

Diego frowned.

"The time it takes for North Korea to send a missile over to Hawaii." She grinned.

"Jesus." Diego winced, feeling for her young students. "That's a bit much."

She shrugged. "Maybe, but it's also reality. They're living through a new Cold War, and these issues need to be written about. I'm adamant about my students confronting the truth of the world and recording them."

Diego processed her answer before asking, "What kinds of responses did you get?"

"I got a lot of drug use and drinking," she laughed. "No surprises there."

"What would you do?" he asked quickly.

"I'd probably get wasted, too. You?"

Diego arched his brow. "No one said that they'd be fucking?"

Her eyes widened as she slapped her hand against her mouth.

Fuck… He should not have said that. It was a completely crass and inappropriate thing to say to his professor. "Sorry," he said.

Mickey shook her head and waved a dismissing hand. "No, you're fine." She busied herself with a sip of her latte as Diego internally kicked himself. "No one shared that with the class, but yes, it definitely makes sense."

He should stop talking for a while…

"I mean, if it's the end of the world, why not get all the pleasure you can?" she said, wiping foam from her lip. Even that simple movement made his heart race. Or maybe it was her words? Was she agreeing with him? "Anyway, that's what I usually teach."

"I'm impressed," Diego admitted. "You put a lot of creativity into your classes. I just thought I'd be learning how to put a sentence together or something."

Her smile dipped slightly as she glanced away from him. "Yeah," she sighed heavily before resting her chin on her fist. "Sometimes I wonder if I put a little too much work into these classes for the money I make."

The way her shoulders slouched as she spoke made him sit up and pay attention. "What do you mean?"

Her smile returned as she waved a dismissing hand. "Oh, nothing, I shouldn't talk to students about this. Anyway, I'm sure I'm not the only one teaching you," she said, switching subjects. "What are you majoring in, Diego?"

He was willing to follow her to the next topic, but Diego was still curious about Mickey's teaching. "Business Management."

Her brow wrinkled in the middle. "Really? Why?"

"I, uh…well, because I think I need it," he stammered. "I'm a business owner."

"Sure," she said, taking another sip. "But I thought for sure you'd be in the humanities. You're a good writer."

Diego didn't realize how badly he needed a compliment. "You think so?" he said with hesitance. "Like, I might pass your class?"

She laughed. "Don't worry about passing, just enjoy the process."

"I worry about passing," Diego admitted.

"You seem like you worry about a lot of things."

He did. He woke up that morning with the usual Saloon anxiety, and then when he remembered how passionately he'd kissed his employee, he barely wanted to leave his bed. "I haven't done school in a long time."

"How long has it been?"

He shook his head. "Years. I dropped out when my mom got sick. Life kept happening after she died."

Mickey nodded, but said nothing. He wondered if he should say more…

"My wife, Lucía, died about five years ago, this past April. Breast cancer." He averted his gaze. "Anyway, Lucía wanted me to go back to college. She said something like… I'd spent so many years *in stasis*. She was really perceptive like that. So, here I am," he said, gesturing at his computer. "Starting from the very bottom. Older than everyone else, trying to do college."

When he finished, he gained the courage to look at her. To his surprise, Mickey's expression wasn't pitying in the way women look when they hear about dead wives. He'd seen that expression more than he had cared to and didn't need anyone's pity. Instead, her back was straight, her dark gaze piercing and her smile broad. "Gotcha," she said with a resolute nod.

Gotcha?

"First, your age shouldn't be something to worry over," she said, letting her eyes roam over his face and body. The way her lips curled as she stared made him hot beneath his shirt. "Non-traditional students bring so many skills to the classroom—I should know."

"Like knowing about *Gunsmoke*?" he asked.

"Exactly, my pop culture references won't be wasted on you," she laughed. "But more importantly, you have more experience than they do. And that's going to help you when you need to solve problems. It's called crystallized intelligence, and you have it. Second, you've already got a business. When you take those classes, you're going to run into young students who only have a theoretical understanding of running a company."

Diego hadn't thought about it like that.

"Try to have fun while you're taking your prerequisites," Mickey said. "You never know where they might lead you. You might find out you're really a history buff."

"Maybe..." When Diego had thumbed through the Hargrove University course catalog, he skipped past everything and went to Business Management. He hadn't seen any sense in wasting the remainder of Lucía's life insurance money on Art History...even though he really enjoyed art. He was secretly relieved that one of his prereqs would be an art survey course.

"You'll see," Mickey said with another nod. "You might not enjoy trying new things, but this is your second shot, Diego."

Every time she said his name, a shiver of pleasure whipped through his body. But how did she know he hated trying new things?

"Your journal entry," she answered, sensing his confusion. "When you wrote about your mother in the kitchen, you mentioned it. Although, I think I picked that up from working beside you yesterday."

He didn't know what to say.

When he opened his online class portal, he read her comments on his work, and blushed. She called his memory "delightful" and said that "there's always time to bring pasteles back into your life." He glanced up to see her typing rapidly and taking quick sips of her coffee. He wanted to thank her for her encouraging words but didn't know how.

So, he followed her lead and went to work. They could talk later if he ever got the nerve to open his mouth.

10

When Mickey found a good place to pause her work, she closed her laptop and stretched her stiff muscles. Diego glanced up at her as if waiting for her to say something. "How's it going over there?" she asked.

"Fine." He looked back at his screen. "I finished another journal entry for the class."

"Ooh, would you like me to read it now?"

"No!" he snapped. His face went red as he looked around the coffee shop. "I mean, you can read it when you grade everyone else's work."

Mickey recognized the tension in his face and neck. Diego was still really nervous about being in her class, being in college altogether. After he explained how he'd promised his wife to return to school, her heart broke for him. She wished she knew the woman who encouraged him to smile, who pushed him to get those adorable wire-rimmed glasses that kept sliding down his nose. "No problem," she said easily. "I look forward to reading it later."

The tension in his shoulders relaxed a little as he hunched

forward. "Thanks. It's just… I might want to edit it again. I don't want to send you a mistake."

"It's a journal entry," Mickey said with a smile. "They're low stakes."

He grunted.

We're back to that…

He checked his watch. "We're going to have to get to work soon."

"I guess so," Mickey replied, suddenly reminded of last night's kiss. She was a little worried that he hadn't brought it up. She was still struggling to say, "I'm so sorry for diving onto your face, *twice*, while screaming at you about decorum." Mickey wondered if he was being polite or if the kiss meant nothing to him. Somehow, the latter hurt her feelings.

"I have to ask you something…as your employer," he said in a low voice.

Her gaze flew to his face. *Oh, god, this was it. He was firing her.* "Okay."

"Jeanie's mother is recovering from surgery. She's doing well, but she definitely can't be active right now. And Jeanie won't leave her side. Not that I blame her…but she's not coming back until her mom's out of the hospital and she finds a home health-care worker."

"Oh," she breathed, relieved Jeanie's mother was out of the woods. "Okay?"

Diego rubbed his cheek and blew out a sigh. "Irene always has the floor covered…" He hesitated before adding, "But I'm going to need help behind the bar."

Mickey waited for more information, but he looked like he was struggling to find his words. Was he asking her for help? Was that why he looked like he was going to explode? She watched as he pushed his glasses up the bridge of his straight nose before impatiently tapping on the table. "Yes?" she said, urging him to say more.

"So, you'll do it?"

Mickey frowned. "Do what now?"

Diego returned her frown. "You'll be my bar partner."

"Did you ask me or did you just assume I knew what you were talking about?"

"I think I asked."

Mickey tried not to let this bother her, but the man really had a problem with expressing himself. He was definitely a better writer than this. "That really depends, Diego. Are you going to behave yourself behind the bar?"

The crease between his brows deepened. "Behave myself? I was training you last night."

"You were a little mean," she said in a tight voice.

"That's how I teach people."

"Then I don't think I want to help you," she said, throwing up her hands. "I'll stick with Irene, and we'll help you from the floor."

Diego let out an exasperated sigh. "You can't."

"Why not? That's what you hired me for."

"Jeanie hired you."

"Well, maybe we should call her," Mickey challenged.

"I own the damn Saloon," he growled.

She leaned back and crossed her arms over her chest. "Of all the people to help you, why not Irene? She's been here longer. Or what about a barback like Ramón or Ollie?"

Diego clenched his jaw as he stared her down. "If I can hire another server, Irene will need to train them. And now that I have two barbacks, I'm not splitting them up. I need the cleaning and basement operations to work smoothly."

"And?"

"And what?"

Mickey gestured to herself. "And is there anything about me that would be helpful to your cause?"

He took a deep breath as his eyes left hers and roved over her body. Goose bumps sprang up on her arms as she followed his eyes. "You're…friendly," he finally said.

"And?"

"And customers seem to like that."

It was as if he'd *just* learned about being nice to patrons. "Anything else?" she asked, knowing that she was pushing it. After all, she couldn't pull a pint that measured up to his standards. She probably talked to the customers too much as it was. And she was still slow on the register. But Diego Acosta wasn't the only person at the table who appreciated a kind word. She noticed the brightness in his eyes when she spoke about his work.

"You're a good kisser, Professor Chambers," Diego said. "But I don't think that will help the customers."

Mickey's mouth fell open, but nothing came out.

"She's finally speechless," he murmured with an arched brow. "I really thought you'd be the first to address the elephant in the room."

"I was angry with you," she blurted out.

"If that's what anger looks like…"

Mickey squeezed her eyes shut and shook her head. "I'm sorry that I did it and it won't happen again," she said. "I don't want to talk about it."

Diego pursed his lips. "How do I know you won't get angry again? I don't exactly have an HR department to report you to."

Mickey's face was on fire. Diego could barely speak when it came to the bar, but when it came to embarrassing her, he was a regular stand-up comic. "I'm usually very good at controlling my temper," she said evenly. "But you were being more than a little obstinate last night. If you're going to keep being a bossy grump, I don't know how I'll react."

He went silent for a moment, his face unreadable. But then his eyes crinkled at the corners as he smirked. "With another kiss?" he asked.

"That's not what I meant," she muttered under her breath.

"Do you find yourself trying to control your temper often?"

"I rarely get angry," she said, puzzled by the question.

Diego frowned. "Rarely? So, you just walk around with that pretty smile plastered on your face all the time?"

Pretty smile? She tried not to linger on the backhanded compliment, but it was a weird snag in his usual gruff nature. "I don't have a lot to be angry about."

She felt very warm under his gaze. In the low lights of the room, she noticed all the things about Diego that made her fling herself onto him. The shine of his black hair and streaks of gray, the light dusting of stubble along his strong jaw, stopping just at his powerful neck. He wore another T-shirt this evening: navy blue V-neck, giving her a small peek at his honey-tanned chest.

"Here's what we'll do—I'll put you behind the bar, and I'll train you right. You're free to correct me any time I step on your toes. But you'll stay there right next to me."

Mickey narrowed her eyes at him. "You won't make me pour the same pint six times to prove a point?"

"Well, shit, if you're not pulling it right, I'm gonna say something."

"You could say it nicer."

He rolled his eyes. "Fine."

"Okay."

Diego drummed his long sturdy fingers against the tabletop again. "Just a reminder—we've got the Riverwalk Blues

Festival next weekend. Jeanie won't be here, so I need you to be on the ball."

Mickey grew excited at the thought of being in the middle of the music festival. Last year, she missed it because she was presenting at a composition conference in Atlanta. There were a couple local Georgia bands she wanted to see live. "I can't wait!"

He shook his head. "Nope, you're going to be working that weekend, and harder than you've ever worked. The bar crawling is going to be out of control. More drunks wandering in than usual."

"And you really think I can help?"

"I know you can," he said in a resolute tone. "So long as you don't get angry."

He was teasing her.

"About that," he continued, slipping his glasses from his face. "Aside from anger, what drove you to do it?"

She would rather the floor open up and swallow her whole before answering his question. She did it because they were in a small stuffy office, and the way he stared at her as she chewed him out turned her on. Diego Acosta was undeniably hot, but she wasn't ready to tell him that to his face. "Because I wanted to," she said defiantly.

With his elbows on the table, he leaned closer to her. A broad smile stretched across his face, revealing a row of perfect white teeth. His playful Cheshire grin made her stomach dip as she squeezed her thighs together. "Maybe you don't mind my firm hand behind the bar," he said, tilting his head to regard her.

She exhaled as quietly as she could, trying not to think of his firm hands. "You don't have to worry about it happening again," she said in a strong voice. Even if he was being a bit of a dick, she didn't take her new responsibilities lightly.

Being promoted to bartender was a big deal and Mickey didn't want to mess that up.

He arched a brow as he packed up his computer. "If you say so, Professor."

Mickey bit the inside of her cheek to keep from snapping on him. Because that would make her sound *huffy*, wouldn't it? "You're safe from my lips," she said in her haughtiest voice.

Diego scoffed rudely before his gaze returned to her. "And is that what you're wearing tonight?"

"It is," she said cautiously. "Why?"

"You look pretty," he said lightly. "You'll probably make more tips than me."

Mickey's face burned. "You'd make better tips if you smiled at the ladies."

Diego shrugged. "Jeanie's already told me as much. But I'm not a smiler."

"Then I guess I'm your most valuable asset," she said confidently.

One corner of his mouth turned upward into a lopsided smile. "I guess you are."

"How was your first day of being a barback, Ollie?" Mickey asked while chopping limes in the kitchen.

Behind her, Ollie hoisted a rack of freshly dried glasses onto an empty counter before loading the next batch into the washer. "Surprisingly well," she said with a chuckle. "Ramón's great to work with. He kinda let me have the run of the basement, taking stock and keg work."

"Where did you learn all of that stuff?" Mickey asked as she filled the lime container. "Have you worked at a bar before?"

"Just one other, when I lived in Indianapolis."

"Ahh, okay. I knew you didn't sound like a Southerner."

"Born and raised in Indiana," she said, leaning beside Mickey.

Mickey was about to get started on another lime, but she took a moment to look at Ollie, who lounged gracefully against the counter with her hands in her low-slung jeans. Tonight, her purple hair was swept back in a short topknot, revealing black gauge piercings in both ears. They were dime-sized in diameter and added to her overall badass appearance. "What on earth brought you to Columbus?" she asked.

"You want the long story or the short?" Ollie asked with a grin. Her maroon lipstick was a fierce slash across her pale face, matching her smoky eye makeup.

"I always like a long story," Mickey said, starting on the next lime. "Diego put me on garnish duty, so please regale me with a tale."

Ollie laughed. "Fair enough."

"Out with it," Mickey urged. "What's an Indiana kid doing in Georgia?"

"I was Amish, or I am Amish," she said with a frown. "I still don't know what to call myself, I guess. Anyway, I grew up in the Amish community in Goshen, Indiana, and I left home during Rumspringa."

Mickey nodded. "I've read about that. You get a little release before you get baptized, right?"

"Right," Ollie said, her mouth curving into a grim smile. "I had plans to leave before Rumspringa, though. I met a girl from town who went to the local high school..." Ollie faltered in her storytelling.

Mickey gave her an encouraging nudge with her shoulder. "Yeah?"

"I had a crush on her, or I was in love with her. I don't know. Maybe I was exploring stuff I couldn't really name. I just knew I couldn't name it out loud in front of my family. So, I just left. I went to Indianapolis and stayed there with a group of ex-Amish kids who'd already set up shop. I lived with them for a few years—" she took a breath "—and then I came down here last year to be with a girl I met online. She was really cool, but I don't think I was ready to be in a real-life grown-up relationship."

"What was she like?" Mickey asked.

"Fort Benning girl, super confident and badass." Ollie dipped her head and bit back a grin.

Mickey chuckled. And here she thought Ollie was the badass. As she gazed at the tall, slender girl before her, Mickey realized how young she was. Beneath the black rings of eye makeup was a girl who was barely twenty-five. "Do you miss your family?" she asked in a soft voice. Regardless of how her people felt about her sexual orientation, Ollie still probably felt the pain of separation.

"I do..." she said carefully, her voice dipping lower as if she were sharing a secret. "But I still communicate with one of my little sisters."

Mickey's eyes widened. "Really?"

Ollie's mouth turned up into a half smile. "I send emails to the girl from high school and Rebecca gets back to me."

Mickey couldn't help taking Ollie by the hand as her own heart swelled. The young woman blushed as they stood there holding hands. "I'm glad to hear it," Mickey whispered. "It's always nice to get a letter from home."

Ollie squeezed her hand. "Yeah," she said, averting her eyes. Her face turned toward the dishwasher. It beeped, letting her know that the next drying cycle would start. "But this is better for me."

Mickey released her hand and patted her back. "Yeah?"

Ollie moved away from the counter and started the next tray of glasses. "My family could have never stopped my curiosity," she admitted. "So even though I had a late start to life, I'm glad I took the first step."

Mickey knew all about late starts, and she'd also taught more than a few students who'd struggled to find their identities. They would enter her class, wary of expressing themselves, but by the time they left, their confidence was inspiring. "Better late than never, Ollie."

"Better late than never to give me these glasses?" Irene said, standing at the doorway with a grin. "Yoder, if you're in here jerking around…"

"You'll get your glasses, Cho," Ollie said with a raised brow. "Try not to drop any more?"

Mickey looked between the two women. Tiny Irene flipped one of her pigtails over her shoulder and narrowed her eyes. "You're still giving me shit about yesterday?"

"You like it when I give you shit," Ollie said with a wink.

Irene's face reddened. "Shut up."

"I know you didn't come in here to bitch about glasses," Ollie replied. "What do you need?"

Irene rolled her eyes and turned to Mickey, who was trying hard not to spy on their flirting. "Boss man wants to see you at the bar."

Even as she nodded, Mickey felt her heart tumble about in her chest. She quickly gathered her lime wedges. "Is it busy out there?" she asked, her voice trembling slightly.

"There's a blind date at a two-top. It's going awkwardly," Irene said with a chuckle.

"Okay," Mickey said.

Irene must have noticed her pensive expression because her eyes softened as she offered a smile. "Diego just wants to get you prepped for the evening."

Mickey exhaled a shaky breath. While she was happy to get "the kiss" out of the way, she was still nervous about working alongside him. "You're probably right."

"He's a grumpy son of a bitch because he worries about

every little thing," Irene added. "He was always a worrier, but it wasn't this bad when Lucía was running the place. Back then, he kinda hid in his office and dealt with accounting and inventory."

That information was as useful as it was heartbreaking. Based on his journal entry, Diego was still hurting from the loss of his wife. And if she were to guess, he conflated Lucía's death with his mother's. Mickey couldn't imagine experiencing that kind of loss in one lifetime. She was so close to her own mother—the thought of her getting sick made her eyes tear up. "I would imagine," she said.

"But if you stick it out longer than our last new girl, I think he'll come around to you," Irene said. "Or you could just be like me—when he gives you shit, you have to give it right back."

Mickey gave her a tremulous smile and nodded. "Sure."

"Good luck!" Ollie said, pulling another rack out of the dryer.

She'd need it.

11

Be nice.

Be polite.

Just pretend she's Jeanie.

She's your old friend, whom you've never kissed.

Diego watched Mickey fill the garnish box with new limes while steadying his breathing. If she peeked over her shoulder and caught him staring at her, she'd probably be shocked. So, he stopped, because it was getting ridiculous. This wasn't the coffee shop, where his anxiety limited him from being direct with her.

He needed to suck it up and put on his boss hat. A slightly politer version of his usual boss behavior… "Mickey," he began, "I want you to work on these before tonight's rush." He pulled a set of laminated cards from his back pocket and handed them to her.

"An assignment?" she said, with that familiar look of excitement in her eyes.

"If that helps you," he said.

Mickey flipped through the cards. "These are drink flash cards," she said brightly. "Who made these? They're lovely!"

"My wife made them," he said gruffly. Diego rubbed the back of his neck as he stared at the cards in her grasp. He hadn't wanted to hand them over to her, but they were the only things that helped him when he started working alongside Lucía.

"Some of these are specialty cocktails," she murmured, examining each card. "Did she invent these? Do you ever serve the El Torro or the Gaucho Juice?"

She was veering them off course with her excitement, and Diego's irritation spiked with each question. "I don't," he said stiffly.

"You know what you should do?" she asked, tapping the stack of cards against her open hand. "You should turn these into a book! Wouldn't it be nice to have a Saloon-based cocktail guide for customers? It's a part of your wife's legacy that's so much more meaningful than Cuervo shots, right?"

"You don't know anything about Lucía," he snapped, his patience hanging by a thread.

Mickey's eyes widened as she stopped fiddling with the recipe cards. When she held them close to her chest, next to her heart, in a protective gesture, Diego felt like an animal for lashing out. "I'm sorry," she said in a low voice. "You're right, I don't."

Diego took a deep breath through his nose. If Mickey *had* known Lucía, she would have been correct. Make a little book, serving her customers her special Mexican drinks, ones she'd spent her evenings concocting… Yeah, Lucía would have done all of that. "You're fine," he said with a sigh. "Don't apologize. Just make me a drink."

Mickey's face softened. "Which one? Can I make an El Gato Negro?"

He shook his head. "No, you need a pot of coffee for that one.

Let's start with something recognizable. Make me a Cosmopolitan."

"Bit of a girlie drink, don't you think?" she asked with a laugh.

"You've got five minutes," he said, glancing at his watch.

"Seriously?"

"Four minutes, fifty-eight seconds."

Mickey pursed her lips and read through the card. "Where's the triple sec?"

"On the shelf, behind you."

She spun on her heel and sought the ingredients. "Should I use well vodka?"

"I'd rather you not," he said to his watch.

"Grey Goose?"

"Better."

Mickey bent to find a shaker and shoveled far too much ice into it. "Oh, shit," she muttered, rereading the card. "Ice goes last." She dumped her ice in the sink and started over, carefully measuring the vodka, triple sec and cranberry juice. A little too carefully.

"Four minutes, nine seconds."

She eventually dumped them in the shaker. But paused. "I need fresh lime juice?"

"Preferably."

She sighed. "I need a whole lime and they're in the kitchen."

"Clock is ticking," he said as she ran away.

"Comin' in hot!" she shouted to Ramón, who passed her on his way to the front.

While he and his brother-in-law waited for her to return to the bar, Ramón gave him a look.

"It's training," Diego said in a clipped tone.

"Be nice," Ramón said. "We need her for more than a week."

"Got it!" she cried.

Back behind the bar, Mickey quickly rolled her lime on a cutting board before slicing it in half. Her technique impressed Diego. "Three minutes, two seconds."

Mickey squeezed like her life depended on it. He almost forgot to monitor the watch. Staring at her using a firm hand on the lime was shockingly arousing. He wondered what those soft hands could do wrapped around his dick.

Fuck...

And it didn't get much better. Once Mickey added her ice, she closed the lid on her shaker and vigorously shook for what was supposed to be thirty seconds according to Lucía's instructions. It would be the slowest thirty seconds he'd ever experienced. Her full breasts bounced with every shake, steering his attention away from being a taskmaster.

Fuck.

When she finished, Diego eventually tore his eyes from her and returned to his watch. He didn't know how much time had passed, but for her sake, he added a few seconds to the clock.

"I need a martini glass," she muttered.

Ramón was right behind her with one. "Here you go."

"No helping, Ramón."

"Thank you," she said, pouring the cocktail to the rim. She set the shaker down on the bar and stepped away with her hands in the air, like this was a reality cooking competition. "I'm done!"

He stepped forward and inspected the drink. "Are you sure?"

A flash of anxiety marred her features as she glanced at the recipe card again. When she spotted her mistake, she scrunched her face in the most adorable way. "Shit."

"Time's up."

"I didn't garnish it," she said with disappointment.

"You did not," he said.

Ramón chuckled. "People don't care about the garnish," he told her. He turned to Diego with another silent warning. "Neither does Diego."

Diego returned Ramón's warning with a glare. "Do you need something?"

"Just wanted to see if Ollie got enough glasses for you."

"She's taken care of everything up here."

Ramón rolled his eyes as he wandered off. What his brother-in-law didn't know was that while Diego *wanted* to be nice, he also wanted to avoid all the things that came with his kindness. At that moment, he wanted nothing more than to run his thumb along Mickey's cheek and over her lower lip until she lashed it with her tongue. He certainly didn't want to admit to Lucía's *brother* that the new server made him hot with desire. It was too disturbing to admit to himself.

She looked up at him with a defeated expression. "I messed up," she said.

"You didn't pay attention."

The corners of her mouth dipped downward as she turned her gaze to what he was certain was a perfectly fine Cosmopolitan. "You're going to dump it down the sink, aren't you?"

"Not with that amount of Grey Goose."

"You'll taste it?" she asked, her face lighting up with hope. He almost hated how expressive she was. Every emotion flitted across her face, informing him of every misstep he made with her. Diego wanted to see more of her lovely smile, but he didn't want to be the one who encouraged it.

"I'll taste it," he said, wishing she could drink it and that he could taste it from *her* tongue. *Jesus Christ.* He busied his own mouth with a sip before he could say something foolish. It tasted like a Cosmo, not his preferred drink, but it was perfectly fine. "It's good."

Her beaming smile unfurled something in his chest.

"But it could use a citrus garnish on the rim," he quickly added.

She deflated only a little.

"Would you like to try?" he offered.

She shook her head. "Too frilly for me. I like my spirits to be straight with me, not dressed up to impress me."

The comment rocked Diego harder than he anticipated. He refused to think too hard about it, but the way Mickey gazed at him with her dark bold eyes made him wonder if she meant something more. "I'm assuming your end-of-the-night drink won't be a cocktail, then?"

Mickey shook her head. "I'll probably have a whiskey and soda tonight."

His preferred drink.

He finished the rest of her cocktail in two gulps. This was going to be another long night, he decided as he washed out her glass. "Why don't you get started on an Old-Fashioned."

"Five minutes?" she asked hesitantly.

Diego shook his head. If he had to watch her make more drinks, he wouldn't be fit to work the rest of the evening. "You're off the clock, Professor. Take your time."

Army rangers were laying siege to their bar.

Mickey had to put a pin in her cocktail training in favor of straight spirits and beer. With Diego at her side, they took care of the first wave of soldiers who were taking a quick R & R from ranger training at Fort Benning. The second wave proved to be a little more challenging. She couldn't fill beer nor could she start tabs fast enough. Some people paid with cash, which was easy enough, but Mickey got flustered quickly.

"Gin and Tonic," said a tall blond man. The noise level was incredible as the jukebox blared some '80s tune she couldn't afford to focus on. A Gin and Tonic was easy enough, but she also had to pour a beer for the last guy. She made both drinks at the same time.

That was a mistake.

As the beer filled with foam, she eyeballed the pour of her gin directly into another glass. Well gin splashed haphazardly, a bit more than the shot a jigger would measure. While she let the foamy beer settle, she squirted tonic into the blond man's drink and set it before him. "That's four dollars. Would you like to start a tab?" she asked, silently praying he wouldn't.

"Yeah, sure," he said, handing over his credit card.

Mickey buried her groan. While holding the man's credit card she filled the rest of the last customer's beer to the brim and set it before him. "That's three dollars. Would you like to start a tab?"

"Yeah."

Jesus Christ.

She wasn't the best at the cash register, so she'd have to take her time. She juggled two cards, making certain that they belonged to the right owner. Blond guy was Matthew, the other guy was Harry. Four dollars, mixed drink, three dollars, IPA. As she stood over the register, her brain fought to keep the details straight. She didn't know how long she stood there, but after a while, Mickey felt the warmth of someone standing behind her.

"Breathe," Diego said, his voice cutting through the confusing cacophony. "Slow down and take care of one thing at a time."

"I am," she breathed.

"And I don't ever want to see you make two drinks at the same time again," he said in a low voice.

She couldn't bear to look at him. Mickey knew she'd tried to cut corners more than a few times. She'd just hoped that he hadn't noticed. Mickey was on the verge of tears, anxious about her failures amid the pandemonium. Diego had warned her of this madness, and this wasn't even as wild as the upcoming blues festival. The register screen blurred as she sniffed away her tears.

"Nope, you're not gonna start crying," she heard him say. She was still afraid to look at him, knowing she'd only see disappointment on his stern face. "There's no crying in bartending."

"I'm not crying," she said, dabbing her eyes with the back of her arm.

"Pick your shit up, Professor, put on that pretty smile and keep serving the boys." Suddenly, she felt a warm large hand on her back, rubbing small circles. Mickey sniffed again and picked her head up. If she weren't so distressed, she would have leaned against his touch. But Diego only offered his warmth as a quick pick-me-up. Something to get her head back in the game. Nothing more. "One thing at a time," he reminded her.

Okay. Harry's IPA went first. Mickey printed out a receipt and jotted his name on it before wrapping it around his card. Then Matthew's mixed drink. As soon as she stepped away from the register, Diego took her place, ringing up his own customer. Her eyes cleared up, and she pinned a smile on her face just as she was told. Her chest shuddered at the near meltdown she'd experienced.

"How can I help you?" she asked the next customer.

The man who stood at the bar was almost a foot taller than Diego and twice as broad. His dark hair was army-issued buzzed and his green eyes hooded as he stared down at her. "Hey, honey," he said in a silky voice. His eyes shone in a devilish drunken haze as he looked her over.

Great, he's already been drinking. "What can I help you with?"

He leaned closer. "You're so fuckin' hot..." he murmured. "How's 'bout you help me with a phone number?"

Diego had warned her about this. "I can help you with a drink," Mickey said.

Green Eyes gave a lazy smile and flexed his muscles through a tight white T-shirt. "Aww...that ain't fun, sugar."

This interaction was different from last night's table of "business bros." They were drunk, a little rowdy, but respectful. This man was *predatory*. She opened her mouth to reply but didn't get the chance to speak because Diego was at her shoulder.

"It's kinda hard to have fun when she's working right next to her boyfriend," he said, pulling a beer. He leaned down to give her a quick peck on her cheek before delivering a fresh beer to his own customer.

Before she could confirm or deny the lie, Green Eyes blinked in embarrassment. "Dude, I'm sorry," he said to Diego. "I didn't know."

Where was her apology?

"No worries," Diego said in a light tone. "What can we get you?"

"Uh...yeah, I'll take a Corona, and maybe you can put on the Braves game?" The man's bravado had worn off by now, and he turned, shamefaced. While Diego searched the cable channels for baseball, Mickey grabbed his beer, popped the top and handed it to him. He left a five-dollar bill and took his leave. Fantastic. A two-dollar tip for sexual harassment.

Mickey took a few more customers, made Irene's drinks and wiped the bar while a quiet fury brewed in her chest. Only when the second wave died down and the rangers were enjoying themselves did Mickey feel like she could take a deep breath.

"You okay?" Diego said, pulling her out of her head. He leaned against the bar, staring at her with a searching gaze. "Do you need a break?"

She shook her head, still too angry to speak. Yes, she probably did need a break to rest her feet and back. Her entire body felt like it was drenched in sweat and her heart raced under the constant stress. She had no doubt that her hyperthyroidism was the culprit and could imagine how angry her parents would be if they saw her in this condition. But she stayed where she was. She had a job to do and wanted to feel in control of herself behind the bar.

"You look upset."

"I'm fine," she muttered, twisting her towel in knots.

When he laid a comforting hand on her back, Mickey let out another deep breath. Aching tension unfurled in her chest and dissipated when he touched her. "Don't look at the jukebox, but the big guy is still making eyes at you," he said in her ear.

She kept her eyes on the bar, pretending to take an inventory of their spirits. "Thank you for that, by the way."

His hand slid to the small of her back as she tipped bottles to read their labels. "I've been everyone's boyfriend here at one time or another. Jeanie gets a lot of attention, but she's pretty good at holding her own." Diego's words were low and deliberate. "If you feel okay to stand on your own, just lemme know when to back off."

"Is he still watching?" she asked.

"Intently," Diego said. "If he's thinking about trying again, I'll ask Stevie or Jerry to get him out of here."

"He was a little extra," she said, taking care not to lean against the warmth he offered her. Diego was very good at playing the fake boyfriend, so good she almost believed in the gentle strokes along her back. Pleasure radiated from the pressure of his palm, spreading to the rest of her body and making her knees weak.

"You're very hot, Professor."

"Thank you," she breathed, "but you don't have to call me that."

"I mean, you're burning up," he said. "Are you sure you're okay?"

Oh, my god…

"I should drink some water," she said quickly, hoping that she didn't sound like a complete weirdo. How had she possibly misinterpreted his words? It was one thing for her boss to stand guard against an aggressive customer, but a whole other thing for him to call her *hot*.

"I've got it," Diego said. Before she could lift a finger, he began shoveling ice into a plastic cup. "You need to stay hydrated throughout the night."

She didn't want to tell him, but Mickey tended to overheat because of her thyroid condition. She'd taken her medication that morning, but she still needed to watch how she exerted herself. Standing on her feet in this stifling hot bar wasn't the best idea, but she noticed how cranky and tired she felt once he suggested water.

"Drink."

Mickey took the cup from him and drank deeply. "Thank you," she said, feeling refreshed from the cold liquid on her tongue, but missing the heat of his hand.

"Now put on that pretty smile," he said, moving on to the latest customer. "We can't have two grumps behind the bar."

12

Diego's luck was changing.

The Newest Girl title now belonged to Gina Perry, a graduate student from Hargrove who needed a job during the summer break. She was a quiet girl who mentioned something about being a chemist.

He nodded along as she explained how she waited tables at a restaurant in Atlanta. She could have traveled with a circus for all he cared. He only sat up with attention when she mentioned that her former professor Michelle Chambers told Gina to put her name down as a reference.

"Wait," Diego said. "Mickey told you we were hiring?"

Gina's large blue eyes widened. "Was that okay?" she asked in a nervous voice. She swept a blond lock behind her ear and sat even straighter.

He shook his head as he looked at her application. "Yeah, that's fine. When can you start?"

"As soon as possible," Gina said.

"Tonight, then?" Diego asked. While wondering how many more Hargrove people he'd get on his doorstep, he was grateful Mickey sent him *someone*. With Jeanie gone, he couldn't afford to take Todd off weekday bar shifts. And even if Irene couldn't admit it, she needed help on the floor while Mickey worked with him.

Gina's perpetually wide-eyed expression grew even more surprised. "Of course," she said. "Thank you."

"Thank *you*," he replied with a relieved smile. "Your trainer, Irene, will be here in a few minutes. In the meantime, fill out this paperwork."

He left her in his office to check on the bar and found another relieving sight.

Mickey sashayed in wearing a pink sundress. This one was just as cute as her other outfits, flouncy and girlish. The ruffled neckline sat just above her breasts, revealing both shoulders, while the hem came to her knees. She wore a pair of platform sandals he could have sent her home for, but he held his tongue, and his breath.

When she caught him staring, she smiled brightly and gave him a wave. "Hey, Diego." She hurried past him, carrying a gentle waft of floral perfume that made his nose follow in a cartoonish manner. "I'm gonna clock in and start on the garnish," she called over her enticing bare shoulder.

"I took care of it," he said.

Her shoulders dropped with a sigh. "Oh, thank god. I hate prepping garnish."

Then I'll prep the garnish forever.

Christ, where had that come from? He hurried to the bar and stayed there while she clocked in. Another evening of stuffing his confusing feelings down into his belly, pretending not to be affected by every single movement she made. Diego didn't know how much he could take.

After pulling that white-knight routine, he realized he didn't mind putting a possessive arm around her while the army ranger pestered her. Anything to stop her from tearing up from the stress of the cash register.

Fuck.

If she couldn't handle working a cash register, she wasn't long for this job. As he wiped down Todd's afternoon bottles, Diego grimaced to himself. Today, they needed to go back to being bar partners. He didn't have time to coddle Mickey. She needed to be a big girl and hold her own.

All those thoughts quickly dissipated as soon as she fluttered back to the front of the bar. As she tied her apron behind her back, she flashed him a double-dimple smile and announced, "I think I feel a lot better about the register."

He raised a brow.

"I've been watching a ton of YouTube videos," she said, getting right to wiping down the bar. "I also saw this brilliant system for organizing tabs," she continued, wiping each beer tap handle. Diego tried not to focus on her vigorous up-and-down rubbing. *Just stare at her face.* "This bartender had this plastic thing that held all the customers' credit cards. I bet you can find one at an office supply store. He wrote the customer's name on each free slot with a dry-erase marker, that way he could go straight to the name to add receipts. As it is, we're kind of wrapping receipts to the customer cards, which isn't really secure. Remember how you even got those two guys' cards mixed up the other night? If we have a more organized system, it might make things move more efficiently. What do you think?"

What did he think?

Dry-erase markers? What on earth? Had he mixed up customer cards? Diego didn't remember doing that. "Um, I'll look into it," he muttered.

"Anyway, I tried to remember which kind of register this thing was, and found some helpful restaurant manager videos," Mickey continued. "I think I have the hang of the machine now."

"Then you don't need my help," Diego said in a voice that was more annoyed than he expected. Now why were *his* panties in a twist? Wasn't he hoping that she'd pick up the register faster?

He needed a reprieve from her.

Luckily, the front door swung open, and Irene walked in. "Hey, Boss. Hey, Newest Girl."

"She's not the newest anymore," Diego said.

"I'm not?" Mickey said.

"Gina Perry is in my office filling out paperwork. Can you train her?"

Irene rolled her eyes as she tied her apron. "Can you give me a raise?"

Diego grunted. That was something he would need to consider. Irene had been with Lucía from the start, training every new server that stepped foot in The Saloon. "Remind me to have a meeting about that tonight."

"Will do, Boss," Irene said as she walked back to the kitchen.

"You hired Gina?" Mickey asked in a hushed voice. "She's here?"

"I did and she is."

Mickey shook her hands as she bounced up and down. "Oh, that's so exciting!"

Too many things excited Mickey Chambers. The thought of figuring out all those things made Diego unexpectedly tingly. "Thank you for suggesting The Saloon."

"Of course," she said. "I had Gina a couple years ago for a postcolonial lit class. I jumped in to teach it at the last minute because the professor got in a car accident. He's fine, by the way, but I had such a great time with Gina's class. She's in grad school, doing something with chemistry. She made a post about needing a job on Facebook and I gave her your information."

Again, Mickey's habit of talking too fast and too much made Diego strain to pick out the important information. "You're Facebook friends with your students?"

She shrugged. "I only accept their requests when they're done with my class."

Before thinking, he asked, "Is that professional?"

Only when she glared at him did Diego realize his mistake. He gave a cough and immediately set about stacking glasses. "Right," he muttered.

You fucking fool…

Diego was growing irritated by the same group of twenty-somethings taking up Mickey's time while he worked the other side of the bar. They ran her ragged with their requests: more bar mix, more water, more Vodka Red Bulls.

Even while she tried to help other patrons, they refused to move from their perch and let her work in peace. Even if her smile never wavered, Diego could tell they were bothering her. Theoretically, there was nothing for him to worry about. Getting pestered by the same customer came with the territory. But he found it difficult to mind his business when it came to Mickey.

When a small voice interrupted his thoughts, he wheeled around to see young Gina standing at his elbow. "Yeah?"

"Can I have—"

"Imma need you to speak up, Gina," Diego barked over the noise.

The girl squared her shoulders and tried to make herself taller. "Can I have two Vodka Tonics?" she asked in a voice not much louder than her first attempt.

Diego got started on them just as Mickey approached the register. "You wrapping up those kids' tabs?"

She heaved a loud sigh. "Yes."

"They had a lot to drink?" he replied, cutting his eyes away from her pretty décolletage. A light sheen of perspiration covered Mickey's shoulders, neck and upper chest. And although he couldn't see her face at the register, he assumed it also glowed. He purposely stepped away from her to resume a professional distance.

"Lots," she muttered. "I'm gonna need Ollie or Ramón to restock these Red Bulls soon."

He had a bad feeling about those kids. All too often, Hargrove students blew into The Saloon to drink their fill and did not leave tips. Irene had complained about it enough times for him to take notice. Diego wondered if this bunch was cut from the same cheap cloth. He kept an ear out as he set Gina's Vodka Tonics on her tray. "Are you able to get through this crowd?" he asked her. She didn't seem like a server who could shove through patrons like Irene.

She nodded as she hoisted her tray high above her head. "I've done this part before," Gina tried to shout. She spun on her heel and made a quick path through patrons, ducking under tall guys and sidestepping drunk dancers. The young woman made it to her table in record time, impressing Diego.

Back at Mickey's end of the bar, the boys signed their slips. The last kid tossed his in the spill gutter, grabbed his drink and joined his friends near the jukebox. Mickey gathered four receipts before fishing the fifth out of a puddle of liquor. All five receipts must have disappointed her because her jaw fell open as she sifted through them. A frown creased her brow as she read what was on the back of one of the receipts. She mouthed a curse.

Fuck.

She stuffed the papers in her apron pocket and moved to the next customer, but her pitiful smile dipped with every nod of her head. She made a show of listening to her customers, but her eyes kept darting back to the group of laughing boys. She eventually produced her jigger and got to work. Her hands shook as she handed the glass over to a woman who greeted her with cash. Something had rattled his bar partner, and Diego was certain that it was the absence of a tip.

When there was a pause in service, he whipped his towel over his shoulder and approached her. "Let me see those receipts."

Mickey's gaze flew to his face; her expression was pensive. "What?"

"Those kids." He nodded to the jukebox group. "I want to see their tickets."

Her shoulders dropped as she fished them out of her apron. He wanted to see how large their collective tab was. "I've been waiting on them for two hours," she said in a terse voice.

The group spent close to two hundred dollars that evening. And not one bothered to tip Mickey. He flipped the slips of paper over to investigate the source of Mickey's anger and found a crudely drawn penis on one ticket. His face burned on her behalf.

There were two ways he could play this—one: he could tell her that this was just one way she could expect to be dehumanized while working in a bar, or two: he could march right over to the jukebox, grab the kid by the scruff of his neck and kick him out of the bar. "Which one of them did this?"

Mickey's face tightened. "What are you going to do?"

He didn't know just yet. But it pissed him off that customers could treat his employees however they wanted without repercussions. That shit wasn't fair. Whether it was Ramón or Irene, it didn't matter—Mickey was now a part of The Saloon family, and he intended to lay down the law tonight. "Which one?" he asked again.

"The kid with the mohawk haircut." She pointed. "Please don't make it worse."

"As your employer, I'm responsible for your safety," he said.

"I'm perfectly safe," Mickey protested.

He marched away before he could hear her objections, heading straight for the faux-punk kid. He wore a faded Metallica T-shirt, jeans and a smug-ass grin on his face. "Hey!" Diego barked. Before the kid could figure out who was speaking to him, Diego shoved the piece of paper under his nose. "Did you draw this shit?"

Mohawk took a startled step back, sloshing his drink down his hand. "What?"

His friends also took a step back, giving Diego enough breathing room to whoop ass if it was necessary. "Did you draw this shit and give it to my employee?"

The young man's face blanched as his eyes darted from the dick drawing to Diego and then to Mickey behind him.

"No, don't look at her," Diego said, drawing closer to the boy. "Look at me."

"I'm sorry!" he said as his shoulders came up to his ears. "It was a joke."

"A joke?" Diego raised a brow and cocked his head to the side. "I've been told that I don't have a sense of humor. So Imma need you to explain how this is so fuckin' funny."

The boy fell silent.

"That woman waited on your sorry asses for two hours, so the five of you could leave without tipping one fucking dollar." He wheeled back to the artist. "Except for you. You thought it was funny to leave this for her. Now tell me how any of this is funny."

“It’s not funny,” Mohawk sputtered. His terrified eyes darted for an escape. “I’m sorry!”

“Oh, no, this dick wasn’t for me. You drew it for her, right?”

The kid nodded jerkily.

“So why the fuck would you apologize to me?” Diego asked, stepping away from him. He pointed to the bar where Mickey was pouring drinks for other customers. “Take your narrow ass over there and apologize to *her*.”

The kid ducked away from him and made a skittish path back to the bar. Mickey glanced at Diego with a confused expression. He couldn’t hear the words being exchanged, but judging by the kid’s tense shoulders, they must have been contrite. When Mickey nodded at the boy, Diego turned to the rest of the friends.

“If y’all ever come in here again to waste my employees’ time and service, I’m banning all of you,” he said, jabbing a finger at them.

The friends nodded with the same nervous energy that Mohawk had. “Okay, yeah,” said one of them. Diego didn’t put too much stock in their fear, but he was a firm believer that if people didn’t have enough money to tip their servers, they didn’t have enough money to go out and eat or drink.

By the time he made it back to the bar, the young man was already reaching into his pockets to pull out several bills. His trembling hand slapped about fifteen dollars onto the bar.

“I’m really sorry,” he said. “I didn’t mean it.”

Mickey pursed her lips as she glanced at the money. “I accept your apology.”

The kid hurried back to his friends without looking at Diego. Soon after, the entire group left the bar with their tails tucked between their legs.

Mickey took the money and put it in the tip jar behind

the bar. "You've just lost five customers," she said, trying to hide her grin.

Just seeing that faint glimmer of a smile made his heart beat faster.

He shrugged. "Sounds fine to me."

"You really scared him, Boss," she said as she pulled a pint for the next customer. "You didn't need to shake him down for his lunch money."

He watched her pull a perfect pint and tried not to let out a groan of satisfaction. She was learning, and it made him strangely…happy. "He'll live."

Mickey glanced over her shoulder at him, her double-dimple smile turning into a laugh. "You're crazy."

He was starting to feel like it.

After the riffraff had exited the bar, it surprised Diego how quickly he acted a fool over her. He tried to convince himself that his actions were based purely on principle, but seeing her hurt expression jarred something loose in his heart. He wanted to protect Mickey and her soft hands. The thought made him cringe as he returned to his side of the bar. Mickey nor her soft hands were his to protect.

This was how he'd behaved when his wife was behind the bar. When she and Jeanie worked, he enjoyed staying in the back of the house where he could stack boxes and manage the books in peace. But on the days he'd had to work the bar, it shocked him to see how much Lucía put up with. What he would call obnoxious, she had simply laughed off while moving on to the next pint.

Guilt set in and drove him for the rest of his shift. As he made drinks, cleaned up spills and cashed out tickets, he kept his eyes on his own work. Meanwhile, Mickey went back to laughing with new customers as she pulled her pints.

13

After only a few shifts at The Saloon, Mickey felt proud and exhausted. She watched the bouncers, Jerry and Stevie, stack chairs on tables while Gina and Irene swept the floors. Ollie was in the kitchen washing glasses while Ramón restocked the bar with beers and Red Bulls Mickey had used up for the rowdy group of kids.

Her shoulders were in knots and her calves were stiff, but as she wiped down the bar, she felt an overwhelming sense of pride. Even with the minor setback of a dick drawing, Mickey felt powerful.

Had Diego stuck around long enough to listen, she could have explained how she'd dealt with worse while being a barista and TA in graduate school. When a distinguished professor screamed at her for mixing up his order, she had to stand there and take it. Her coffee shop boss hadn't exactly come to the rescue when Dr. Whitman threw his tantrum. But Diego had. Perhaps he would have done it for any of his employees, Mickey reasoned. But even that made her feel a part of The Saloon family.

"Dammit," Ramón muttered, squatting in front of the beer refrigerator.

"What's wrong?" Mickey asked.

"Oh, nothing, I think I forgot the Service Pale Ales," he said, searching the bottom shelf. "Or I need to order some… I can't remember if we've got any left."

"I can check for you," Mickey suggested. "I'm already done with the register."

Ramón glanced up with a frown. "You don't have to do that."

"It's not a problem, Ramón. Do you need Rally Point?"

His expression shifted to surprise. "You know it?"

Mickey draped her towel over the edge of the sink and chuckled. "My brother and I had some in Savannah last year. I'm not a fan of pale ales, but he loved it."

Ramón gave her an appraising nod. "Okay, then. Check the basement—the far-left wall next to the deep freezer." He rose from the floor. "If we're out, make a note of it and give it to Diego. I'm outta here."

"Where are you off to in such a hurry?"

He closed the fridge door and toweled his sweaty face off with a handkerchief. "Hurry? It's one in the morning. I'm going to watch the Braves game, drink a beer and go to sleep."

Mickey chuckled. "In that order?"

"In. That. Order," he said, patting her shoulder. "And then plan to wake up very late tomorrow."

"Have a good day off, Ramón," Mickey said as she followed him from behind the bar.

"Y tú también."

Mickey left the bar and walked to a dusty stairwell she'd never been down. As she carefully descended in dim lighting, she heard the faint clanking of bottles knocking into one another. She paused midway and strained her ears for more.

A man's grunt and curse punctuated the silence. The familiar sound made her smile. "Diego?"

There was a pause before she heard him growl, "What?"

Mickey rolled her eyes. "I'm just making sure you're not a basement monster," she said as she continued down the stairs. When she found him, his back was to her as he leaned over a keg. She took a step forward but faltered when she got a good look at his body.

Oh, my god, he's shirtless. Mickey wondered if it was too late to turn around and run back upstairs where there were no shirtless men. Where men's pants didn't hug their long sturdy legs and cup their asses in such a pleasing manner… She didn't know how long she had stood there, watching the cords of muscles in his damp back, but when he finally straightened up with an irritated grunt, Mickey blinked in embarrassment.

"I'm just here to find some beer," she blurted out in a voice much louder than she intended.

And then he turned around.

Jesus in heaven… Her mouth may have gone dry, but her panties experienced something quite different. The man's torso gleamed in the low light of the basement, giving her a full inventory of every muscle that a man could possess. Even those hip ones that dip into waistbands and point directly to dicks. Four—no, six—abs dented his flat stomach, each the size of those delicious chocolate croissants served at Fountain City Beans.

She licked her lips and tried to think of something smart to say but got distracted by the dark dusting of chest hair that charted a lovely course down his torso, and disappeared into his pants. *Oh, Christ, the pants.* With his shirt on, she hadn't seen how his waistband hung dangerously off his hips.

Everything in Mickey's body clenched.

"Beer?" he must have asked. She wasn't listening.

"Huh?" Her eyes finally focused on his face. Mickey dashed a hand over her mouth. "Yes, I'm looking for a beer for Ramón. I mean, not for him to drink. He wanted to know if there was any more Service Pale Ale and I said I would come down here and check it out. He's gone for the night, but he told me to let you know if we were out of Rally Point, so that's what I'm doing down here."

Diego pointed his chin at the wall to his right. "They're over there. By the deep freezer."

"Great," she said, hurrying past him.

He went back to work, fiddling with the keg. While searching for the IPA, she tried to steady her thumping heart. Flashing images of his chest didn't help. It was relatively cool down in the basement… Why would he need to take off his shirt? Maybe he just ran hot? Mickey suppressed a groan as she continued her search.

She didn't need to think about her student/boss's hot body. Not when she was getting just as hot under her sundress. As a feverish blush hit her cheeks, she reminded herself that she had, in fact, taken her meds that morning. This wasn't a thyroid-related hot flash… It was Diego.

"Fuck," he cursed. Seconds later, she heard a metallic clatter.

When she spun around, Diego clutched his arm away from his body. "What did you do?" she asked.

"It's nothing."

In seconds, she was by his side, examining the angry scratch on his forearm that began bleeding. "You're hurt," she said, her hands on his bicep, extending his arm into the light.

"It's nothing," he repeated, but he didn't pull his arm away. He stood still enough for her to press her fingers around the injury. The cut wasn't terribly deep, but it needed cleaning and dressing.

"Is there a first aid case down here?"

He sighed, blowing warm breath above her hair. "There are extra kits on the shelf over there," he said, pointing behind her.

Mickey retrieved a fresh first aid kit and a roll of paper towels. "Come over here," she said, pulling his good arm toward the deep freezer. He followed with an annoyed scoff. Mickey set her supplies on top of the freezer and got to work on his cut. "It's nothing?" she asked, pointing at the running blood. "You nicked it good."

"Not enough to call emergency services," he said.

Mickey rolled her eyes. "No, but you've got to be careful with all the metal down here. The kegs and pipes can get damp and rust easier." She dabbed the blood around the wound, without touching the cut, before digging into the kit. "Is your tetanus shot still up to date?"

"I have no idea."

She gasped. "Are you kidding?"

He rolled his eyes. "I'll look into it."

Mickey poured a bit of rubbing alcohol on a sheet of paper towel. "This is going to sting," she said, pressing it against his arm.

"Goddammit!" he growled. His arm jerked from her grasp, but she gripped it tighter.

"I said it would sting!" She kept the alcohol-soaked paper towel pressed to his arm long enough to get distracted by his nearness and scent. The heat coming from his body made her stomach flip-flop and her heart pound harder. He smelled like some intoxicating blend of cedar cologne and clean sweat. "Trust me when I say that this is better than lockjaw."

His dark eyes twinkled beneath heavy brows. As close as she was, Mickey couldn't help but notice his smirk creased the wrinkles at the corners of his eyes. "You've had tetanus?"

"No..." she said. "I've read about it, though." She had done quite a lot of reading about serious medical conditions when she was younger. She needed something to do while stuck at home, sitting in emergency rooms or lying in hospital beds. Learning about tetanus, snakebites and Ebola made her feel less anxious about her own illness.

"Of course my English professor reads medical journals," he said in a low voice. "She does it all."

Mickey could feel his pulse under her fingers. It was about as fast as hers. "Can you be still enough for me to apply an antibacterial cream?" she asked.

"Go ahead, Professor," he said, his voice dipping lower. Was that possible? Also, was he standing closer?

The bleeding seemed to slow as she slathered a bit of ointment on his cut with a clean napkin. "What were you doing with that keg?" she asked, taking care not to touch anything but his arm.

"There's something wrong with the Coke line. I thought I could fix it myself, but I think I fucked it up more."

Mickey swiped the cut gingerly before returning to the kit for a bandage. "You should get Ollie to work on it. She knows about that kind of stuff."

"Yeah, I'll have her look at it on Monday," he breathed. She glanced at his chest and noticed how it rose and fell with each breath.

Mickey knew that once she placed a bandage on Diego's arm, she'd lose her excuse to touch him. So, she purposely slowed down. After years of people fretting over her, she didn't mind helping someone else feel better. And, of course, it was just wonderful to touch a man this hot.

She couldn't believe she was this thirsty over a man who was her student. The guilt was there, just further beneath the surface than she had expected. Her arousal now took precedence, and it was a five-alarm fire that made her thighs clench and her mouth water. She wondered if Diego could see the naked desire on her face.

Because he wore it on *his* face.

His eyes seemed darker, and his nostrils flared as he stared down at her. After a deep breath, he asked, "Am I all patched up, Professor?" His voice was so quiet—so deep—it vibrated in the space between them, drawing her close like a magnet. Her knees trembled under his stern gaze. She wondered if he could be just as stern in bed as he was behind the bar. She wondered many things as she held on to his perfectly fine arm.

"I think you'll live," she whispered with a shaky breath. "And you don't have to call me professor… I'm an adjunct instructor."

"I don't give a fuck about that," he scoffed as his eyes roved over her face. "You're teaching me at college. That makes you my professor."

She didn't feel like explaining the details of higher education hierarchy to him. "Okay, but—"

In an unexpected move, Diego pulled her closer to his chest. "What are you really doing down here?"

To steady herself, she planted her hand on his bare chest and looked up at him. When she met his piercing gaze, she lost her train of thought. Mickey had her hands on his body; they'd crossed the line yet again. "Beer. I'm looking for beer."

"And what are you doing now?" he asked.

"Helping you," she whispered.

His head cocked to the side and he narrowed his eyes. Mickey immediately felt foolish. She had made him sound like a sea turtle stuck in plastic rings, struggling in an oil slick. But her words hadn't stopped his good arm from snaking around her middle and drawing her even closer. "I don't need your help, Professor," he said in a hoarse voice.

Of course not. But when he pressed her against him, she felt *something* that needed tending to. Mickey's mouth fell open as her soft belly pushed against his hard erection. The sensation and promise sent shivers throughout her body. "What do you need?" she dared to ask.

Diego's jaw clenched, but he said nothing. She desperately wanted him to speak, to say anything. Instead, he dipped down and took her by the hips. Before Mickey knew it, he hoisted her in the air and placed her on top of the deep freezer. Diego held her thighs apart and stood between them. "I don't know," he said as he crept the hem of her dress upward. "You confuse the fuck out of me, Mickey."

His calloused palms pressed into her flesh, but his eyes searched hers with indecision. Diego was on a precipice—he'd come too far but wasn't willing to take the leap. His chest rose and fell as his eyes landed on her mouth.

She knew, right off the bat, what they were about to do was dangerous. Him standing between her thighs was wrong, and it would ultimately get her into trouble. But she couldn't bring herself to push him back and close her legs. "What do you want?"

His fingers moved before his lips had. They inched beneath her dress to the sides of her biking shorts and gripped the edges. Diego let out a long, ragged breath as he held her still. "I want *you*," he rasped, dropping his head.

"Okay," she said.

He lifted his head and frowned. "Okay?"

She nodded. "Yes, okay."

Diego paused. "You don't mean that."

Didn't she? Mickey suddenly felt confused by this conversation. "Yeah, I think I do." After all, his roughened fingers still gripped the edge of her shorts, just waiting to pull downward. Everywhere his hands touched, heat followed, making her shiver in the damp, cool basement.

He was giving her a taste; she needed a mouthful.

When Diego's hands left her hips, she almost let out a pained whimper, but they skated upward and around to her lower back. "God help me, but I want you, Mickey," he whispered, not so much to her, but to himself. "This is so fucking wrong."

Mickey wasn't trying to get hung up on the right or wrong of it. She simply felt good; she wanted to feel *better.* "Maybe we can—"

"Yo, Mickey!" called a voice from upstairs.

Diego quickly removed his hands from her dress and stepped away. She closed her legs and fought the urge to scream. "Just grabbing beer," she replied in an annoyed voice.

"It's me, Jerry. I'm walking the girls to their cars… Do you want us to wait on you?"

She looked at Diego, but he was already back to the boxes of wine, slipping his shirt back on. "I'll walk her to her car, Jerry," he called out.

"Sounds good, Boss."

In the quiet of the basement, Mickey could only hear their breathing. Hers sounded shallow, his ragged. "I'm sorry about that," he muttered.

Mickey scooted herself from the deep freezer and adjusted her dress around her legs. "It doesn't look like we have any more Rally Point Pale Ale. You should order more."

Diego turned away from her and rubbed the back of his neck. "I'll do that."

She quickly climbed the stairs and clocked out.

Diego Acosta wanted her badly enough to tell her, which must have been a feat for him to admit aloud.

What she would do with that information was still a mystery, but it excited Mickey to see him become completely undone before her. She hung up her apron with the others and waited for Diego to emerge from the basement. They didn't have to do or say anything tonight. She just held on to the fact for another day.

14

Just push the submit button.

Diego hadn't planned on letting the first assignment get the best of him, but after reading his paper for the third time, he no longer felt confident in his work.

It was Mickey's fault, really. She barely gave instructions for this assignment. He read it several times before he sat down to write it. It had to be 750 to 1000 words; no citations necessary... Where was the stuff about font size? How was the line spacing supposed to go? He had to Google what passed for a decent header in college courses these days. Or was he supposed to use a title page for APA format?

And her rubric was only more bullshit. Something about holistic assessment? What did that even mean? "Writer entertained their audience by being attentive to pathos, ten points." He'd read the statement a dozen times and nearly put it to music so he could sing it. Was his paper *entertaining* enough? Diego had little time to think about it because his paper was due in about three minutes.

He held his breath and pressed submit.

Nothing happened.

The web page flickered and an error warning appeared on his screen. "Session timed out?" he muttered.

He tried navigating to the last page, but another screen popped up. "Sign in again?"

Two minutes until noon.

He scrambled to get to the log-in page to try uploading his document all over again. But he couldn't remember the overly complicated password he'd only come up with a couple weeks ago. Why couldn't he remember it? Capital letter, special character, number.

Lucía80!

Account/Password incorrect.

LucíaA80!!

Account/Password incorrect. You have one more attempt before lockout.

"Shit!" Diego had to slow down. Most of his online passwords were some variation of his wife's name. But when he was forced to deviate from what he knew, it always screwed him up. He had one minute left…

Why had he waited so long to upload his assignment? A paper that probably wasn't that great to begin with, but Jesus, why had he waited?

LucíaAcosta80!

You have been locked out. Contact Helpdesk for assistance.

"Fuck."

12:01.

And now he was late turning in his first assignment. He would rather chew his own hand off than call Mickey for help...

He didn't know what he would say to the woman who he'd pawed at in his bar basement. After he locked up the bar, the walk to her car was quiet and awkward. She didn't say anything about what happened on top of the deep freezer, and he could barely look at her. How could he possibly come back from that?

While sitting in his home office, he palmed his phone and wondered how long he'd put off the inevitable. While he waited, he stared at the people who jogged around the perimeter of Lakebottom Park. Lucía had picked out their house based on the park and made a habit of rising early enough to jog around it. He'd accompanied her on most mornings, racing her from the massive oak on Forest Street, to the freshly planted copse of saplings. After five years, the saplings now resembled young oak trees. He only saw them grow from his office window; he didn't jog Lakebottom Park anymore.

"Oh, god..." he murmured. It wasn't just that he needed to call Mickey, but he'd have to see her again. The Riverwalk Blues Fest was this weekend, and Jeanie was still with her mother, post-surgery. He'd have no choice but to work with Mickey behind the bar.

Perhaps this was meant to happen. Maybe he was supposed to fuck up his paper submission to atone for his sins. Playing grab-ass with an employee...

He called her.

After six rings, a husky voice answered. "Hello?"

Diego tensed at the sound of Mickey's sleepy grumble. She didn't sound as bubbly as he was used to; she was more sultry and intimate. "It's Diego," he said.

There was a pause on the line before she spoke again. "What's wrong? Is it the bar?"

"Nothing's wrong with The Saloon," he said quickly, though he found it interesting that that was her first thought. "I messed up my paper."

"What paper?" she mumbled.

"The Personal Narrative paper."

"When is it due?" she asked.

Diego frowned. "Eight minutes ago."

She paused again.

"I couldn't turn it in," he continued. "Something went wrong with this portal, and I couldn't remember my goddamn password. I can't submit it if I can't log in—"

"Diego, it's really not that big a deal," Mickey yawned. He could hear blankets shifting in the background. "Just email it to me."

Had he really expected Mickey to be a hard-ass professor who'd need to see evidence of his screwup? "I thought—are you sure?"

Her throaty chuckle tickled his ear. "If you email it to me in the next hour, you're good. I'm not suspicious of my students." She shifted in her bed again and let out a satisfied sigh.

Was she stretching like a cat in her bed? If so, what was she wearing?

Diego cleared his throat and his dirty mind. "Thanks."

"You're welcome," she said. "How did the first assignment go? Did the journal entries help you get comfortable with the topic?"

He hadn't realized that the journal entries were supposed to aid in the first assignment until she mentioned it. But when it clicked, he suddenly felt silly for being angry at her prompt. Diego had received positive feedback on his other work; why would he be so bent out of shape over this one paper? Because he was insecure as fuck. "I think it went well," he said. "Journaling probably helped."

"Oh, good," she said with a bright voice. "What did you end up writing about?"

"I'd rather you just read it," he said with hesitance, before adding, "But I can give you a hint, I guess."

"Please do!"

"I wrote about mofongo. I made it for my wife, and I wrote about the personal experience of eating it, but also added some history to the dish. I don't know if you'd need that or not." He paused. "I hope that's okay."

"That sounds wonderful," Mickey said. "I know about mofongo, but you should always think about the audience outside of your professor."

Diego nodded, feeling a little pride in his work. "It ran a little longer than what you asked for," he said.

"That's fine."

"I wrote it using APA," he added. "I googled that second semester composition classes usually used that."

"I didn't specify," Mickey said offhandedly. "It's not that big a deal."

"Don't you think some students need a few more specifics?"

Another chuckle. "Are you saying *you* need more specifics, Diego?"

He rolled his eyes. "Some students might want to know what their professor wants from them so they can get a good grade."

"I'll grant you that. But I don't ride my students hard about the little shit like formatting. I'm more interested in their ideas. Do they have them? And do they need more help to shape them?"

That was fair.

"Did you want to discuss anything else, Diego?" she asked in a cautious tone.

He closed his eyes and pushed his glasses to his forehead. "Um… I guess I should say something about last night."

"That might be helpful," she said. "It wasn't like kissing in your office. This was different."

Diego took a deep breath. "Right."

"We said and did some things that were—"

"I know," he exhaled. "I'm sorry that I touched you like that. I crossed a line. I was being impulsive, which isn't like me. I don't usually… What I mean is that I wasn't planning to do that to you. It just happened. I acted like a fool all night, starting with those kids who stiffed you. I could have just let it go, but when I saw how upset you were, I just—I don't know—I felt like I should stick up for you." He was rambling, but he nearly got everything off his chest by the time he cut himself off. Nearly everything.

The pause on the line lasted long enough for him to wonder if their call got dropped.

"Are you still there, Mickey?"

"I am," she said in a soft voice. "I'm just thinking."

Diego pressed his palm across his forehead and waited for her to think. In the meantime, he thought the worst of himself. He was probably making her work environment a living hell. She would probably quit.

"I didn't mind it," she finally said.

"Huh?"

"I didn't mind it at all," Mickey continued. "Now what are we going to do with that information?"

Now it was his turn to pause.

"Are you still there?" she asked.

"I am."

"Well, I guess we're doing the right thing by addressing

the obvious—we're clearly attracted to one another," she said hesitantly.

"We are," he agreed. "I find you…very attractive." His face flushed as soon as the words left his mouth. This was the most he'd spoken about feelings since Lucía. "I think I felt something when I first met you," he admitted.

"Same," she breathed.

"Okay," he said in his steadiest voice, hoping shock didn't color his tone.

"So, what comes next?" she asked.

Diego wasn't sure about that part. Telling her she was attractive seemed to roll off the tongue so easily. Making good on that desire was a whole other thing. "I would imagine that Hargrove University has a policy about relationships with students," he said cautiously.

She chuckled. "You'd be surprised to know that Hargrove doesn't have an explicit policy…but I do, I mean did. I'm sure it didn't seem like it last night, but I just want you to know I've never thrown myself at any student. I'm assuming The Saloon has a similar policy?"

"We don't," he replied.

Her laughter ended abruptly.

"What I mean is that I'm not in danger of losing my job like you are," Diego said. "I understand that you have a code to uphold as a professor. I don't want to mess that up for you."

"I really appreciate that, Diego."

If she could see his face, it would be beet red. "I would never want to do something that would get you in trouble with your bosses. I'm just saying that if we did, it wouldn't get you in trouble at The Saloon." What the fuck was he saying?

"If I kissed you again, you wouldn't tell your HR department," she teased.

This drew a smile from him. "No…because I don't have an

HR department," he reminded her. "I don't want to scare you off, Mickey. I don't want you to quit because of my actions."

"I told you I wouldn't quit," she said with force. After a beat, she took a breath, and he heard her covers shift. "I like The Saloon. I enjoy working behind the bar with you. It's something different and refreshing."

"Even the dick drawings?" he asked in a dry voice as he set his glasses on his desk. He leaned back in his office chair, getting comfortable with this conversation. Talking to Mickey on the phone was easier than he'd expected. In person, her beauty overwhelmed him and made him sound like an ass. *This*...this was just nice.

"That's not a big deal," she laughed. "I was going to tell you I've dealt with worse, but you took off after that kid before I could say anything."

"No one fucks with my employees."

"I see that now..." Mickey said. "Thank you."

His heart flip-flopped in his chest. Everything she said made him feel happy and relieved. Diego even felt confident to continue this conversation in person, where he could see her smile. "You're welcome."

They settled into a pause that would normally stress him out, but today, he didn't feel rushed to fill the silence.

"So, you're going to Ramón's birthday party tomorrow, right?" Mickey asked abruptly. "I think Irene said it was going to be at the Riverwalk Park..."

Diego had been so focused on his schoolwork he nearly completely forgot about Irene and Stevie's plans. While he hated attending parties, it would be nice to celebrate Ramón. He loved his brother-in-law and needed to spend more time with him. And it would be even better to hang out with The Saloon family outside of a stressful work environment. "Yeah, how about you?"

"I'll be there!" she said in a bright voice. "I'm just a little surprised I was invited."

Diego frowned. "Why wouldn't Irene invite you?"

"No, no, it's not that." She paused. "It's just that the bar is like its own little family. I've only been working with y'all for a week."

"That doesn't matter," he said. "I—we want you there."

Another awkward silence filled the line. He should have told her that any member of The Saloon was welcome to join. Of course she was welcome to celebrate. It was only right to include everyone. Even Gina and Ollie would be there. Perhaps that would have been overkill, but it would have certainly prevented him from saying the obvious: I want you there.

"Well, I guess I'll see you then," Mickey said. "Irene assigned me chips and dip."

Diego nodded to himself. "She usually puts me on beer duty."

"That makes sense."

He could feel the conversation winding down and he hated that he might have to let her go. He enjoyed talking to her about non-Saloon stuff. "So...what are your plans for today?" He glanced at the clock on his laptop and remembered she was still in bed at noon.

Mickey yawned. "My friend Cleo is coming over for Sunday Funday."

"What's a Sunday Funday?"

"It's pizza, booze, reality TV and girl talk. She and I try to meet up every week to give each other a rundown while getting drunk."

"And you'll catch her up on all the bar happenings?"

"Not all of them," she said with a scoff.

Right... The reminder of the tight hold he'd had on her

last night, in the bar basement, legs parted, breasts rising and falling with each breath… Perhaps it was time to let her go.

"Well… I guess I'll go ahead and email you my paper, then." He pressed the heel of his palm to the bridge of his nose and silently cursed himself.

Mickey chuckled into his ear before sighing. "Please do. I can't wait to read it," she said before hanging up.

He set his phone on his desk and glanced back at the grove of young oaks in Lakebottom Park. He wondered if a walk around the park was what he needed to steady his nerves and get back in touch with his past. Lucía was out there, and he'd been avoiding her for years. "Am I making a mistake, Lucía?"

Just as he expected, there was no answer in his empty house. Diego had received no signs from his wife, but he had hoped for something small. Anything to tell him that falling headfirst into something new was a good idea.

15

Mickey had just taken cupcakes out of the oven when Cleo knocked on her front door. She hoped a girls' night in with her best friend would help her make sense of the Diego problem. "Come in!" she called from the kitchen.

Cleo let herself in, carrying two pizzas and a bottle of red wine. "Sunday Funday," she called back, kicking her shoes off near the door.

"Girl, am I glad to see you," Mickey said, fanning the chocolate cupcakes on the stove.

Cleo dressed casually today, wearing her long twists in a ponytail and sporting a loose-fitting pair of denim overalls. "And I'm ready to open this," she said, holding up the wine.

"You know where the corkscrew is."

"Tell me how your first week as a bar girl went," Cleo said as she rifled through Mickey's junk drawer.

"Well, where do I start? The first kiss or the—"

The shrill ring of her cell filled the kitchen, cutting her off from spilling the tea. Cleo's mouth dropped open as she clutched the corkscrew. "Bitch, what?"

Mickey found her phone and groaned. "It's my mom..."

No doubt, she would question her absence from yesterday's Saturday dinner. She still hadn't informed her parents of her new job, and she knew they'd have a million concerns. None of which she wanted to deal with. "Hey, Mama," she answered in her customary chipper tone.

"Hey, Michelle, what are you up to?"

"Cleo just stopped by for a girls' night in."

Her mother chuckled. "You tell Cleo I said hey."

Mickey relayed the message to Cleo, who was still shook.

"Now tell me why you missed dinner yesterday?"

Instead of outright lying, Mickey said, "I was working. I meant to call you and Daddy, but I just let time get away from me."

"You were working on the summer class?"

"Mmm-hmm."

The micro-pause her mother took made Mickey wonder if that would be enough to skate by. "And you're feeling good?" her mother asked.

"I'm feeling good," Mickey said, smiling into the phone. She was a firm believer that people can hear smiles, and she wanted to reassure her mother even while lying about work. "I gotta go, though, I need to see about these cupcakes."

"Okay, then. I love you, Michelle."

"I love y'all, too!"

When she hung up, she bit her lip and closed her eyes.

"Now why are you lying to Mama Chambers?" Cleo asked, finally uncorking the wine. "You're not grown enough to work at a bar?"

Mickey leaned against the counter and sighed. "I am, but I don't want them to worry. If they knew how much physical work I was doing…on my feet, all night, they'd panic."

Cleo found two wineglasses in the cabinet. "How do they expect you to make money if you're not on your feet?"

"You know them." And while that didn't excuse how overbearing they were, Cleo knew enough about her family to understand. Since they were kids, and Cleo came over to play, she saw firsthand how Rita fretted over Mickey's health.

"I do, but you're not tender-headed," Cleo laughed. She poured wine for them both and sat at the kitchen island. "And you protecting them from the fact you've grown up isn't helping them. Is it something else?" she asked, raising a brow.

"Like the fact that it's a bar?" Her parents were working-class folks who believed in making honest money, but Mickey knew they couldn't picture either of their children working in a bar. Not a place where folks fell down drunk, cussed and fought. "I'll eventually tell them. I'd just like to get my bearings first."

"And that brings us back to the kissing. Please, girl, I've had a long week dealing with the mayor, who's working my very last nerve… I need to hear something spicy."

"What's the next minor holiday you will need to prep for?" Mickey asked, swirling her wineglass around before taking a sip.

Cleo groaned. "National Handshake Day… He's going to want to pull some 'reach across the aisle' bullshit, I just know it. But no, we're not talking about that right now. Spicy, please."

"Diego and I are in an entanglement," Mickey admitted.

Cleo nodded. "Okay, that makes sense…because he was watching you like you were the only woman in the bar with that intense I'm-gonna-fuck-that-woman sort of stare."

"Really?" Mickey asked, leaning forward. "You saw all of that?"

Her friend shot her a look. "Of course. Now give me the rest of the story because I am currently *not* in an entanglement."

Mickey explained things as best as she could, careful not to linger on her passionate experience in the basement. By the time she finished, Cleo had polished off her first glass of wine and poured the next.

"Goddamn, Mick..." she said after a gulp. "Y'all were doing alla'dat in the basement?"

"What do you think I should do?"

Cleo tapped her chin while she thought. Mickey was equal parts embarrassed and proud of her retelling. But if there was anyone who wouldn't judge her, it would be Cleo. They'd swapped stories like this since they were teenagers, laughing and cutting up over boys was standard. "It sounds like you're the first woman he's talked to since his wife, which is kinda heavy."

"Maybe, and yes, it is."

"You like the job enough to keep playing with fire? Because that's what you guys are doing."

"I like it more than I thought I would," Mickey said with a smirk. "And the tips are incredible. And so far, he's doing well in my class. He keeps up, turns his stuff in on time, and I plan to grade him accordingly."

"You're not gonna give him an A for that D?" Cleo joked.

Mickey rolled her eyes. "Har-har-har. I know you're being funny, but I don't joke about grades. In my class, you get what you earn."

"So, you know you're both in the wrong," Cleo said, standing up from the kitchen island and grabbing a box of pizza. "Bring your ass over to the couch so we can talk straight."

Mickey reluctantly took her ass to the couch, preparing for the inevitable chastising. "Give it to me straight."

Cleo flipped open the pizza box, revealing sausage and onions, and took the first slice. "Don't fuck this man—"

"That's your advice?"

"Let me finish," Cleo admonished. "Don't fuck this man *yet.* You're his professor and you're on the hook for his grade for how long?"

"Another four weeks," Mickey said.

"Be careful… I work for a man whose ethics commission jumps down his throat if he accepts anything that looks like a gift. Be it a fruit basket or a meal at Penny's BBQ Shack, people are always watching. You think you're being slick, but that shit catches up with you."

Even though Mickey rolled her eyes, her friend was right. There was no reason to jeopardize her teaching gig for a man. "Am I supposed to just be horny for four weeks? Do I have to work right next to him while he's shaking drinks with those forearms?"

Cleo ignored her by pulling her phone from her back pocket.

"What are you doing?" Mickey asked, craning to see her friend's phone.

"I'm sending you a link to one of my favorite sex toys…" Cleo murmured. "Here. Get this clit-sucker and hush."

Mickey buried her head in the couch cushion and screamed.

"Are you done?"

She lifted her head and sighed. "Yes, and you're right. I'll dial it back for the sake of my two jobs."

Cleo wiped her hands and returned to her wine. "Do you really enjoy working there? Could you see yourself continuing for the rest of the month?"

Mickey had thought it over during her phone call with Diego. She *did* enjoy working at The Saloon. It was a place where everyone pulled their weight, ragged on each other in a friendly way, and she was actually being paid for the labor she put in. "It's rough and fast, but no one is trying to take it easy on me," she said. "I like how I never know what's coming through the door. I had a great time at the bachelorette party."

Cleo grimaced.

"Yeah, that was the same face Diego made. He doesn't like them, either."

"No, it's not that," she said, shaking her head. "It's just that you've reminded me of an obligation I've been putting off. You know Beth from work?"

Mickey took a pizza slice from the box. "The mayor's secretary?"

"Yup. She's getting married and I'm a bridesmaid. I accidentally agreed to help her with her bachelorette party. Keaton has been riding me so hard about campaign stuff that I've pushed back planning."

"You should have it at the bar!" Mickey said. "We'll make a night of it."

"But your boss—"

"Will get another shot at being nice to people."

Cleo eyed her suspiciously. "A Saloon bachelorette party?"

"There's a room near the back that's large enough for a party of eight. We could decorate it and, oh, my god, what if I make those specialty cocktails from Lucía's recipe cards? She has one for a Mexican coffee that would go perfectly with a dessert." Mickey's mind spun with so many ideas that she needed to grab a pen and paper. "We could get my friend Patrick to do karaoke. Beth loves that, right?"

"Hold on a minute," Cleo warned. "Mexican coffee? Karaoke?"

Mickey searched her desk for a notebook. "Diego's wife made these beautiful recipe cards, but he doesn't serve her drinks anymore." She spied an ink pen and snatched it up. "I took pictures of the cards and was thinking about turning them into a book for him."

When she returned to the couch, Cleo's eyes narrowed in

suspicion. "You don't think your boss will mind that you're trying to resurrect his dead wife's drinks?"

Mickey frowned as she started her party list. "I don't think so," she said. "He lets me practice with them all the time."

"Fine," her friend said with a sigh. "But karaoke?"

"Patrick used to do it in Atlanta. He has the equipment, and he owes me a favor."

"I don't even know who all is going to be there," Cleo protested.

"Let's plan it tonight," Mickey said. "That way it's off your plate and you won't have to worry so much."

"We're really spending Sunday Funday in on this?" Cleo asked. "It feels like you're assigning me homework."

"It won't feel like that," Mickey said. "We've got cupcakes, wine and pizza. That's an automatic party right there." She snuggled into the couch with her best friend and felt quiet relief take over her body. Talking to Cleo was the best thing she could have done. She was mature enough to keep her hands to herself and continue doing her job. And now she had a new project for the bar: Bachelorette Destination and Karaoke Station.

16

"You came!" Irene cried as Mickey strolled up to the picnic benches. The young woman greeted her with such a tight hug Mickey almost fell back from the force.

Mickey was relieved to see her coworker's excitement. She'd had her apprehensions about being invited to Ramón's party, but Diego assured her—in his way—that she would be welcomed. Just about everyone was there: Ollie and Jerry were messing around with speakers for music, while Gina kicked around a soccer ball with Stevie, and Ramón handled one of the park's grills. The only person missing was Diego.

"I'm sorry I'm late," Mickey said, hugging Irene. "I forgot to get ice for the dips."

"You're right on time," Irene said, guiding them to the picnic pavilion. The table had been decorated with balloons, and a cake box sat at the center. "Ramón is still grilling even though RAMÓN SHOULDN'T BE GRILLING AT HIS OWN PARTY," she said, yelling that last part.

Ramón waved his tongs at her. "Hey, hey, calm down… I didn't like how Stevie was treating these patties."

Irene blew out a sigh. "If Stevie can't watch the door at work, I can't expect him to watch the burgers."

Mickey chuckled as she set out the various bags of chips and small plates. "Is boss man on his way?" she asked, hoping to sound nonchalant. Regardless of her oath to Cleo about "not fucking this man," she was still rattled by her last phone call with him. They had awkwardly shuffled around the subject of their kiss before eventually settling into polite conversation. No matter how conflicted she felt, she needed to stick to her guns.

"He ran to the bar to get some more ice," Irene said. "Do you want a beer?"

"Please, and then I want to hug the birthday boy."

Mickey popped the top of a lager and wandered to the small grill station where Ramón cooked. "¡Feliz cumpleaños, Ramón!"

He swung a meaty arm around her shoulders and squeezed. "Gracias, Mick. How was your day off?"

"Pretty good," she said. "It's weird getting used to this new schedule. I didn't expect to have a party right before going into work today."

The music finally settled on a booming Reggaeton beat that got Ramón nodding his head. "Working nights is like that. You still gotta find time for fun, though."

"I support having fun."

"Of course you do," said a voice from behind her. Mickey glanced over her shoulder to find Diego right at her back, holding a large bag of ice to his chest. He wore the same strait-laced, humorless expression from work. The impulse to roll her eyes was too powerful to ignore.

"Will you be having fun today?" she asked, genuinely curious.

"It's a birthday party," he said with a sigh. "I guess it's required."

She and Ramón looked at each other with widened eyes. "Oooohh," they intoned together. "Boss man might relax today?"

Ramón laughed as he rocked his hips to the music. "Maybe he'll even dance?"

Diego shook his head as he emptied the ice into a cooler. "I didn't think dancing was required."

"Dancing is included in revelry!" Mickey said.

He threw the bag into a trash bag and smoothed his T-shirt down over his belly. He wore his standard issue bar uniform: T-shirt and dark blue jeans. His dark hair was already plastered to his sweaty forehead. He almost cracked a smile, as if the simple act was killing him. "If it comes to that… I guess I'll comply."

"That sounds promising."

"So how was your Sunday Funday?"

"What's a Sunday Funday?" Ramón asked, grabbing himself another beer.

Before Mickey could explain herself, Diego was on it. "Apparently, you get together with your gal pals and eat pizza, drink and gossip?"

He was teasing her. Her heart still sped up with the anticipation of teasing him back. "I had a lovely time with Cleo. We had a good gossip session and managed to fit in even better reality TV."

"Ah, should we be having Sunday Funday?" Ramón asked Diego. "I don't have gossip, but I can bring the pizza."

The question seemed to catch Diego off guard. He blinked at his brother-in-law before answering. "Uh…sure. I guess."

Ramón patted him on the shoulder before joining Ollie and Irene at the picnic table.

"So..."

"So..."

They'd spoken in unison before breaking out in laughter. He gave a genuine chuckle that she had rarely seen. Mickey realized that she loved the way his eyes crinkled in the corners when he smiled. She appreciated the light in his eyes, the easiness in his face. When all his muscles seemed so trained on remaining serious, Diego almost appeared to be made of stone.

"Sorry," he tried again, his smile dipping. "I was going to ask, are we cool?"

Mickey nodded. "We're cool."

"Good." He looked around. "I didn't want to make you feel uncomfortable or anything."

She waved him off. "It's water under the bridge, Diego. We don't have to talk about it." It was for the best. They didn't need to unpack the desperation they'd both felt in the basement. The way his fingers curled around her thighs. According to her best friend, it was best to let all that go. If in four weeks she still felt like exploring that part of their relationship, she knew where to find him. But for now, she needed to hold fast to her convictions: You don't get involved with your students or your boss.

"You're right," he said. His eyes fell to her body. "You look nice today."

"Thank you."

"You look nice every day," he quickly corrected. "I don't think I've seen that outfit. Is that new?"

She was wearing denim shorts and a white off-the-shoulder peasant top. "I don't know," she chuckled. "You've only known me for about a week. I'm sure I'll still have surprises for you."

His face reddened as he rubbed the back of his neck. "Right, sorry."

"Okay, we're playing a game!" Irene interrupted.

"That's your cue for fun, Diego. Think you can handle it?"

His dark brown eyes crinkled with another blessed smile. "If I have to."

Like many low-stakes games, cornhole often brought the worst out of participants. The Saloon crowd was no different. By his third beanbag toss, even Diego felt himself loosening up. It was probably because his partner was Mickey. Every time she scored, she launched herself into a silly dance and trash-talked with Stevie and Jerry. Like his Lucía, Mickey was a sore winner. While the comparison made him grin, it also exposed him to a strange mix of feelings. He enjoyed the reminders but didn't want them coming from another woman. After five years, was he ready to believe there were other women who could make his heart race again?

She told him that their basement incident was water under the bridge and he was glad to hear it. The last thing he needed was to distract himself with that heart-racing question. There were other important things on his mind: getting the bar to work consistently, starting his schooling off correctly. Fucking Mickey was not on that list.

Still…whenever she flashed him that easy grin or teased a smile from him, the thought of kissing her grew too strong to ignore.

"WE WIN!" Mickey screamed after his beanbag flew through the opposing team's hole. She took him by the hand and raised it over their heads. He couldn't help himself. In a moment of revelry, he scooped her into his arms and hugged her tight.

When he set her back on her feet, she looked up at him with a puzzled smile. "Whoa…the boss man is having a fun time? I never thought I'd live to see it."

He was.

"Maybe I am," he said cautiously.

"Well, good for you." Mickey wiped her forehead with the back of her hand. "I'm gonna seek some shade since the sun's back out."

"I'll join you."

He followed her to the shaded pavilion and sat opposite her at the picnic table. Stevie took over the grill so Ramón could play cornhole with Ollie against the waitresses. Mickey fanned her face, which had turned pinkish in the time they'd spent out in the open.

"You doing okay?" he asked. "Need some water?"

"I'm covered," she said, closing her eyes and breathing through her nose. "But I could use a cup of ice, if you don't mind."

"Sure." He grabbed a plastic cup and scooped as much ice into it before quickly returning. "You sure you're okay?"

Mickey chuckled lightly as she pulled a couple ice cubes from the cup and rubbed them against her neck and chest. "I'm sure. I just need to watch how much sun I get," she said, then quickly added, "Like anyone."

While he was concerned by how red she'd gotten, Diego's attention was pinned to the glistening streaks of water left behind each stroke of ice on her hot skin. When one melted cube slipped from her grasp and tumbled down the valley between her breasts, disappearing beneath her blouse, his eyes followed its trail. With more concentration than needed.

"So, what did you get Ramón?" Mickey asked.

Diego blinked as he ran a hand over his mouth. "Cigars. He likes the Double Ligero from La Flor Dominicana. Got him a box."

"That sounds lovely," she said, shaking her wet hands. "I've never smoked a real cigar before. My uncle let me take a drag on a Swisher Sweet, but that was it."

He smiled. "What flavor?"

She scrunched her nose. "Vanilla. I begged him and he relented."

"And you hated it."

"Yep."

"But you're glad you tried it."

Mickey cracked a grin. "I guess so."

She seemed like a person who enjoyed trying new things. He suddenly wanted to know what else she'd tried, what other interests she had…what her life was like outside of his little bar. He regretted not being able to sit in her classroom, in one of those uncomfortable desk chairs, taking notes. He'd sit in the back, of course. Couldn't let her know how intently he studied her. Then perhaps he'd stay behind, after class, talk to her about her lesson. Ask her more questions. This fictitious version of himself was probably more charming than the Diego sitting at the picnic table.

They eventually fell into what Diego might call a *comfortable silence*, watching the two teams, Waitresses vs. Barbacks, sling beanbags. While he knew he'd be on duty later that evening, hanging out in the park with his friends felt nice. After polishing off a couple beers in the warm air, he was glad that Irene had come up with the celebration. The waitress team won their cornhole bout before people strolled back to the table to eat. Burgers were dressed, more drinks were poured and there was a serenity that blanketed the table.

After singing, cake-cutting and opening presents, the party began to die down and it was time to pack it in. Nearly all of them, except Jerry and Gina, would have to work that evening, so they slowly drifted toward their respective cars near the downtown strip. While the rest of the gang chattered near Ramón's truck, helping him put away his leftover cake and gifts, Diego followed Mickey to her car, which was parked next to his.

"This was nice," he said as the first drops of rain hit his face.

Mickey must have felt the rain as well, because she looked up and immediately gathered her loose fluffy curls into a tight ponytail. "It was! I'm glad I came."

"I'm glad you did, too," he admitted. When she looked back at him with a curious smile, Diego let the statement stand. He didn't try to cover it up with something gruff or prickly. He simply smiled and said, "We'll have to do this again."

Fat raindrops fell faster, and he knew he had to let her go. "I'll see you tonight," she said.

"You will."

He watched her get into her car before giving her a wave and retreating to his own driver's seat. As she pulled out into the street, he let out a sigh. "Give her space," he muttered to the empty car. "Let her be."

Diego hoped his resolve was stronger than this.

Because currently, after one nice day with Mickey, the desire to be next to her grew more intense. Sure, he'd see her tonight, work beside her at the bar, but that was different. The companionable silence they shared stuck to his bones and made him feel comfortable in his own skin. A feeling that was hard to let go of.

17

"You're late," Diego said from behind the bar.

Mickey stopped herself from rolling her eyes as she breezed past him, heading straight for the time clock. "I wanted to enter grades before coming in," she called over her shoulder.

"Grades are up?" he shouted in a nervous voice.

She grinned as she punched in and tied her apron around her waist. "Yup."

When she reappeared, Diego furiously wiped an already-clean bar with a white rag, determined not to meet her gaze. Even after yesterday's lovely birthday celebration, and last night's easygoing shift, it appeared that Diego was back on defense, looking gruff as ever. It didn't matter, though. Mickey was happy to come to work all the same. Even if she still had a couple more weeks to prove she wouldn't quit, yesterday's birthday party helped her feel at home with the bar family.

"You gonna check your grade?" she asked coolly.

His shoulders tensed mid-wipe before slouching. He hung his head and let out a sigh. "Do I want to?"

Mickey opened her mouth to speak but was interrupted by

Ollie, who rushed through the front door. "I know I'm late," she said, half running to the time clock. "I had a thing."

When Ollie disappeared in the back, Irene rushed in behind her. "Sorry I'm late, Boss!" she called, cutting the same rapid trail as Ollie had.

"Seems like all the women of this bar are losing all sense of time," Diego barked to the kitchen.

"I had a thing!" Irene shouted back.

She and Diego caught each other's curious gazes. She could tell he wanted to know more about the two women but wouldn't speak on it. Mickey filed it away for another day. Right now, her student needed another pep talk about his studies. "You should check your grade," she said, standing beside him. "It's your first grade in how many years?"

He furrowed his heavy brow. "That's why I'm not in a hurry," he replied in his customary stiff tone. "I just have a feeling I fucked it up."

"You won't know until you find out," she said, bumping his shoulder. "Until then, you'll just stress yourself out, wondering if you've got the chops."

Something flickered in his eyes before they softened. He scoffed before resting his elbows on the bar. "You think I got chops?"

He had what it took to finish her class and go on to the next. Diego Acosta was a solid writer. She wanted him to work on a few things, but he already had insight and eloquence. "Let's just say, I wish you expressed yourself *verbally* as well as you do when you write."

He raised a brow. "Yeah?"

Mickey nodded.

Diego finally pulled his phone from his back pocket and visited the grade portal for her class. While he did that, Mickey worked on serving one of their customers, a woman in her forties, who sat at a two-top with her laptop.

"Can I get another Bud Light. My tab is Keller," she said, brushing her blond curls from her face. She placed her empty bottle on the bar before them.

"Coming right up," Mickey said with a smile. "Are you really able to work on stuff in this space? I can't imagine how distracting the bar is."

The woman's green eyes lit up. "I can write anywhere," she said, returning Mickey's smile. "I grew up in a crowded house, so I guess I need the noise."

Mickey popped the bottle cap before handing the beer over. "What are you writing?"

The woman hesitated for a second before answering. "I'm trying to write a novel," she said with a half shrug. "I don't know if it's any good, but I think it's finally time to try…so why not?"

"How wonderful! What kind of novel are you writing?" she asked, leaning against the bar.

"It's a crime thriller."

"I can't believe I'm meeting an author tonight," Mickey said. "What's your name?"

The woman let out an abrupt laugh before taking a sip of her beer. "I'm Tara Keller, but I don't know if I'm an author."

Mickey shook her head. "If you're writing, you're a writer. So, you might as well be an author."

Tara blushed furiously as she held her beer bottle close to her chest. "I mean, I'm probably starting all of this writing business too late," she reasoned. "I'm a forty-six-year-old paralegal…"

"Which means you already know law jargon for your books," Mickey finished. "Oh, my god, you probably know all about sentencing times, jury selections and all that stuff.

I wouldn't even know where to start. And murder? I can't imagine how many details you'd have to keep in order. Suspects with the right motives, staging the crime scene, hiding a weapon… You're probably perfect for this genre!"

Tara blinked in shock. "I mean…yeah, I guess you're right. No one's ever put it quite like that."

Mickey shrugged. "You gotta write what you know, right?"

The woman nodded, as if she were sorting it out in her head. "Right."

"Okay!"

Tara continued nodding as she wandered off. "Right," she murmured to herself. Mickey caught her smile when she returned to her computer. Tara went right back to typing at high speed.

"How do you do that?" Diego asked, wearing a rare, curious smile. He laid his phone on the bar, his grade visible to them both.

"Do what?" she asked, glancing at his B+.

"Make a total stranger feel…special."

Mickey frowned, not understanding his question. She was genuinely interested in the woman's work and encouragement seemed like a natural response. "I don't want to sound corny, but everyone's special in their own way."

He rolled his eyes. "Yeah, that's corny."

"Do you have questions about your grade?" she asked, changing the subject. "We could have a quick office meeting."

Diego shook his head. "I think we probably need to stop having office meetings, Mickey."

His words would have been a disappointing blow if she hadn't spotted his tiny smile before he turned away. "You're probably right," she muttered, remembering Cleo's warning.

"Until we figure out how to stay out of trouble," he chuckled, "maybe we can meet at Fountain City."

"That's fair," Mickey replied, straightening up the well bottles. It wasn't a date, but her heart beat faster with the anticipation of sharing another small table with him. Maybe he'd wear his glasses again…

"But I don't have any questions," he said, referring to his phone. "I earned better than I expected, and I understand your comments about structuring my ideas. I feel good about it."

"You feel proud?" she asked.

Diego reached behind her for a bottle of Hendrick's on the top shelf. "Proud enough to treat myself to a gin and soda," he said. "I hear it's the best way to drink Hendrick's."

After he mixed his drink, and added a twist of lime, he held it up to the light, examining the contents. She watched him take a healthy gulp before offering the glass to her. Mickey was slow to accept it, wondering if it was appropriate. She was probably playing with fire, but the desire to try this dance with him was powerful.

"It's good?" he asked in a dark voice.

"Delicious."

His brow arched as he gazed at her. "So, we're ready for another professional night of working together?"

Mickey set his glass on the bar. "Absolutely."

And prayed that she told the truth.

I'm a B+ writer… Fuck yeah!

Even while serving drinks to a man who wanted to talk about IPAs, Diego had enough patience to listen to him. As the man in the striped polo yammered on and on about the merits of hops, Diego nodded along, thinking only about Mickey's comments.

She'd pointed out phrases she found entertaining. She enjoyed the subject he wrote about. He realized he should outline his papers in the future because he jumped around too much. But he could correct his mistakes. He could get better. For the first time in a long time, Diego wanted to *try*.

"So, anyway, Jumpin' Jack Flash is pretty good," said Polo Shirt. "But I keep telling people about your Purple Prose. It's definitely a superior IPA and the citrus notes are amazing. You know, you guys have a lot more local beers than the other places around here. You should really advertise. Get into that indie vibe."

"Uh-huh," Diego murmured, not remembering if he'd asked the man for advice. Someone tugged on the back of his shirt, saving him from more beer lectures. He turned around to find Mickey's hundred-watt smile beaming at him.

"I don't want to interrupt, but I wanted to ask you something."

"Of course," he said, following her to the other side of the bar. "What's up?"

She sneaked a peek at Polo Shirt before chuckling. "Nothing really, I'm just rescuing you from your customer. You had this blank look on your face that didn't match his level of enthusiasm."

Diego exhaled a relieved laugh. "Was it that obvious?"

"You're not the only one who can save people," she said with a wink.

That wink…must have rattled something loose in the machinery in his chest because his heart suddenly felt lighter. He couldn't help the growing smile on his face, or that she might witness it. "I—thanks."

"I also have a favor to ask you," she said, her eyes brightening as she bit her bottom lip. Diego fooled around with wiping down the bar to avoid staring at her mouth. Mickey was his employee, and a full nine years younger than he. This strange flirting they engaged in was incredibly inappropriate, and went against his vow not to get distracted by her. After

Ramón's birthday party and their shift together, he went home feeling hot and frustrated.

"Go ahead."

"I'd like to organize a karaoke night."

The request immediately disturbed him. "The bar's not busy enough for you?"

When the light flickered from her eyes, Diego knew he'd fucked up. Mickey opened her mouth before clamping it shut and diverting her eyes. "I just thought—"

"No, no, go on," he cut her off. "Give me your business plan."

He wished he hadn't been so abrupt because her hesitance to explain made him feel like an ass. She shrugged her shoulders and peeked up at him. "I just thought that it might be cool since we'd be the only bar who's doing it. Also, you have this stage but don't invite bands to perform. It might be nice to let patrons use it."

"I don't have any idea how to set up a karaoke system," Diego admitted.

Mickey sprang on it. "You wouldn't have to! My friend Patrick is a DJ, and he's got all the equipment you'd need. I'm pretty sure he could hook things up to your speakers and TVs."

"How much would I have to pay him?"

"I'd have to ask him," she said, her eyes already shining with excitement. "But I bet if you threw in free beer, it would sweeten the deal."

"So, where did this idea come from?" he asked, stroking his chin as he stared at her.

Mickey twisted her fingers in the ties of her apron. "Well, it's related to the next favor I need to ask for…"

Her nervousness was as adorable as it was concerning. "Do I look particularly generous today?" he asked, raising a brow.

"No, but I figured it wouldn't hurt to ask," she admitted.

A small smile crept onto her face. "I'd like to host a bachelorette party here. It's for my best friend's coworker, and I would take care of everything. I'll have them in the back with premade drinks, champagne and wine."

Diego rolled his eyes. "How are you going to find the time for that when you're teaching and behind the bar?"

"You forget, I've already taught your class," Mickey said triumphantly. "My PowerPoint lectures were recorded last year and don't need updating. All I do is answer emails and grade. Also, if I make the drinks ahead of time, the women will serve themselves, freeing Irene and Gina up to work the room."

Oh, she's thought of everything…

Diego's mind battled itself. The genuine fear of losing control of anything in his bar, in *Lucía's* bar, nagged him nightly. What if giving Mickey more responsibilities turned out to be a mistake? But her excitement was…contagious. She had a way of painting the bar with an optimism that he hadn't felt in years. Had Lucía come up with the idea, he wouldn't have given it a second thought.

"Let me think about it," he finally answered. "Maybe we can talk about it when we get coffee tomorrow."

Her eyes widened in surprise. "What makes you think I'll be at Fountain City tomorrow?"

Diego's hands itched as his heart jittered wildly in his chest. "I don't—I just—I planned to work on your next assignment, and I figured you might wanna share a table." His hands clenched on the bar's edge, waiting to hear her speak. He hoped he hadn't made a damn fool of himself…but also hoping she'd say yes.

"Alright, then," she said. "I'll be there."

He gave a curt nod before tapping the bar with his knuckles, checking to see if the polished wood was in working order. "Sounds good."

Diego wandered back to his side of the bar where Polo Shirt waited, but quickly busied himself with another customer.

Another coffee date? To what end? Hadn't he told himself to dial it back? He wanted to give Mickey her space, make her feel comfortable enough in his bar. A coffee date, if he could even call it that, was just him toeing the line before stepping over it again. But she'd asked for a favor and he relented... Perhaps he wanted to do himself a favor.

He looked down the bar at Mickey.

She was talking to that woman from before, the writer. They were laughing as if they were old friends. Mickey treated everyone like they were old friends. She could do the same for him if he would lighten the fuck up. The thought almost pushed his doubt away, making room for hope.

18

It's not a date.

It's not a date.

So why did Diego take care in getting ready that morning? When he stood in his bathroom mirror, styling his hair, he grew frustrated by the amount of gray he kept spotting. No matter which way his comb ran, a silver strand appeared. He finally concluded that he hadn't paid attention to his appearance after Lucía died. His formerly black hair had been carefully invaded by silver sideburns when he wasn't looking. Diego had simply aged. And while forty-two looked good on him, the reminder was still a small shock.

"¡Mano!" Ramón snapped at him from the driver's seat.

They sat in the downtown parking lot near the Riverwalk before Diego realized where he was. "What?"

"You gonna be here all day?"

"Yeah, yeah," he said, returning to the present. "Until my shift."

Ramón had helped Diego take his car to the shop for brake maintenance before giving him a ride downtown. Now, as they sat in the cab of Ramón's pickup, an uncomfortable silence settled over the two men. Diego was almost tempted to talk to his brother-in-law about his feelings, but had stopped himself twice on the drive over. It was easier to settle into rumination mode instead.

"How's school going?" Ramón asked.

"Why?"

Ramón arched his brow. "Why do I want to know?"

Diego shook his head. "Sorry, it's fine."

"You're on edge," he chuckled. "How is it really going?"

Diego leaned back on his headrest and sighed. "It's actually going better than I expected. I'm glad I started with one class… I think that's all I could have handled for the summer."

"Your teacher is okay?"

His gaze slid to Ramón's. He'd almost forgotten that no one knew Mickey was his professor. Diego tested the waters. "Mickey Chambers is my professor," he said carefully. "She's teaching my writing class."

His brother-in-law's eyes widened before he let out a braying laugh. "Dios mío… I wish I could have seen your face when you found out."

Diego's face broke into a grin. "Yeah, I was a little shocked, I guess."

"You better be extra nice to her, then," Ramón joked.

Diego couldn't bring himself to join in the laughter. His behavior toward Mickey had oscillated between asshole to… well, a little too intimate. He probably confused the hell out of her. "What do you think of her?" he asked.

"I like Mickey," Ramón said, nodding as he stared at the brackish waters of the Chattahoochee River before them. "She's a really nice girl. Pretty funny, too. She's always in the kitchen with the jokes, you know?" He paused. "There's something about her… She brings a different energy to the bar."

He knew what Ramón meant. "What do you think of karaoke in the bar?"

"¿Qué?"

Diego shrugged. "I don't know. It was something she mentioned last night. She suggested using the stage for karaoke."

"That might be fun," he chuckled. "Lucía would have loved that."

"I kinda thought that, too…"

They went silent again, thinking about Lucía. He and Ramón didn't talk about her as much as they should. The loss had stunned them silent for the first couple years. Only recently did it feel okay to speak of her, laugh about her, remember all the funny things she had done. And then his brother-in-law said something that jolted him out of his thoughts.

"You think it's time for you to start dating again?"

Diego's heart hammered against his ribs. "What?"

Ramón shrugged, still gazing at the river. "We don't talk about it, and maybe that's my fault…but don't you think Lucía would want you to move forward?"

Diego ran a hand over his mouth. "I don't know."

Ramón turned his body in his seat, resting his hand on Diego's shoulder. "Hey."

He forced himself to look his brother-in-law in the eye. "Yeah?"

"You were a good husband, Diego." He squeezed his shoulder. "You made my sister very happy. Maybe it's time for you to make yourself happy. Take care of yourself."

The heaviness in Ramón's palm, the reassuring squeeze, was enough to leave Diego speechless. After caring for his mother, and then his wife, Diego couldn't remember the last time someone told him to take care of himself.

All he could do was nod.

"Anyway, just think about it. Forty-two is probably too young to live alone."

"Speak for yourself," Diego protested. "Who are *you* dating these days?"

"Shit… I'm talking to ladies here and there," Ramón said with a laugh.

"Okay, okay, let's change the subject."

"I'm gonna let you go so I can get home. I'll see you tonight."

Diego grabbed his satchel. "Get some rest, man."

Once he left the truck, his walk to the coffeehouse was brisk. Just that brief talk with Ramón validated him, made him consider the possibilities. He checked his phone, making sure he wasn't late for Mickey. He still had a couple minutes to find a table, get his shit together and prepare himself to focus on his schoolwork.

Once he reached Fountain City, he took a deep breath and stepped inside.

"Hey there," said the kid at the counter. It was Mickey's student Kevin.

"Hi," he said absently as he searched the space for Mickey. He found her standing by the counter, mixing sugar and cream in her coffee. She wore another cute outfit, a blue-and-white-striped sundress that hung to her knees. All her looks were adorable; Mickey just knew how to wear clothes.

Feeling unusually playful, Diego slowly approached Mickey, hoping to surprise her. When he came right up to her, he was about to say something funny, but didn't expect her to turn around with her coffee in hand.

Before he could open his mouth, Mickey bumped into him, sloshing hot coffee onto his shirt and khakis. He hissed in pain as he doubled over, clutching the counter beside him.

"Oh, my god, Diego! Are you okay?" she cried, grabbing

a stack of napkins and immediately pressing them against his stomach. "I didn't see you standing there."

"I know, I know," he breathed, trying to avoid the burning liquid against his skin. Mickey tried to pat his clothing with her napkins as best as she could, but as her hands trailed down his front, Diego jumped back. "It's okay."

Her blush hit her cheeks as she realized how dangerously close she'd gotten to his crotch. "I'm so sorry."

They were attracting attention from customers around them, and he didn't want to embarrass her further. "I'm just gonna step outside," he said, backing away from her.

"Kevin, do you have some paper towels?" she asked.

"Sure, hold on."

Diego went back outside to wring his shirt onto the sidewalk and noticed how wet the front of his pants were. He'd have to change his clothes before his bar shift, and he had no car to get home. Ramón was most likely on his way back to his house for a nap.

Mickey rushed out of Fountain City Beans with a wad of paper towels ready to dry his groin. "Oh, no," she said. "You're wet all over. Does it still burn?"

He stood up straight and grimaced. "Not anymore, but it's pretty uncomfortable."

"I would imagine," she said, handing him the paper towels. "Maybe we can put off our coffee thing so you can go home and change."

Diego paused mid-wipe. "About that... Ramón dropped me off because my car is in the shop."

"I could drive you," she blurted. "Let me just get my bag and I'll take you home."

Before he could object, she disappeared, leaving him to worry. He couldn't spend alone time with her. The whole point of meeting in public was so he wasn't tempted to do anything foolish.

And now she was taking him home…

"It's the red house on your right," Diego said, pointing to the street. "That's my driveway."

Aside from directions to his house, he had remained quiet during their drive. She frowned as she approached the gravel driveway. Diego lived in her favorite house? The red house she always took time to admire? Now the disappearance of the porch rocker made sense. The other one belonged to his wife. *Jesus…* "Your home is lovely, Diego. I don't see very many red houses," she said, trying to make conversation.

He peered out her windshield and nodded. "That was my wife's idea," he said. "She wanted to stand out."

"I like the way she thought," Mickey said with a smile.

He caught her gaze and returned her smile, but his was a little sad. "Yeah, she liked bold stuff."

For a moment, Mickey's car went quiet. She wondered if he was going to ask her inside.

"Would you like to come inside?" he asked, breaking the silence. "I asked you out and now…"

"Sure," she quickly replied. "Do you have coffee?"

"I do," he said, opening his door. "It's not as fancy as what your student makes, but I've got fresh milk and some sugar."

Mickey reached toward her back seat for her bag at the same time as he did. Their outstretched arms bumped into each other, and her breath caught in her throat as she came face-to-face with him. She immediately retreated from his space, apologizing as she went.

Diego quickly retrieved his bag and exited the car, leaving her to get herself together. She took a few deep breaths, grabbed her bag and followed him up his walkway. "You have a really lovely porch, too," she said. "It's a lot like my parents' wraparound."

"I like it," Diego said, unlocking his front door. "It's nice to sit out here in the evenings."

"Do you yell at kids to stay off your grass?"

He led her inside a vestibule, where she slipped off her shoes and nudged them against the wall. "You think I'm the man who yells at children?" he asked with a frown.

Once they passed through the foyer, she found a spacious living room to her right and a tidy office to her left. She tried to take in as much as she could without appearing nosy. "I've seen you do it," she murmured as she glanced at a bedroom; sheets and a comforter were strewed about the bed. Did he sleep downstairs?

"If you're referring to those knucklehead college students, they deserved it. And I would hardly call them children," he said, leading her down the hallway to an impressive kitchen. He'd painted the walls a sunny yellow and his appliances were vintage. There was a cute breakfast nook next to a large bay window that looked over a spacious backyard. Mickey barely listened to him as she basked in the warmth of his kitchen. "You're not a kid if you're buying liquor in my bar."

Mickey waved him off as she wandered the space. "Okay, fine, you yelled at young adults, then."

He scoffed but didn't argue. Instead, she watched him pull coffee from his cabinet. Was he really about to start a fresh pot while wearing his soiled clothes?

"Diego, shouldn't you go get cleaned up?" Mickey asked as she stood near his kitchen table.

"I thought I'd get you started first," he said, rinsing out the decanter and jamming it under the drip. "It only takes a minute."

Anxiety vibrated throughout her body. They were alone,

in his house, where no one could stop them from kissing one another. Surely, he understood the danger in waiting just a minute. Mickey cleared her throat and set her bag on his table. “Okay, I’ll watch the coffee,” she said.

“That was your first beverage job, right?” he asked as he turned on the machine. He wiped his wet hands on his khakis, which were still damp from her spill, and leaned against the counter. “You told Jeanie that you worked at a coffee shop... Where was it?”

“In Athens,” she said, sitting at his table. “I did it while I got my master’s degree.”

“You like it?”

She shrugged as she thought back to that time. Her coworkers were alright, mostly checked out and barely cleaned after their shift. Her manager was a former hippie who enjoyed talking about and drinking coffee more than he liked running a business. “Let’s just say it was better than working at Men’s Warehouse.”

Diego raised a brow. “Really? You styled men at one time?”

Mickey laughed. “Styled is a strong word, but I’ll remember that the next time I update my résumé.”

He cracked a smile and shook his head. “You’re an interesting woman, Mickey,” he said, pulling away from the counter. “I’m just going to change my clothes and I’ll join you. The Wi-Fi password is Lucia80!, capital L, all one word.”

She watched him wander down the hallway and disappear into the bedroom she’d spotted earlier.

As she set up her computer, Mickey heard him close the door behind him and move around the room. The drip of his coffee machine drew her attention back to the kitchen. What was she doing here? What was she hoping for? Cleo’s words drifted back to her: do not fuck this man...yet.

She didn’t have long to think about her friend’s warning

before Diego padded back to the kitchen wearing a new forest green T-shirt and a pair of khaki shorts that came to his mid-thigh. She'd never seen him wear shorts but was delighted by his muscular brown legs and bare feet. Mickey was probably thinking too much into it, but a shorts-wearing Diego seemed more relaxed.

Of course, he was in his home… Why wouldn't he want to be comfortable? "So, did you get a chance to look at this week's lecture on review writing?"

Diego gave an affirmative grunt as he set up his laptop. "I thought I would be ready to throw a review together until I saw the lecture," he said on his way to get coffee. He pulled two mugs from his cabinet and gathered the milk and sugar. "You take cream and sugar?"

"Yes, please. What was wrong with my PowerPoint?"

"Nothing was wrong, I just underestimated what you wanted from us." He brought her coffee to her. "What you're asking is a helluva lot different from what dicks post on my Yelp page."

Mickey ducked her head to hide her grin. "Pretty rough reviews, huh?"

He sat down with his coffee, drinking it black. "If you call *the bartender is an asshole* rough, then yeah," he scoffed. "I never see anything about criteria backing up their claims."

While she was happy that he'd completed her forty-minute PowerPoint lecture, she was even happier that he'd applied what he learned to real-world examples of writing. "No, Yelp reviews aren't well written, but you don't think that that reviewer had a point?" she asked, peeking at him from behind her computer.

His eyes flickered to her before narrowing. "You calling your boss an asshole, Mickey?"

"Nope," she said, shaking her head. "As far as I know, only Irene gets to do that without getting fired."

The corner of his mouth quirked. "When you work with me as long as Irene has, you'll earn the honor, too. Until then, keep it under your hat."

"Will do, Boss."

She opened the grading portal for the students' latest journal entries. The Five Senses exercise asked her writers to reflect on an eating experience that employed each of their five senses. Again, all her students hit the mark; some even took the opportunity to write funny anecdotes about unpleasant experiences. When she clicked on Diego's entry, she read it carefully.

It's nothing to look at, the turkey mole at La Nacional Restaurant and Grocery, but I think it's the best dish they serve. The stewed meat is so tender it hangs loose from the leg bone. Translucent slivers of onion sit atop bright yellow saffron rice. The dark brown mole sauce is a steaming hot glaze filling every crevice of the turkey.

If Yara is in the kitchen cooking, she's so liberal with the sauce that it can drip off the plate. I like to run my finger along the edge and taste it before I tuck in. Just the sauce alone: the bittersweetness of the chocolate mixed with the smoky spice of the ancho chili makes my mouth water every time I think about it...

By the time Mickey finished reading his entire entry, her stomach grumbled in disappointment. Wherever this restaurant was, she needed to go there and order the turkey mole. But his descriptive way with words also made her swoon. She could almost imagine his smile as his plate was brought to him, licking sauce from his fingers, moaning from the sweet and savory flavors... "Good lord," she murmured to her computer screen.

"What's wrong?" Diego asked.

Her gaze darted up. “Oh, nothing,” she said, face suddenly feeling flush. “It’s just an annoying email.”

“Mhm.” His eyes roved over her face, making her even warmer.

As he silently appraised her, Mickey turned Cleo’s warning into a mantra. *Don’t fuck this man yet, don’t fuck this man yet, don’t fuck this man yet…* But it was so damn hard. They had the gift of privacy—no one would interrupt them, he was wearing shorts, she’d just read how he licked sauce off his fingers. It truly wasn’t fair.

“Can I use your bathroom?” she blurted out.

“Of course,” he said, nodding toward the hallway. “It’s the first door on your left.”

She hurried off in that direction to get away from his piercing stare, his muscular calves and whatever sexy cologne he wore. Mickey just needed to throw some cold water on her face and remember the mantra: *don’t fuck this man yet.*

19

Once she patted her neck and chest with cold wet hands, Mickey stared at herself in the mirror. "Get a hold of yourself, Chambers." She was going to go back into the kitchen, do more class prep and not study Diego Acosta's every move.

She steeled her nerves as she opened the door to the hallway. Maybe before she had to face him, she could do a little first-floor exploration. No harm in scoping out his living space while getting herself together. Mickey drifted into the living room.

His living room was cozy with proper furniture, not the Ikea pieces she'd had to Allen-wrench together. A large flat-screen television was the focal point of the space. He positioned two navy blue easy chairs and a matching sofa around it. Wood accents filled the rest of the space, dark stained end tables and a coffee table. "Your decor is really nice, too," she called out.

"Also my wife's doing," his muffled voice replied.

She slid her sock-covered feet against the dark hardwood floor as she ran her fingers along the back of his couch. "She had a good eye," she said.

"She was a stylish lady," he said, his voice much closer.

Mickey jumped at the sound and glanced at him over her shoulder. "I see…"

He stood in the hallway, leaning against the wall, staring at her. "What are you doing?"

Mickey's heart thumped hard against her ribs as she turned toward him. Her exploration was over, and it was time to return to the kitchen where she should mind her own business. She suddenly felt silly spying on his life. "I just wanted to see how you lived," she said with a laugh. "Not even my best friend, Cleo, has such an adult setup."

He ran his fingers through his hair and gazed around the living room. "Adult setup," he intoned softly. "I guess that's what it is."

Okay, enough of this, Mickey decided. She walked toward him, heading back to her computer, taking care to maintain a wide berth around Diego. He straightened away from the wall just as she crossed her path, nearly bumping into her. "Sorry," she said, as he caught her by the elbow.

That's all it took, really.

Once his large warm hands pressed against her bicep, Mickey's resolve broke. She froze and he didn't release her. Their eyes locked, sharing the same frightening realization at the same time. "No," he murmured. "I'm sorry."

Since that night in the bar's basement, there were too many things left on the table. He'd said he wanted her. And while his statement could have meant a whole host of things, Mickey desperately wanted him to put a finer point on it. "Diego," she whispered, taking a step back from him.

His fingers tightened, forcing her still, but only for a few seconds before he realized what he was doing. "I'm sorry," he repeated, shaking his head, as if he were shaking some idea loose from his brain. But when he looked at her again, it was still there. Whatever thoughts plagued him darkened his eyes and made his cheeks flush.

Together, they stood awkwardly, wondering what to say that wasn't another apology. Mickey wondered if she should run back to the kitchen, toward something safer: coffee, lesson plans, mundane chitchat. Or stay here and stoke the fire in Diego's eyes.

She didn't have long to decide before he took a step toward her, raised his hand to her cheek and let his thumb stroke her face. "What are you doing?" she asked, leaning into his touch.

He stared at her mouth as he traced the calloused pad of his thumb down her jaw. "I don't know," he finally whispered. He took another step until he stood over her. "But I don't want to let you go."

Heat flooded her face as his fingers played along her skin. A tingling sensation buzzed in her chest and in her belly, while her breasts rose and fell with each breath. Mickey wanted to reach out and grab him, her mantra long forgotten. She wanted to kiss him, searching his mouth with her tongue, to bury her hands in his hair. "You don't have to let me go," she told him. "We talked about this."

He raised a brow in recognition as he gave her an uncertain nod. "I didn't—I never gave you an answer."

Diego hadn't said anything during their phone call about acting on his desires, but perhaps this moment was his answer. With her back against the wall and Diego right on top of her, Mickey had hoped he would find her through the haze of doubt and lust. "Talk to me, Diego."

His hand shook as it drifted down to her neck. He used his thumb to stroke her riotous pulse, looking between that spot and her face. "Call it luck, but I'm glad you spilled coffee on me. I'm glad my car's in the shop today. And I'm glad that you're standing right here."

Mickey's brain glitched as she stared at his lips. "Why's your car in the shop?"

"Brakes," he said, planting his hand on the wall above her head. "I wore my brakes down."

"Oh," she breathed. "That could be dangerous."

"Very," he agreed. "I feel like I'm driving without them right now."

Mickey was also barreling toward a cliff and had no intention of slowing down, either. "Why are you glad that I'm standing here?"

His other hand tipped her chin upward. His calloused fingers were cool against her warm skin as he splayed them along her neck. "Because, Mickey," he murmured, "I've waited too long to touch you. Do you mind if I touch you?"

"No, I don't," she said dreamily. His fingers caressed her thrumming pulse delicately, pulling her toward him like a moth to flame. She held the wall behind her and pushed forward until she was only inches from his face.

"Can I kiss you?"

She nodded.

"Talk to me, Professor," he commanded with a quiet rumble.

"Yes," she whispered.

Diego studied her lips while she waited impatiently for him to do something. It was as if he wanted to commit the terrain of her mouth to memory before tasting it.

"Please?" Mickey added.

His dark brown eyes cut to hers. "Of course," he said before slowly dipping downward to kiss her. His lips brushed lightly against hers, but the grip on the back of her neck tightened.

She raised up to meet his lips, pressing hard against him and feeling the softness of his mouth. He angled his head to take more of her, licking at her until she opened her mouth and accepted his tongue. He released the wall behind her and pulled her soft body against him.

Mickey gasped between his devouring kisses, trying not to drown in them, but soaking in pleasure that wet her through and through. She clutched his biceps and kissed him back, spiraling in a maelstrom of sensations. She tilted her head back as he kissed down her neck to her chest. His hands cupped her breasts through her dress, pushing them upward. Diego kissed through the fabric as he squeezed. "Mickey," he whispered. "Can I taste you?"

She blindly parted her legs in response as she stared at his face. She needed to feel his touch everywhere. There was no way she would tell him no. "Yes," she panted.

Diego slowly inched the hem of her dress up her thighs as he kneeled before her. He ran one hand along her inner thigh until she leaned back and widened her stance. "I want you," he choked out in a hoarse voice. "I meant what I said in the basement, Mickey. I don't—I can't think of a better way to say it, but it's the truth."

Her eyes followed him to the floor and found a starved man. What Diego needed, she could only guess. Affection? Intimacy? Passion? Mickey could give him those things; she wanted them, too. She helped him by hitching her dress up to her breasts. "I heard you the first time, Diego," she said. "I want you, too."

On his knees, he gave her a half grin before pulling her panties to her knees. "You're already wet for me," he murmured against her thighs, almost amazed by the observation. He marveled at her nakedness for a moment before meeting her gaze. "What have you been imagining, Mickey?"

"This," she said in a halted breath. "I've wanted this."

"Open up for me," he said in a quiet voice, pulling her panties down to her ankles. She stepped out of them before her skin broke out in goose bumps at his command. "I want to see all of you."

Mickey complied but gestured to the dress bunched in her fists. "You haven't seen all of me."

He sat back on his heels and gave her a rare tremulous smile that lit his entire face, like a boy in a candy shop uncertain of what he could have. "Do you want to undress for me?"

She quickly pulled her sundress over her head and cast it inside the room.

"Your bra, too, please," he said politely. "I want all of you."

Mickey reached behind her back and unclipped her bra, letting it drop to the floor. When she fully revealed herself to him, she stood straight against the wall and pushed her breasts outward as if to say, *This is all of me*.

He gazed up at her in wonderment, his eyes searching her body. "You're so beautiful…" Diego whispered before kissing her inner thigh. His lips crept upward until his nose hit the crease between her thigh and pussy. Mickey inhaled sharply as he kissed the sensitive skin at her juncture. He teased her by not touching her clit directly, but it was enough to rattle her.

"Thank you. A man hasn't done this in a long time. Some guys are a little *meh* about going down, so I don't press the subject. But for some reason blow jobs are—"

"Mickey," he cut her off as he lifted her leg over his shoulder.

"Yeah?"

"I can't really talk while I'm eating," he said in a low voice, his hot breath fanning against her skin, causing a shiver to run through her body.

Her jaw fell open. Oh, he's *serious* serious… "Go ahead then," she breathed.

"Thank you," he said.

With one thigh hitched over his shoulder, Mickey exposed

herself to Diego's undivided attention. He kissed the inside of her thigh, licking the plump flesh before rubbing his lips across her folds. The quick brush sent a jolt throughout her body, making her grasp the wall behind her. Diego spread her lips open and ran a finger between them, grazing her clit. She gasped at the sensation and tried not to double over, but she had to hold on to something.

"Hang on to my head," he whispered as if reading her mind.

"Okay."

And then Diego ate.

He started with a simple move: flattening his tongue while licking up and down. But something so elementary shouldn't have made Mickey shudder like she did. Her head lolled against the doorjamb as she gave herself over to waves of sensation. Each stroke against her wet softness was slow and deliberate, as though Diego was committing her taste to memory. As his hot tongue lapped at her, she floated through every pitch and fall of arousal, unable to catch her breath.

"Could you use your fingers, too?" she asked. She needed something to fill her as his tongue stroked her. Diego groaned against her pussy, sending delightful vibrations right to her womb, before gently pushing one finger inside her. She clenched around his intrusion, letting out a sigh as her shoulders sagged. "Yes..."

His finger started off slowly, curled toward him, rubbing against her G-spot. As if planned, Diego moved to the next stage of attack: circling his tongue around the hood of her clit, but not making direct contact with it. Now both of her hands were in his hair, and she breathed through each teasing caress that came close, but not quite there.

Mickey felt a carnal thrill as she rode his face while watching it shine with her wetness. "Please," she panted.

One finger quickly became two, and his tongue finally

zeroed in on the primary goal. Once he made contact with her sensitive clit, he went to work with a rapid flicker of his tongue. Mickey whimpered as she felt the rising crescendo. "Oh, god," she moaned, tears wetting her lashes. "Diego… Oh, god, Diego."

He didn't let up.

As she fell forward, her fingers slid through his hair until she touched the back of his neck. He held her up with his free hand while suctioning her between his lips, and applied more pressure. The last part of his well-crafted plan now included briskly alternating between strong sucking and languorous licks. Mickey chased the surge of a mounting orgasm, writhing against Diego's insistent mouth. Her breath came in ragged pants until the dam broke and she spilled into an abyss, a bright expanse of spasms and waves that swept over her until her body weakened and her cries became groans.

Mickey floated on that high until she caught her breath. Diego's tongue gave her a few playful swipes before pulling away. When he finally sat back on his heels, his expression was a mix of arrogance and arousal.

She slid her leg from his shoulder and tried to lean upright against the wall. "That was…"

"Alright?" he asked, standing before her.

She rested her head against the wall and breathed deeply. "You weren't just alright, Diego, and you know that."

"I guess that clears up the basement situation?"

Mickey forced herself to ignore her current vulnerable state and met his piercing gaze. He pressed his clothed body against her nakedness and ran his fingers along the curve of her hip. She gave a wordless nod. Diego's nearness, his scent, which now mingled with hers, overwhelmed her senses. All she could do was lean back and take his kisses, hoping she wouldn't pass out from the pleasure.

"You realize this changes everything about our working relationship," he said with a heavy sigh. "I've licked my employee's pussy and you've let your student go down on you."

His observations pulled her right out of her swoon and back into the real world. "No shit," she said with a startled laugh. "We have some stuff to figure out."

20

Had he planned this?

Diego, who had undressed before getting into bed, glanced over at the woman sitting beside him, drinking coffee. Mickey was naked, of course, with blankets tucked around her breasts, but she seemed very much at home…in his bed. As if they wouldn't have to go into work together in a few hours and pretend to—what were they pretending? He could barely remember.

It was hard to recall why he hadn't wanted sunshine in his life now that he'd finally warmed his face against it.

"You're staring," she said into her coffee mug.

"I am," he admitted, taking the cup from her hands and placing it on the nightstand behind her. "It's nice to do it after denying myself for so long." He brought her wrist to his mouth and kissed along her arm until he reached the inside of her elbow. She shivered under his lips before sinking into the pillows. He delighted in how soft her skin was as he rubbed his cheek against her bicep.

She leaned closer as he placed a gentle kiss on her shoulder, angling herself to face him. "Why did you deny yourself?" she asked.

Diego ran his tongue along her throat, eliciting a chuckle from her. Her laughter soon became a groan as he kissed her jaw, licking behind her ear. "I think the reasons are obvious," he whispered. "This is very inappropriate."

She gasped as his teeth closed around her earlobe. "Yes, it is," she breathed.

"And I haven't thought about another woman like this in about five years," he admitted, pulling her against his naked body.

Although she let herself fall into his arms, Mickey pulled her face back to peer at him. "Is that true?"

He nodded, nervous to hear her reaction to the news. "Not since my wife."

Mickey rested her hand on the center of his chest and bit her lip. It took her a moment to speak as she searched his eyes. "Thank you for trusting me," she finally said with a smile.

Her smile wasn't pitying, and he appreciated that about her. Mickey didn't feel sorry for him; she just listened. He tangled his legs with hers and pushed an aching erection against her soft thighs. "You don't mind this?" he murmured. "Being kissed by an asshole widower who makes you cut garnish?"

Her eyes softened. "You can't help being a widower, but you can probably do something about being an asshole." She shifted against him, slipping her thigh between his. "You could just be nicer."

He caught her under her chin, nudging it upward to kiss her neck. She let out another satisfied sigh. "I think you like it when I'm a dick," he growled in her ear.

Her breath hitched in her throat as he climbed atop her, pressing his hips against her. The wetness between her thighs returned as he positioned himself between them. A gentle blush marked her nut-brown skin as he ground against her. "I don't like cutting the garnish," she panted, raking her nails against his back.

Diego shuddered, losing himself in the sensation. The feeling of her stiff nipples, pressed against his chest, the sheen of sweat sliding between them. Even the coconut in her hair was as fun and playful as a piña colada, but her lips…they tasted better than any aged scotch he'd ever had the pleasure of drinking. All of Mickey was meant for overindulgence and intoxication. "I'll prep the limes tonight," he muttered.

She caught his mouth and kissed him roughly. "Are you trying to exchange labor for sexual favors?"

He rocked his pelvis slowly, savoring every bit of her slickness sliding against his dick. He was so hard he could barely think. "Is it working?"

"Yes," she panted, raising her hips.

The intense pleasure of his dick at her entrance almost made him move forward with instinct, but a sudden thought made him pause. "Shit," he breathed, remembering he didn't have condoms on hand. He hadn't needed them in years…

"What?"

"Uh…unless you're carrying, we don't have protection."

She flashed a wide grin as she bucked her hips again. "It's been a minute for me, but I'm on birth control."

"Thank god," he said, kissing her. "Because I want to fuck you so badly, Mickey."

"How badly?" she goaded.

Diego reached down and guided himself at her entrance. With his head, he rubbed between her lips, grazing her clit. The gasp she let out made him grin through the intensity. "About as much as you want it."

She widened her legs. "I want it," she whispered.

He nudged just the tip inside, grunting at the pressure of

her tightness. Mickey arched her back from the mattress to meet him. "You'll take this dick?" he asked, lashing his tongue across her nipple.

She nodded as she squeezed her eyes. "Yes."

As Diego sank into her, he lost himself halfway through the journey. Overwhelmed by every touch and sensation, he groaned in pleasure, squeezing the globe of her breast. "Oh, god, Mickey," he said in a hushed voice as she pushed forward.

"Yes, yes," she whispered back.

Once seated inside her, he paused. "Are you okay?" he said, looking down at her.

"Yes," she said, her brow furrowing. "And I'll be even better when you fuck me."

"You sound a little huffy, Professor," Diego said, sliding back in roughly, bouncing Mickey slightly.

Her eyes widened as she yelped in surprise. "Okay, then," she squeaked.

"Hold on, honey," he said before kissing her again.

She wrapped her legs around his hips and rode through the rough thrusts, gasping and moaning with every plunge. "Di—ego, oh, god…oh, yes…"

He couldn't call what they were doing *fucking.* That sounded much more crass than the sensations he drowned in. The tightness of her walls surrounding and massaging his dick was too deep. The way her hips rose and fell in time with each stroke was like a stormy symphony. Each of her whimpers and moans mingled with his grunts and growls, punctuating the music beautifully. He wasn't just a rutting animal desperate to spend himself; he was making love to Mickey. The thought almost pulled him out of the act, reminding him how long it had been.

"Oh, right there," Mickey hissed. "Slower, please."

He slowed his pace, increasing the grind against her clit. She let out a long moan while arching her back once again.

"I wanna be on top," she panted, pressing her hand to his cheek. "I want to ride you, Diego."

He didn't stop to question it. He quickly rolled them over until he was on his back. He shoved pillows out of his way and kicked the covers to the floor. "Ride me, baby."

From this vantage point, she was even more of a sun goddess, pinning him in place with her thick thighs, an exultance that made his breath stutter. Diego had no choice but to lay back and let her radiance shine over his body. "Oh, god," she breathed through the pleasure. "You feel so good."

He was about to tell her the same as he ran his hands along her stomach, up to her breasts, but when she began moving, all words died on his lips. He tried not to hold her hips in place and let him drive into her, as the urge to control the pace was overwhelming. Instead, he focused on pleasuring her from his position.

Diego circled her clit with his thumb while squeezing her breast with his other hand. The way she moved, slow and deliberate, withholding and giving, drove him crazy with want. She held the pace, not at a gallop but a steady stroll, milking pleasure from him and making Diego growl as he tweaked her nipple. "Good god, Mickey," he moaned. "That's it, honey."

"I'm close," she whimpered. "I'm so fucking close..."

She *was* close. Her walls twitched around his dick as she rode him. She changed her tempo and picked up a little more steam. He released her breasts to let them bounce while he gripped ample handfuls of her ass. He'd help drive her to the finish line if he needed to.

Mickey pressed her palms against his chest as she let her head drop. "Oh, my god," she chanted. "Oh, my god..."

"Come on, baby," he urged her. "That's it... Give it to me."

"Yes, yes…" She rocked hard against him; a droplet of sweat landed on his chest. "Yes, yes, oh, god, yes!"

Her pussy fluttered around him as she doubled over, jerking and spasming toward climax. "Yes…good," he said, holding her tight against his chest. As he rose into her like a well-oiled piston, she whimpered in his ear, riding her own orgasm and holding herself still through the storm.

Diego felt her wetness leak down his length, covering his balls as he drove in and out of her. The sounds of her juices and their flesh slapping joined the chorus, making him delirious with desire and his balls tighten.

Mickey had all but gone limp in his arms, but she was still there, urging him on. "Do it," she whispered. "Fuck me."

Her dirty command nestled in his brain; it was enough to make him lose control, let go of the reins. Diego squeezed his eyes shut and gritted his teeth as an intense orgasm rolled through his body like a tidal wave. His toes curled as his muscles clenched and his stomach dipped. "Aye, fuuucck," he growled, tightening his arms around Mickey's body. The wave rolled out to sea, leaving him breathless and tired, but unable to separate from her. Subtle tremors shuddered through him, but he never let her go.

Mickey was the first to lift herself up. She looked down at him with a sneaky grin. "Alright?"

Diego took her smile in, let it shine through the rough exterior of his heart, and sighed. "You know that was more than alright," he said. "You were brilliant."

She pushed herself to a seated position, his dick still inside her. He let out an involuntary moan as she shifted atop him. "You and I have very dirty mouths when we fuck," she chuckled. "I didn't expect that."

He shrugged. "It felt right."

Mickey threaded her fingers through his chest hair to pinch his nipples until he hissed.

"Ahh, come on..." he warned, feeling warm all over again. He slapped her ass in response.

Her laugh was music to his ears. "Where's your shower?"

"You have to go upstairs."

"This is a guest room," she said, looking around the room.

"I rarely sleep upstairs," he admitted. When he came home from the bar, it was easier to work in the office and then fall into bed in this room. He tried not to think about it too hard. That would mean having to admit he didn't like to sleep in the bed he once shared with Lucía.

"Can I use your shower?"

"Of course."

"You know I can't go to work smelling like you, right?" she asked with a grin.

Diego gripped her ass possessively. "Why not?" he asked. "Would that be a bad thing?"

"Are you trying to save me from the next army ranger who hits on me?"

The thought thrilled and frightened him. After being alone for so long, the urge to take ownership of a woman, to make her his, made his heart thud with worry and anticipation. "Are you worried about my cum dripping down your thighs while you serve beer?" he asked in a soft voice while rubbing her ass.

Mickey let out a startled laugh before her eyes went hazy with lust. "I wasn't...but now I'm thinking about it."

"It could be our little secret," he murmured, running his hands along her thighs. "My handprints on your body. My kisses burning your skin. My...staining you. You think you could work like that for the rest of the evening?"

Her thighs trembled around him as her fingers touched his

chest idly. "No… I can't work like that. And I don't think you'd want me to."

Mickey was right. They still had a shift at The Saloon to get through. He needed her on her toes, ready to deal with any disaster that came their way. "The bathroom is upstairs, third door on your left. Towels are above the toilet."

She lifted herself from him and planted a sweet kiss on his lips. "Just you wait, Diego Acosta. I'm going to bring so much sunshine and rainbows into your life you're going to get sick of me."

He tugged her closer to deepen their kiss. When he finally released her, letting her climb from the bed and leave the room, he had a sudden bereft feeling that startled him.

Get sick of her?

He didn't see that happening. Mickey Chambers and her soft hands had left an impression on him that would be difficult to shake.

21

Okay, we're trying this again.

As Diego pulled into the student parking lot of Hargrove University, he tried to reassure himself that meeting up with Mickey a day after banging her brains out was a good idea. That simply spending a little time with her outside the bar was perfectly fine. At the same time…he worried about intruding on *her* world. The rules were different in college. One of those rules was probably "don't sleep with your professor," but he needed to be mindful of how things worked at places like this.

Because, one day, this would be *his* world, too. He undid the top button of his shirt and blew out a nervous breath as he walked to Grazer Hall. She'd said that was the best place to meet since it was where she worked and closest to student parking. He decided to dress up today with a pair of navy blue slacks and a white button-down. But it was already getting too hot and long sleeves now seemed like a mistake. He quickly rolled those to his elbows and raked a hand through his hair.

For some reason, Diego got it into his head that he should look professional while walking around for Mickey's unauthorized campus tour. If he was going to start classes here, he'd better put his best foot forward. As he looked around, at students half his age, he realized he was performing a little too hard. The kids either looked like they'd rolled out of bed and ran to class, or they were more focused on life *after* class. He did not look like a student. Nor would he, not in his forties. That time had long passed him by. Oh, god, the regular sweat was transitioning into nervous sweat. Before he could worry about soaking his nice shirt, he spotted a woman waving at him in the distance.

Mickey stood from a bench located just outside Grazer Hall and waved him down. Today's outfit was a white tank top and denim shorts. Good lord, the woman sure could wear a pair of denim shorts. He pulled at his collar again as he tracked the curve of her thighs pressed together. He didn't realize he was a legs man until he met Mickey, but now it seemed he couldn't get enough of hers.

He walked faster, not wanting to keep her waiting, and not wanting to spend another second without her. Diego returned her wave and called out, "You haven't been waiting too long, have you?"

"Oh, no," she said, securing her purse strap over her chest. He couldn't help but glance at where the skinny strap of leather settled: right between her breasts. "I just got here. You look nice."

Her appreciative smile made Diego feel like he'd made the right choice. "Thanks. I thought I'd try something a little more professional."

"Very professional, indeed," she chuckled. "And very handsome."

He rubbed the back of his neck as he averted his gaze. "Thank you, Mick."

"So…we'll start with my building and then we'll hit up

some places where you'll likely spend time. The library, the athletic center...business department?"

He shook his head. "I can skip business for now. If there's a place where they do arts or sciences or something, I'd like to go there."

Mickey raised a brow and nodded. "That sounds fine to me."

"Lead the way." He gestured to Grazer's entrance. The air-conditioning inside was a huge relief. Even more, the building was nearly empty of onlookers as Diego took that moment to slide his arm around Mickey's waist and kiss her on the cheek. "I've been waiting too long to do that," he murmured in her ear.

Her gaze darted up to him and her smile was bright. "Since yesterday?"

"Like I said, too long," he said, removing his arm. As much as he'd have liked to show more affection, he had to remember that this was *her* workplace.

"How do you think our shift went last night?" she asked. "Considering..."

"We're going to have to do a better job at talking about this kind of stuff," he said in a low voice. "We had sex, Mickey."

Her face flushed dark as she teethed her bottom lip. "We did."

"And now you're showing me your university," he chuckled.

"I am. And now I feel like we're flirting with danger by doing this. Hopefully we don't run into my—"

"Mickey!" called out a woman's voice. Down the hallway to their right, a white woman in her forties started toward them. Her blond bob haircut shook as she waved energetically. "Just the woman I needed to see."

"Oh, god," she muttered under her breath. Mickey's smile

dipped for a split second before she turned up the wattage. "Hey, Lara!"

Diego looked between the two women, wondering what to do with himself. Lara gave him a quick scan before smiling. "I was actually gonna call you today, but, my god, you're here. Do you have a minute?"

"Sure," Mickey said quickly. "Can I introduce you to a student? This is Diego Acosta and he's in my online class this summer."

Her words tumbled out in a hurry with a slight shakiness.

"Of course." Lara stuck her hand out. "It's nice to meet you, Diego. Are you enjoying Mickey's class?"

"Mickey's been great."

"Mind if I take her off your hands for a second?" Lara asked. Her green eyes squinted in a way that told him she wasn't asking for permission. He took a step back, making himself scarce. Mickey glanced at him over her shoulder as she followed Lara. He wondered if the woman was her boss. If so, Mickey's nervousness made more sense.

The two women disappeared into an office, where they remained while Diego pretended to read a bulletin board about study abroad programs. By the time he scanned the Ireland program, Mickey was back in the hallway, speaking in low tones. He heard her assure Lara. "No, no, it's fine, really."

"Are you sure?"

"Sure," Mickey said with a strained chuckle. "I'll figure something out."

If he was worried if the woman thought anything amiss about the nature of his and Mickey's relationship, his fears were quickly assuaged once Lara waved. "Nice to meet you."

Once they were alone again, Diego tried to search Mickey's face for something. Her expression was unreadable as she faced the bulletin board.

"Huh, I was looking at the Ireland program a while ago," she said in a flat voice. "I'd love to go, but the chaperones are always tenured professors."

Diego didn't really give a fuck about the school's travel opportunities. He was more curious about what had been said in Lara's office that made her sullen. "Yeah?"

"You wanna see the office I share with three other people?"

The tone and suddenness of her question caught him off guard. Something had shifted in their outing. "Uh, sure."

He followed her down another corridor, walking past several classrooms and offices. Grazer Hall's quiet was punctuated by the occasional open office door. Not many people seemed to be working in June, which was just fine with Diego. He wasn't sure if he wanted to meet anyone else who might spoil Mickey's mood further. When they arrived at an office with several cubicles, he ducked his head inside.

"This is where you work?"

She stood in the doorway and sighed but didn't step inside. "Yep."

"I guess I assumed everyone had their own office."

Her mirthless laugh made him glance at her. "You seem to keep forgetting that I'm an adjunct, not an actual professor."

"Do you want to be?" he asked.

"Not really. It requires about four more years of school, and a crushing job search in a field that's quickly filled up by people with more prestigious degrees."

"Do you want to continue being an adjunct?"

"No."

"Really?" he asked.

"Huh? I mean, I don't know," Mickey quickly answered. "Sorry, I wasn't thinking."

"Yes, you were," he said, stepping inside the empty office. "It sounds like you said exactly what was on your mind."

She reluctantly followed him, closing the door behind her. "Lara is the department chair. My boss."

Diego found her desk immediately. Compared to the other cubicles, Mickey's space was decorated with dozens of motivational quotes, colorful silk flowers and cute stationery. It seemed like she was good at leaving her mark wherever she went. "And what did she need?"

"To let me know that I've only got one class to teach this fall. She wanted to break the news sooner so that I'd have some time to prepare," Mickey scoffed. "She felt bad that she kept me waiting about this summer course."

"So, you get paid per class. You're not a salary employee."

"I get paid by credit hour," she corrected.

Diego frowned. "Jesus..."

She slowly approached him. "I don't want to ruin your tour with this stuff."

He took her by her shoulders and forced her to meet his eyes. "This *stuff* is your life, Mick. I'd like to know more about it."

"I don't know if I can keep working here," she admitted. "I feel like I'm wasting time, holding out hope for something that's not going to pan out. In the time I could have been making actual money, I spent it teaching."

"And that's admirable," Diego said, rubbing her arms. "You're a good educator. Your students love you—"

Her eyes narrowed. "Do they?"

"Don't be a smart-ass, Mickey." He was relieved when she finally grinned. "You're good at what you do. But you have to think practically. Have you gotten as far as you can in a place like this?"

She nodded.

"Then it's time to move on. You need to find out what will make you happier and make you more money." The more he spoke, the more indignant he felt. "The students are gonna miss out, but this system sounds like horseshit. If they want the best for these kids, then they need to pay their people the best. There's no reason you should be scrimping and saving after the work you do."

"Okay," she breathed, staring at him.

He wasn't finished, though. "That's why you have to work at the bar, right? These people only gave you the one class? God knows three credits isn't enough to hold you over until fall. Just let me know and I can give you more hours in August. It's hard work, but at least you'll get what you put in. This—" he looked around the bullpen of cubicles "—might not be it, honey."

Her wide grin tripped him up.

"What?"

Mickey didn't answer. Instead, she yanked him down by his collar and kissed the hell out of him. It took him a second to catch on, but quickly his hands dug into the tight curls at the base of her neck and cradled her against him. Her lips moved urgently against his, pushing and pulling with insistence. Diego tried not to think about their setting or the fact that any one of her colleagues could walk in on them. He concentrated on the softness of her pliant body, pressed against his, and the surge of desire that set fire to his blood. He suddenly wanted to get out of there, take her back to his place and pick up where they left off yesterday.

When she released him, he sighed happily. "What was that for?"

"That's for understanding something that I'm still scared to talk to my parents about. They're proud of me for being a teacher, and part of me doesn't want to let go of that," she said in a soft voice. "Plus, it always feels nice to catch you off guard with a kiss."

He remembered their first angry kiss in his office and smiled.

"I like how you're full of surprises. Are you sure your parents wouldn't be proud of anything you did?"

She pursed her lips. "I haven't told them about the bar because I can't handle the judgment I know I'm gonna get. I figured I still had time to sort out my life before getting to that."

Diego frowned. "Is it that much of a big deal?"

Something flickered in her eyes. "My parents are really protective of my health and well-being," she said carefully. "And they kind of love that I'm a teacher. The bar might be a lot for them to process."

She wasn't telling him something. He could see that much from her eyes. "I hope that you'll be honest with them sooner than later. There were a lot of things I wish I could have told my mom before she passed. Life's too short to not be real with the people around you."

"That's a lot coming from a guy who grunts his feelings."

Okay, maybe he deserved that. "I get that, but this is also coming from a guy who ran out of time with his mom. And his wife… Sorry, I just don't want you to get stuck like me."

Mickey's mouth fell open. "You're not stuck," she argued.

"Believe me, it takes a lot to move me forward," he admitted. "You've had something to do with that."

Blush hit her cheeks as she averted her eyes. "Alright, then… maybe we move forward right now. Would you like to continue the tour?"

"Only if you're okay."

She took his hand and squeezed it. "I'm good."

After seeing Grazer Hall, they moved on to the education building, where she showed him the day-care center used by early childhood education students. The excitement returned to her voice as she described how the Art Department recently received a grant allowing them to make repairs on their building. He learned that another fire kiln would be available by the time he started taking classes. Diego had a feeling she was trying to push him in that direction. He didn't mind.

Eventually they ended up back in the student parking lot, ready to part from one another. "Can I see you again?" he asked.

She laughed. "You'll see me tonight, Diego."

"You know what I meant," he said, waiting for her to unlock her car.

Mickey tossed her purse on the passenger seat. "Of course. If we're discreet, I suppose. I'd like to survive the three-week bet y'all have without everyone knowing I'm involved with the boss."

He tried to bite back his grin. "That sounds fair…though no one's actually betting money on you. But your odds are looking better and better."

She climbed in and let him close her door. "Then I'll see you soon?"

"You will."

Diego let her go before walking to his own car, contemplating her behavior. Mickey seemed to be putting on a brilliant act for these people. She smiled brightly and forgave them so easily when she knew she was in a dire situation. There was a passionate woman beneath the Mary Poppins performance, a woman who enjoyed yanking him into submission for a kiss. Even her request for discretion felt like an act. It seemed important for Mickey to convince those around her that everything was okay.

Eh, Diego could understand that.

He'd been keeping his own act up for five years. Everyone around him knew that he was trying his best to get past Lucía's death. But what was Mickey trying to overcome? What was she trying to keep at bay? He hoped that whatever it was, she'd one day feel comfortable enough to show him that side.

22

Mickey was on a roll tonight.

She set up Cleo's band of bachelorettes and bride-to-be near the back of the bar with their own decorated party table. Mickey also supplied them with bottles of champagne, white wine and several pitchers of the El Torro cocktail she'd prepared the night before. Ollie stopped by every so often to top up their ice supply, ensuring a refreshing mixed drink every time.

Her friend Patrick was on stage working karaoke night with customers who signed up for songs. So far, their older crowd had dominated the night with '80s classics. At one point, Mickey caught Diego mouthing along to "Footloose" as he shook his cocktail shaker.

And Diego…was in good spirits that night, which was strange for his coworkers to witness. He traded his usual scowl for a smile, and *chatted* with customers. But Mickey knew the truth behind his smiles and kept it close to her heart. So long as they were keeping each other's secrets, she was satisfied for the moment. The biggest secret that she was still afraid to reveal had to do with her illness. Yes, she kept it under control with medication, but he was getting uncomfortably close to the truth while they hung out in her university office.

First, it was about the money she made, which was next to nothing. She didn't want to tell him that it wasn't enough to fund her hyperthyroidism. Next, it was her parents. She'd left out the reason *why* they meddled as much as they did. But blessedly, he let her drop the discussion. And she'd leave it for another day. Perhaps after she learned more about him and his family, she'd be open to explaining herself. Until then, she didn't need a man who'd already suffered two major losses to suddenly worry about losing her.

But she refused to deal with any of that tonight. Diego was in a good mood, their customers were on their best behavior with two bouncers working the door, and the kitchen was finally a well-oiled machine.

"Behind you," Diego said, reaching around her for a bottle of the well vodka. His arm brushed against her back, sending a jolt of electricity down her spine. It was purely accidental, but excitement still bubbled in her chest. "When are you going to sing, Mickey?" he asked in a teasing voice.

She took her latest order to the cash register. "I'll sing when you do," she called over her shoulder.

Diego rocked his shaker near his ear as he spoke. "I've never karaoked before," he said. "Is that right? Can I make karaoke a verb, Professor?"

She chuckled as she counted her change. When she took care of her customer, she turned to Diego. "English is a very fluid language, so you do what you want."

"What song would you pick?" he asked, pouring his cocktail into two glasses.

As an amateur karaoke performer back in Athens, she had always started with '90s hits before moving into Motown classics as the night went on. "Probably a Backstreet Boys song," she said, taking his vodka bottle back. "You?"

He shook his head, rubbing the back of his neck. "I don't know."

"You're too scared?" she teased.

"I ain't scared," he said, moving to the register. When he cashed his customers out, he stood beside her and nudged her shoulder. "I just can't carry a note to save my life."

The warmth of his body, standing so close to her, set her skin on fire. She'd been aching for him since they last had sex in his house. Between their shifts at the bar and schoolwork, they'd never decided when the next hookup would be.

She didn't mind being casual, but after a taste of what Diego was capable of, she could barely think of anything else. "The point of karaoke is just to have fun," she said, nudging him back. "You don't have to be a good singer to have fun."

Just then, a man and woman took the stage and began singing "Paradise by the Dashboard Light." Diego groaned. "There's nothing fun about that," he said. "It's a ten-minute song."

She chuckled. "You don't like Meatloaf?"

He shook his head. "I don't."

"The bride wants more white wine!" Cleo shouted as she approached the bar. "And she's actually having a great time."

"We're glad to hear it," Diego said with a smile. He retrieved a chilled bottle from the small refrigerator below the bar. "This one is on the bar."

Mickey raised her brows, wondering if she'd heard him correctly. The man hated being nice to customers.

Cleo took the bottle and flashed a bright smile. "Thank you again for letting us party here," she said. "You should let Mickey plan more events."

Diego glanced at her with a twinkle in his eye. "You think Patrick wouldn't mind being on retainer for once a week?"

"I think so," Mickey said, feeling excited. "Ooh! What if I hosted a cocktail crafting night for women? I could teach them how to make Saloon specials."

"It could raise the age of your clientele significantly," Cleo added. "Have you noticed the distinct lack of college students tonight?"

"A trivia night could do that, too," Mickey suggested.

"I have noticed the missing kids," Diego agreed. "And I don't mind."

"His reputation for yelling at kids might have taken hold," Mickey quipped. "Diego hates kids."

Suddenly, his arm was slung over her shoulders, pulling her closer to his sweaty side. "I thought I told you I don't yell at kids," he corrected. "I yell at college students who don't tip."

Mickey all but sank against his chest, tempted to place her hand on his muscular belly. As she looked up at his bronze face, shining with perspiration, her knees wobbled slightly. "You shouldn't yell at them, either, Old Man Acosta," she said, keeping her tone light. If she teased him, he'd be less likely to see the heat in her eyes or hear the heaviness in her voice.

But when he glanced down at her, his dark brow quirked as a grin slid across his face. "I don't recall you thinking I was an old man the other day."

She playfully shoved him away, but her face burned with desire. "Shut up," she laughed.

"Take your break, Mick," he said, walking back to his side of the bar. "Go sign up for a song."

In a daze, she watched him tend to another customer, not realizing Cleo still stood at the bar. When her friend snapped her fingers in her face, Mickey jumped. "What?"

"Y'all are fuckin'," her friend hissed.

Mickey's eyes widened. "What?"

"Say what again," Cleo said, rolling her eyes. "You heard me."

"We're not—" Mickey started, but quickly shut up. She and Cleo had been friends long enough for Mickey to know better.

"I don't wanna hear it," Cleo said, holding up a hand. "I'll get in your ass later, but for now...your *boss* is letting you take a break. You're singing 'California Love' with me."

Mickey bit her lip to keep from grinning. "You signed us up?"

Cleo nodded to the stage. "I'm getting white-girl wasted tonight because this campaign is killing me and I need a break, too." She shrugged. "So yeah, we're singing after Meatloaf."

"Oh, no, do you want to talk about it?"

Cleo shook her head vigorously. "Absolutely not. I'm just gonna drink."

Mickey ran around the bar. "In that case, I wanna be Dre," she said, following her friend back to the bachelorette table.

"I've had too much to drink to be Makaveli."

"But you know his parts better than I do," she said, grabbing Cleo by the waist.

Cleo passed the white wine to a bachelorette who shouted along to Meatloaf. "I want you to be careful," she whispered in Mickey's ear.

Mickey pulled back slightly to look her friend in the eye. "I will."

"And you'll tell me all about Old Man Acosta later?" Cleo asked, letting a smile slip through her stern facade.

She held up her pinky finger, immediately linking it with Cleo's. "Promise."

He thought he'd gotten used to Mickey being a distraction, but when she and her friend took the stage to sing "California

Love," he couldn't tear his eyes away from them. Nor could the rest of the bar. The two women had everyone on their feet, dancing and singing along, transforming The Saloon into an LA nightclub within minutes.

Mickey sang Dr. Dre's parts well enough while Cleo was too drunk to master Tupac's fast rhyme flow. After a while, the two friends tried their best to rap through a giggling fit but caught up near the end. They finished the song with flourished bows as the bar crowd went wild. Mickey hopped down from the stage and gave high fives to customers as she traveled back to the bachelorette table.

"Hey, Boss," Irene called out, setting her tray on the counter. "I need six shots of Cuervo."

"Coming up," he said, glancing at Mickey, who danced with her friends.

"Tonight."

"Keep your pants on," he said, stacking shot glasses with both hands.

Irene narrowed her eyes at him. "Were you smiling just now?"

He poured the shots. "I don't know," he lied. He probably was and hadn't noticed it. The past few days had been like that. His employees were catching him grinning like a fool with every pint he pulled. If they'd attributed his light mood to Mickey, they weren't saying anything. As far as he knew, no one had noticed how little they bickered at one another. Behind the bar, he and Mickey worked as one. Their partnership was almost as fluid as his and Jeanie's.

"She's making you smile, isn't she?" Irene asked, leaning against the bar. Her cheeky grin was wide and annoying as hell.

"Like Ollie makes you smile," he replied blandly.

"Ollie and I are having fun getting to know each other,"

Irene said with a shrug. "I like the little Indiana girl. She's kind and funny, and gets my unique brand of bitch… We're actually going on our first real date after one of my shows."

Well, this was news to him. In all the years Irene had worked with him, her sexuality never once came up in conversation. She started working for Lucía to make money, supplementing her income as a costume designer at Springer Theatre, and then she just stuck around. Like him, Irene was mum on her life outside of The Saloon, and he wondered why she'd say something now. His eyes flitted to her tray. "Your shots are ready, and… I'm happy for you."

"Thanks, Boss." She flashed a bright smile at him before whisking her tray of drinks away.

Okay, maybe he wasn't being as slick as he thought.

"What the hell is going on in here?" asked a voice from the front of the bar.

Diego let out a surprised laugh when he caught Jeanie leaning over the bar, dispensing herself a plastic cup of Coke. "Hey, what are you doing here?" he asked. "How's Wilma?"

She settled back on her side of the bar and sipped her soda. "She's out of the woods with two stents, but I don't want her to be alone yet."

"You're good to take the time off, you know," Diego finished.

"Could you give me another week to figure out her nurse situation? I wanna hire someone for a night shift so I can work."

"Of course," he said, wiping down the bar. "If you need to work a day shift in the future, just let me know. Mickey and I have it covered for a while."

"Newest Girl?" Jeanie laughed. "Okay, what have I missed?"

"You hired a good one," he said. "She's a hard worker and all of this was her idea."

"I like it." She nodded. "It looks like a good crowd, too. Deputy Rivera might not bust you tonight."

"Jeanie, you're back!" Mickey squealed as she ran to the bar. "How is your mother doing? Is she feeling better?"

Jeanie spoke to Mickey about her mother's condition while Diego added another beer to a customer's tab, every once in while catching snippets of Mickey's voice. Her excitement, empathy and concern punctuated their conversation, dragging Diego's attention back to her. By the time he returned to the women, they were in the middle of exchanging phone numbers.

"Let me know about that trip to Atlanta," Jeanie said, tucking her phone back in her pocket. "I wanna hit up Ikea for some more bookshelves."

"I will," Mickey said. "We can borrow my dad's pickup if you need to get some bigger pieces."

"What's that?" Diego asked.

"Mickey and I are planning a quick trip to Atlanta," Jeanie said before finishing her soda. "Maybe I'll take you up on that day shift, Boss." She sneaked a covert glance between him and Mickey. "It looks like you've got it covered."

"Just let me know," he said, rubbing the back of his neck.

"Yeah," she laughed. "I'll see y'all later."

"You're not gonna sing a song?" Diego asked.

Jeanie continued laughing as she receded into the crowd. "I'll sing when you sing, Boss," she called over her shoulder. Diego watched her leave, doubting he'd ever get up on that stage to make a fool of himself. It was bad enough that he now smiled in front of his crush and made idle conversation with the patrons.

Diego scoffed to himself as he wiped down the bar. *Sing? Yeah, right.*

23

The morning after karaoke/bachelorette night, Mickey woke up to a loud rapping at her front door. She sprang up from her bed, threw on a robe and ran through her apartment to look out her peephole.

Diego stood on the other side holding a box of donuts and two coffee cups. She nearly squealed when she opened her door, but decided on a cooler greeting. "Diego? What are you doing here?"

He blushed as he held the donut box aloft. "I got up early enough to finish my homework, and I thought I'd treat you to breakfast."

She leaned against her doorway, peering into the box. "You got a lot of nerve buttering me up with sweets when papers are due today. Is that coffee also for me?"

Diego stepped closer. "It's all for you, Mickey."

Her face was already burning from his intense stare; his words didn't make things better. "Get in here," she whispered, pulling him inside before glancing around her neighboring apartments. Her landlady was a lovely woman but liked to talk about everyone else's business; Mickey didn't need to give her fodder.

"Did I wake you up?" he asked, setting the donuts on her kitchen island.

She quickly wrapped her robe tighter and brushed her curls out of her face before checking the stove clock. "It's before nine a.m., so yeah."

"I also wanted to wish you luck for the bullshit hurricane that's going to hit you today, and to congratulate you on last night's event." Diego helped himself to her kitchen, searching the cupboards until he found a couple small saucers. When he plated up two donuts and licked the tips of his fingers, Mickey's breath caught in her throat. *Oh, to be those fingers right now...*

"What did I do?" she asked in a voice huskier than she meant it to be.

"You made me try something new," he said. "I talked with your friend Patrick, and he said he'd be our karaoke guy every Friday night. Except tonight—he's performing at the Riverwalk Fest."

Mickey smiled. "You're welcome."

"And I'd like to thank you for being a good teacher." Diego glanced down at his donut and rubbed the back of his neck. She noticed that was something he did when he turned shy. He averted his eyes and found something to do with his hands. "You, uh...you make me see something in my writing—something I hadn't seen before. And it makes me feel..."

"Proud?" Mickey finished as she approached him.

He met her gaze, and his face broke into a wide grin. His eyes softened despite the small wrinkles around them. It was ridiculous how his smile brightened his face. How it lifted the clouds that he continually walked in. "Yes, I feel...proud of myself. It's been a while."

Hearing any student say those words boosted Mickey's spirits. She stopped herself from telling him he'd *had it in him all along* because Diego was still a cynical man in his forties, but his admission made her want to burst. "You *should* be proud," she said, taking her pastry.

It was a regular glazed cake donut, nothing fancy, but just right for a morning coffee. She bit into it and relished in the instant sweetness. "Oh, god, this is good..." she moaned. When she looked up, he was staring at her again. Mickey quickly placed the donut back on its plate.

His eyes darkened. "I like that about you."

Her mouth went dry. "What?"

Diego reached out and swiped his thumb along her bottom lip, starting from the center and moving until he reached the corner of her mouth. "You enjoy everything with such brightness." He pulled his hand away just as she leaned into his touch. Diego licked his thumb until the entire tip disappeared between his full lips. "Why do you enjoy life with such willingness, while I let it drag me forward?"

She couldn't answer that. Not in so many words, while watching him suck his own thumb. She couldn't tell him how she'd spent a little over half her life worried about tomorrow. Mickey Chambers didn't have time to *not* enjoy life. It was finally in her hands. And because she wanted to continue enjoying life, she leaned forward and kissed Diego's sugary mouth.

He grunted as she nearly fell into him but caught her around the waist and tightened his arms. She licked the sweetness from his lips until he opened his mouth and met her tongue with his. Diego pulled her close against his chest and deepened his kiss, setting fire to her entire body. As his hands coursed down her body, her stomach flip-flopped. Her panties went damp with her desire, and she was suddenly aware of her near-nakedness beneath her robe.

When he released her, he blew out a sigh. "You are the sweetest thing I've tasted today, Mickey."

Wetness slicked against her thighs as she rubbed them together. His hands slipped under the folds of her robe, rubbing her skin, cool against hot. "I'm sweet elsewhere," she whispered.

He chuckled darkly. "You're sweet everywhere, honey. And I want to taste all of you."

"Yeah?" she asked.

Diego gestured to her discarded donut. "Take that to your bedroom. We'll both eat."

Mickey grabbed her donut and took his hand. "Let's go."

Mickey did not feel well.

It was only two hours into her shift at The Saloon and she felt…weird.

The Riverwalk Blues Festival was in full swing, bringing every single Columbus citizen through their bar. And because it was busier than normal, she drifted between the outdoor seating area and the bar, helping Irene and Gina with orders. The scorching sun and the running back and forth was making her dizzy.

She couldn't place it on the donuts and sex with Diego this morning. In fact, she couldn't place it at all. Besides the pleasurable haze of her bedroom, she could barely remember eating lunch and driving herself to the bar. Her mind drifted in different places: one moment, she was behind the bar and the next moment she stood outside listening to a band called Whiskey Bent.

Mickey felt herself disassociating, floating in and out of her body with every step she took. Time seemed to slow as she stumbled through a hot haze, her mind speeding everywhere at once.

It meant that she hadn't taken her meds.

Fuck, fuck and fuck.

She took a pitcher of Corona beer to the sidewalk while retracing her steps from earlier in the day. She ate a donut, maybe two, and had a long lovemaking session with Diego. She made them sandwiches for lunch, and they went at it again… She read a book while he worked on school stuff. Later on, she got dressed for work and they took off for downtown Columbus.

Nowhere in that retracing could Mickey remember taking her thyroid medication, nor her other meds that regulated her mood and hormones. She was too busy caught up in Diego. She was too busy being infatuated with him.

"Jesus fucking Christ," she muttered under her breath as she made it to her table. The three men who waited on their order were loud, boisterous oafs. They hooted like owls as she approached them. She tried her best to discreetly wipe away the sweat pouring off her, but the back of her hand came away from her forehead completely wet. She needed to sit down, but there were two more tables that would require her attention.

"About time," her customer barked. He was a balding man who sat with his legs astride grotesquely. "What's the holdup, little lady?"

"There's no holdup," she snapped, slamming the pitcher down on the table, sloshing the surface with beer. "We're very busy, and you're not the only table that needs to be served."

The men looked up at her in surprise.

Okay, that was more emotion than she wanted to show. "The world doesn't revolve around you guys," she said in a calmer voice.

The bald man scoffed. "Okay, honey. Relax."

Mickey paused when she should have walked back inside, escaping the overbearing sun. This man's entitled attitude, his leering friends and all the rushing about made her want to burst into flames and sweep fire down the entire street. “Fuck you,” she said through gritted teeth.

The table went quiet.

She stumbled backward as she brought a trembling hand to her cheek.

“Is she okay?” one man asked in a hushed voice.

“Michelle?” said a familiar voice. She spun on her heel toward the sound, but her mind was too slow to keep up. It was her mother who held hands with her father. Mickey forgot they attended the Blues Festival annually. It took all her remaining energy to muster up the words. She opened her mouth, but the words wouldn’t come.

“Michelle, what are you doing out here?” her father asked.

She was very close to answering, but she couldn’t push the words past her numb lips. As her vision dimmed, her body swayed and her knees buckled. Thank god, someone caught her elbow before the sidewalk rushed up to meet her face.

24

"Boss? There's something wrong with Mickey," Gina said, setting her tray beside him. He was in the middle of pulling several pints when he saw the terrified look in the girl's eyes. "I think she passed out."

His heart dropped as he set his glass down. "Ramón!" he shouted to his brother-in-law, who cleared a table in the distance. "Ramón, take the bar."

Ramón hitched his tub of glassware onto his shoulder. "¿Qué pasó?"

Diego was already around the bar and headed out the door. He squinted against the outside brightness as he searched for her. An older man held Mickey up while his wife flapped a festival pamphlet in her face. They shouted her name as they begged her to wake up. The woman who fanned Mickey furiously looked like an older version of her. He wasn't certain, but if he had to guess, Mickey's parents had come to her rescue.

"Is she okay?" he asked, rushing to her side. The man struggled with Mickey's dead weight while the three gawking men who sat nearby were absolutely no help. He took her other arm and propped her up. "What the hell happened to her?"

The man and woman threw him a confused look. "Excuse me?" the woman asked. "Who are *you*?"

"I'm—I'm, uh…her boss." He shifted his weight to offer his hand. "I'm Diego Acosta."

"Her boss?"

"Rita, let's continue this conversation inside," the man grunted. "Michelle is getting a little heavy."

"Good idea," Diego said, steering the family indoors, where it was only slightly cooler. Stevie and Jerry met them at the door and took over for her father.

"Did she pass out?" Jerry asked as they toted Mickey through the bar.

"Yes," Rita said, following close behind. "She shouldn't have been out in the sun like this."

He didn't know why Mickey couldn't be out in the sun, but that she was still unconscious worried the hell out of him. Diego's heart hammered in his chest as they brought her inside his office. He cleared away the couch that was mostly hidden by boxes and files. When they laid her down, Stevie and Jerry backed out of the room.

"Grab three bags of ice," he called out to them as he kneeled at her side and vigorously fanned her with a manila folder. "Come on, Mickey. Wake up," he whispered.

"You said you were her boss?" her father asked.

"Yeah, I, uh, I own The Saloon," Diego said, fanning hard at Mickey's face. "She's been working here for the last couple of weeks."

Once Stevie was back with ice bags, Diego quickly placed them on various parts of her body. Two went under each arm and the last sat on her chest.

"My daughter works at a bar?" Rita asked. "Did you know this, Virgil?"

"Oh, god…" Mickey finally groaned.

Diego took her by the face, stroking her hot cheek with his thumb. "Christ, Mickey, you scared the shit out of me," he rasped. "Are you okay?"

Her eyelids fluttered as she scrunched her face up. "I thought I heard my parents."

Diego exhaled harshly. "Yes, and they're pretty damn surprised that you're working here." She tried to sit up, but he put a firm hand on her shoulder. "Nope, you need to rest."

"Mom, this is not what it looks like," she murmured.

"Michelle Naomi Chambers, tell me exactly what this is. Because from here, it looks like you are laid out after getting sick in the streets. You're a barmaid?"

"Have you been taking your medication?" Virgil asked. "Why on earth would you be working someplace where you'd be on your feet all day? Do you wanna end up in the hospital again?"

"Daddy, you didn't call the ambulance, did you?"

"We haven't," Diego said. "But you need to tell me what got you so sick, Mickey." He needed to know because he was about to go sick with worry. He had to shove down the anger that bubbled to the surface as he held her face. Had he almost lost her today? Did she have a medical history that serious? And why the hell hadn't she told him about it?

For the first time since she woke up, she met his gaze. He didn't find contrition in her eyes, only annoyance. "I'm not sick," she said defensively. "My parents are overreacting."

"We're not overreacting," Rita said, crossing her arms over her chest. "If we hadn't been walking by, you could have busted your head open. And can you please tell us why the hell you are working here when you should be teaching?"

Mickey drew herself into a sitting position, tucking the ice bags around her chest. "Momma, I needed the money—

and before you say anything—no, I'm not taking any of your money. I just got another job."

Her father's mouth pressed into a firm line as he looked down at her. "Couldn't you work anywhere else?"

"I like it here," she protested.

"And what are you doing to make sure she takes breaks, drinks enough water?" her mother jumped in.

Diego didn't have an answer for her. Until this very moment, he hadn't known one of his employees had a chronic illness. Now her hesitance to be honest with her parents made sense. When she said they were very watchful, he hadn't known it had something to do with an illness. "Everyone is supposed to take breaks," he said weakly.

"Well, our daughter has a thyroid condition that requires her—"

"I'm not required to do anything but take my medication, Daddy," Mickey interrupted.

"And did you take your medication?" Virgil asked.

Mickey's mouth clamped shut as her eyes flickered to Diego. Blush crept into her face as she pursed her lips. They had spent the morning together and all he could remember was her stunning body writhing beneath him as he drove into her. His face also flushed from the memory. "I…didn't."

Diego pushed himself to his feet. "Uh, this feels like a family thing," he said, turning to her concerned parents. "I really have to get back behind the bar. Mickey, if you need to go home, you can…just clock out."

Her eyes flashed in anger. "I'm not going home," she said. "This is the Riverwalk Blues Festival, and I promised to help you."

He needed to get out of the room before he said something impulsive. Something like, *Goddammit, Mickey, I care about you too much to see you face-plant on a city sidewalk.* He backed out of the room instead, leaving her to a tongue-lashing from her parents. It was safer to stay out of family conflicts.

If he didn't know all the facts, perhaps they hadn't reached that point in their relationship yet. When he returned to the bar, he relieved Ramón, who couldn't handle the crowd. Diego tried to keep his mind on orders, but his thoughts kept returning to her and her limp body. It scared him more than he was willing to admit aloud, which was why he was desperate to concentrate on work.

He should send her home.

And he would have, but the solid determination in her eyes gave him pause. After a few minutes with her parents, she returned to the front of the house with her mouth pursed. Mickey rarely appeared angry and today Diego felt heat roll off her in waves as she worked around him.

She wasn't rude to the customers, but the usual brightness in her demeanor had dimmed. When he asked her if she felt better, she offered him a clipped, "I'm fine," and explained that her mother would return with a dosage of her medication. She didn't offer him more information, and he was nervous about pressing.

Sure enough, her mother did return with her meds. He tried to speak to Rita, but she only gave him a tight smile as she saw to her daughter. Before long, she left and Mickey went back to work. Other than his employee losing consciousness, he counted the first day of Riverwalk Fest a success.

Still, Diego should have sent her home.

He could have avoided this exact moment when he needed to speak to her. When he closed the bar for the night and everyone set out to do their end-of-shift duties, he watched Mickey count her drawer from the corner of his eye, waiting for her to finish. She worked efficiently and quietly, not joining in at the end-of-the-night goofing off they usually got up to.

Mickey slammed her drawer shut as he wiped down the last well bottle. “My drawer is off by two dollars,” she said in a tired voice.

“Short or over?” he asked, trying to read her eyes.

She avoided his direct gaze, opting to look at the floor. “I’m short.”

“Aww, you’re at least over five feet,” he said with a chuckle. He wanted to pull a smile out of her, anything to replace this sullen look.

Mickey sighed as she stepped around him. “Take it out of my tips,” she said, walking toward the kitchen.

He followed close behind her. “Office hours,” he said in a low voice.

Her shoulders slumped in resignation, but she bypassed the punch-out clock and went straight to his office. Once inside, he closed the door behind them. Mickey raised a brow and pursed her lips. “I thought we were going to keep the door open.” Her eyes cut to the door.

“We said a lot of stuff,” he said. “But I think we left out some pretty important details. You wanna tell me what happened today?”

Mickey teethed her bottom lip, an action that would normally drive him mad, but her anxiety was more pressing today. “I forgot to take a medication that I’ve taken every day since I was twenty-one.”

“You realize that whatever illness you have is fine,” he said. “I won’t fire you… If anything, I can accommodate you.”

Instead of appearing comforted or appreciative, Mickey scowled at him. “You wouldn’t know what that looks like,” she said. “I don’t even know.”

“So break it down for me,” he snapped, frustration bunching the muscles in his body. "Explain it to me so I can help you."

"Why are you the one who's angry?"

"I'm not angry," he hissed, taking a step closer.

She took a step back and gestured at his body. "I can't tell if you want to kiss me or wring my neck, but this stern-daddy thing is not what I need right now."

Diego looked down at himself and saw her point. Even though his hands were planted firmly on his hips, his muscles felt tense enough to spring. "I'm sorry," he sighed, stepping back.

"And besides, I know enough about HR policies to know I'm not obligated to disclose any illness or disability to you, and you're not allowed to ask."

She had a point.

He rubbed his hand down his face. "I don't have an HR department as you damn well know, but you're right. I can't treat you any differently from my other employees. And I don't want to, but..." He didn't know how to finish his sentence because it would mean admitting how frightened he was.

"But what?" she asked, crossing her arms.

Diego faltered, raking his fingers through his hair. "I care about you. Not just as your employer, but as the man you—" he gestured between them "—you know, as the person who's..."

"Fucking me?" she asked with narrowed eyes.

He heaved a loud sigh and rolled his eyes. "You know what I meant, Mickey. I assume you'd tell your boyfriend if you needed his help."

Now it was her turn to falter. Her mouth dropped open as she stared at him. "I didn't know you were my boyfriend."

Diego's face burned from the admission. He suddenly felt old and out of his element. Based on how many times they'd fooled around, he naturally assumed they were in a monogamous relationship, not an appropriate one, but a relationship, nonetheless. The shock in her voice told him he'd misspoken. "I guess not?"

Her face colored as she averted her eyes. "We haven't talked about it."

Of course. She probably thought they were just hooking up for fun. Diego hadn't been anyone's boyfriend in years, so why had he thought he was Mickey's? He felt like a goddamn fool. All he could do was give a gruff cough and nod as he backed away. "Right," he muttered, opening the door. "We'll just leave it there. I'm gonna try to convince Todd to come in for more behind-the-bar support, but I'll see you at the same time tomorrow."

He glanced over his shoulder at Mickey, expecting her to make an awkward exit from his office. But she approached him with a slow deliberateness that made him stand taller. He wouldn't let her see his embarrassment on her way out.

But instead of leaving him, Mickey stopped just before him and closed the door. "I don't think we're done talking," she said in a firm voice.

25

Mickey closed the door with a soft click.

Tension filled the air of the stuffy little office as electricity crackled in the thin space between their bodies.

"Mickey, I don't want to push," Diego said, pressing his back against the wall behind him.

She took his clenched fist and relaxed his fingers enough to intertwine with them. "You're not pushing," she said in a soft voice. "To an extent, you're right. We need to talk to each other before we make assumptions."

His Adam's apple bobbed in his throat as he gripped her hand. "I think I've already fucked that up."

She opened her mouth to protest but was interrupted by a shadow of someone's profile on the other side of the door. "Hermano, you good to lock up?" Ramón asked. "Everyone's gone home for the night."

"I'm good," Diego said. "Mickey and I are working on next week's schedule."

"Alright, then," he said, giving a final tap on the door. "Buenas noches."

When Ramón's footsteps receded, Diego let out a breath

and closed his eyes. "No wonder we're unsure about this relationship," he muttered. "I keep lying to my brother-in-law about it."

"Thank you for maintaining the secrecy for me," she whispered. "But I wouldn't be surprised if people knew. You're not exactly the same Diego since I started working here."

He narrowed his eyes on her face, glancing at her mouth before settling on her eyes. "I'm different because of you," he agreed.

They still held hands, but his grip loosened slightly. "I like being with you, Diego," she said. "I want to keep being with you."

His eyes widened as he licked his bottom lip. Her eyes went there and stayed. Standing like this, tight against the doorway, reminded her of their most recent lovemaking. The passionate whirlwind of being in his rough hands made her flush with desire all over again. She pushed down the urge to climb him, though. They needed to understand each other first.

"I'm telling you this as my lover, and not my employer—I was diagnosed with hyperthyroidism when I was younger," she said in a rush. "It's a completely treatable illness that I manage with several medications, but it's chronic. I don't plan on having a surgery for it, so the meds are going to have to do. When I don't take them, I get overheated, my heart pounds erratically and my brain gets a little spacey. I've only forgotten to take them a couple times in my life, but today was bad because I was rushing around, and it was hot outside. Please do not use this information against me… Don't treat me like the Newest Girl with soft hands."

As soon as she went quiet, her anxiety returned. Outside her family and Cleo, no one really got the rundown of her illness. She kept it to herself and pretended that her life hadn't started several years after all her friends'. She pretended she hadn't been a burden on her parents' bank account and time.

Diego also went quiet. But his hand fell away from hers and slid up her arm. His warmth traveled over her shoulder and settled onto her neck. "Mickey..." he murmured, drawing her toward him. She sank against his chest, stopping her fall by placing her hands on his pecs. She could feel his heart beating through his T-shirt; it pounded at the same reckless speed as her own. "I like your soft hands. And your soft heart."

She tried not to tear up from his words. His strong, piercing stare broke through any defenses she struggled to put up, just as the calloused pad of his thumb stroked her jaw. "You made fun of my hands from the start," she said in a watery voice. "You told me I wouldn't last."

Diego frowned as he wrapped his other arm around her waist and pulled her flush against his body. "And I was wrong to say that."

"Diego, I—"

"I will never use what you shared with me against you," he said fiercely as he held her tight in his arms. "I'm sorry that I made you feel you couldn't hack it, because that's far from the truth. I just didn't want you to get—" He stopped himself to glance at her mouth.

She swiped her tongue along her bottom lip. "Get close?" she asked.

With his gaze still locked on her lips, he tilted her chin upward. "Yes," he breathed. "I couldn't let you bear that burden."

Mickey understood what he meant because it was on her mind as well. She couldn't ignore what this meant for him: letting another woman into his bed, letting her into his heart. Her heart broke for him. It crumbled into tiny pieces when she witnessed his fears exposed.

But no one had ever asked Mickey to carry a burden.

She'd lived a life of being pampered and protected and coddled. She wasn't there to rehabilitate Diego, but she could offer him something else: possibility. She could show him a life after grief. She had enough experience to know what reinvention looked like. Mickey could show him, by example, what it was like to let life in after being dormant for so long.

She really should have told him as much, but she let her lips speak in a different way. Mickey stood on her tiptoes and lightly kissed Diego. He froze under her touch, but quickly caught up to kiss her back.

She licked at the seam of his mouth, urging him to invite her in. When he parted his lips, she swiped her tongue against his, relishing in the groan that vibrated throughout his chest.

"Mickey," he whispered against her lips.

She kissed away his next words, possibly his next breath. She wanted to inhale everything, suck the air from the room to fill her need for him. Mickey wanted only him, at this moment. All of him.

Diego pushed away from the wall and walked her backward. She followed as if they were dancing, her hands gripping his shirt and her kiss uninterrupted while they moved together. He broke their kiss to sit on the small sofa he'd cleared off earlier. "Come here." He beckoned with his chin.

She settled onto his lap, straddling his legs. "Are you okay?"

He nodded. "I'm okay, Mickey. I just want you to sit with me. Let me hold you for a little while."

She frowned. "Hold me?"

Diego shrugged. "So you can hold me, I guess," he amended, his voice now tired. "I just need you to be with me tonight."

Mickey could do that. She wrapped her arms around him and rested her head on his shoulder. "Like this?" she asked.

He tilted his head against the cushions and closed his eyes. "Like that," he murmured.

She stared at his profile while he wasn't looking, tracing a path from his forehead to his chin. He truly was a beautiful man. "I'm not making you uncomfortable?"

"Nope," he grumbled. "I like it when you wrap your thighs around me."

"Would you like to talk about stuff?"

He opened his eyes and glanced at her. "Okay."

"Tell me about Lucía. How did you two meet?"

He chuckled as his hand ran up her back. "She was the cute teller at my bank in Chicago. I made sure I got in her line every other week so she could deposit my paycheck."

"Were you still taking care of your mom in Chicago?"

He nodded. "My tía Elena helped me while I delivered for UPS."

She pulled back to look at him. "You were a UPS guy?"

Diego cocked a brow. "You look surprised."

"Well, now I'm imagining you in those cute shorts and I like what I'm seeing."

He lightly tapped her butt as a grin spread over his face. "I'm trying to talk to you."

"I'm sorry, go on." She nestled against his chest. "Lucía was the cute teller at your bank."

"Yeah, well, I think she liked the brown shorts, too. Because a few paychecks later, she asked if I wanted to get a drink with her."

"She asked you?" Mickey asked, stroking the hair at the nape of his neck. "I like her boldness."

"I did, too…" Diego whispered. His hands were back to her thighs. "She took me to her favorite bar and then I took her back to my place."

"On the first date?"

"For someone who kissed her boss on the first day on the job, you sound pretty damn judgy," he muttered.

"Not judging!" she laughed. "Again, I'm just impressed by her bravery."

"When you know, you know. We didn't date that long before I proposed. My mom was kind of responsible for that," he laughed. "She loved Lucía and needed me to nail that down."

When it seemed like his muscles had loosened and his tension had melted away, Mickey's hand drifted lower to caress the center of his chest. "I think that's sweet," she whispered. "What were your favorite things to do with Lucía?"

"Oh, god, I liked watching movies with her, but Lucía was always trying to go out and do things. If there was a new restaurant opening, she was there to try it. One time," he began, laughing. "Jesus…one time, she dragged me to this giant laser-tag place. We were running around for at least an hour trying to zap kids at this birthday party." His laughter grew louder. "She was so excited."

"Oh, my god," Mickey said. It totally tracked that a woman had to make Diego do fun things. "What else did you guys do?"

"Ahh, let's see." Diego closed his eyes to think. "She drove us to Alton, Illinois, to stay in a haunted B&B." His laughter was the most delightful thing she'd heard that day.

"Was it really haunted?" she asked.

"No," he said, shaking his head. "It was just fucking expensive. Lucía wanted to wander around the mansion at night to find ghosts, but we got caught by the innkeepers and were told to go to bed."

Mickey joined in his laughter as she imagined Diego tiptoeing around in the dark, trying not to knock over someone's delicate tchotchkes. "She was really fun, huh?"

"She was…" He sighed. "I haven't laughed like that in a long time. I need to think about those fun times more often."

Mickey sat up and slid off his lap. "You do," she agreed, taking his hand. "She deserves it, right?"

Diego gave her a tremulous smile. "Yeah, you're right."

"Maybe we should go home."

"Will you come home with me?" he asked, squeezing her hand. "We don't have to do anything, I just… I don't want to sleep alone tonight."

Mickey nodded. "Sure."

"Thank you for letting me talk," Diego said, rubbing the back of his neck. "I should probably start seeing a therapist."

"Therapy is great actually," she said as she pulled him from the couch. "I had a great therapist when I was in Athens. She was the only reason I got through my master's program."

"I'll think about it," he said seriously. "I'd like to work on some stuff."

Mickey hugged him again. "Let's watch a movie tonight. What's your favorite genre?"

He grimaced as he led her out of his office. "I'm not sure I wanna say…"

Mickey punched out and grabbed her purse from the coat-rack. "Well, now you have to say."

"I appreciate a good romantic comedy."

Her gaze flew to him. "I don't believe that."

Diego shrugged. "Fair enough."

"Which is your favorite?" she asked.

"*Someone Like You.*"

Mickey almost didn't believe him, but ending the day with a romantic movie felt like a good idea. Sitting on his couch, snuggled up under a blanket. That was the evening they needed after such a rough day. "Let's do that, then."

26

When Mickey entered her parents' home, she had braced herself for an inquisition. She hadn't spoken to either of them since Friday, nor had they checked in. She felt guilty for not calling her mother, but she also felt that she needed to get through the Riverwalk Festival before dealing with something else. Saturday went well enough, though. Thankfully, the bar was closed for Sunday even if it meant losing Festival money. Diego said they all needed a break.

"I'm home," she called from the foyer, where she set her purse and slipped off her shoes.

"In here," her brother replied from the living room.

She followed the sound of his voice to find him lounging on the sofa, playing on his phone. "Hey, Junior."

He didn't bother to glance up. "Yoooouu in troubbblle," he teased in a singsong voice.

Mickey froze. "What do you mean?" she asked, looking for their parents. She spied them on the patio: her dad grilling in his red apron and her mom standing next to him, sipping sweet tea.

"Momma called me on Friday and told me all about it," Junior chuckled. "Said you were a barmaid."

Mickey plopped down on her father's easy chair and arranged her skirt around her knees. "I wouldn't call my position a barmaid," she said. She summoned the image of a busty woman in a tight corset serving tankards of ale in an old tavern and laughed. "I'm a bartender at The Saloon."

"You like it?" he asked, still looking at his phone.

"I do," she said. "It's fun and interesting, the people I work with are cool and I like my boss."

Junior looked up from his phone. "You like your boss."

She stared at him. "What did I just say?"

Her brother's lips quirked on one side as he raised a brow. "Yeah, okay."

"What else did Mom tell you?"

"Nothing," he said with a shrug.

"Did she sound mad?"

He shrugged again.

As mature as her brother thought himself to be, he still acted like a little shit sometimes. "Did she sound disappointed at least?"

"You know moms," he said, returning to his phone. "They're always disappointed about something. She'll get over it."

Mickey chewed on her lip. "I guess."

"How's the money?" he asked.

"Very good," she said. "I doubt the paycheck is going to be anything to call home about, but the tips… Those are quite helpful. I've already made a decent-sized deposit this week."

Junior nodded. "That's what's up," he said approvingly. "You'll be okay for the summer, then?"

"I will be."

The patio door slid open. "Is Michelle here?" her mother asked.

"I'm here, Momma."

"Oh, good...you want something to drink?"

"I'll just have some water, Momma," Mickey called back.

"Your dad is grilling chicken, hamburgers and pork chops," Rita said. "I've got macaroni and greens going on in here."

Mickey pulled herself out of her chair and followed her nose into the kitchen. "Momma, you know there's only four people in this family, right?" she joked.

"You've heard of leftovers, right?" Rita retorted.

She walked up to her mother and wrapped her arms around her. "Thank you for cooking," she said.

"Baby, I cook every weekend," her mother said, patting Mickey's arm. "You just have to come home to see."

"You're right. I'm sorry I've been a no-show."

Her father came inside, carrying a tray of hamburgers. "There's the barmaid," he quipped.

Mickey rolled her eyes. "Bartender," she corrected.

"Uh-huh..." Virgil set down the burgers. "You taking your meds?"

"Yes, Daddy."

"That's all I wanna hear," he said, returning outside.

When she and her mother were left alone, Rita handed her a water bottle. "Why didn't you tell us?"

Mickey leaned against the kitchen counter. "I just figured y'all wouldn't approve."

Rita scoffed.

"Well, you don't," Mickey argued.

"You assume a lot," her mother said, leaning beside her. "Your dad and I don't care where you work, just so long as you take care of yourself while you're working."

"Momma, you and Daddy brag on me to anyone who will listen. *My baby's a professor. Michelle's up there at the university teaching kids.* Well, I'm not." Mickey's words tumbled out of her mouth in embarrassment. She was quickly on the path to admitting something that she'd been avoiding all these semesters at Hargrove. "I'm actually stuck in a hamster wheel at that job, teaching whatever they throw at me, and I think I'm only carrying on with it because at least I'm adjacent to a real profession." She paused to take a breath. "At least, at the bar, I can see where my work goes. I get paid what I actually put in. And I like the people I work with."

Her mother went quiet.

"I'm sorry I kept that from you," Mickey said. "I just didn't want you guys to think I couldn't take care of myself."

Rita gave her a weak smile. "How old are you again?"

"Thirty-three," she said, grinning back.

"Alright then, I suppose you're old enough to work wherever you like," she said, wrapping an arm around Mickey. "I'm sorry for not remembering that." She paused, searching her daughter's face. "Sometimes I look at you and think of that skinny trembling child who looked so small in a hospital bed. And the doctors who thought I was just making things up."

Mickey pressed her lips together as she listened.

"I think of that one doctor who asked if you were on drugs," Rita said angrily. "He looked you over so quickly before he told us to leave… I mean, how hard is it to do simple blood work?"

"I know, Momma."

"We wanted to protect you, Michelle," her mother said. "And for years, it didn't feel like we could. Like we just stood there and watched you get sicker. I guess I didn't realize we were still making up for lost time."

Mickey understood where her mother was coming from. She had remembered those years as being hard on the family, but in an abstract way. Hearing Rita's side of the family trauma was like puzzle pieces settling into place. For the first time, she was looking at Rita Chambers, not as her mother, but as a woman who only wanted answers. She took a deep breath. "So, you're not disappointed that I'm a bartender?"

Her mother chuckled. "I sure didn't expect it...but no, I'm not disappointed. You seem like you know what you're doing. I'm proud of my kids because they're mine. You don't have to be a teacher for me to care about you. Do you think you'll quit Hargrove?"

Mickey pursed her lips and sighed. "I'm not sure. I love being in the classroom... But being a good teacher can't save me, and it can't keep me fed."

"Listen, as long as I'm your momma, you don't need to worry about eating," Rita said with a raised brow. "You gonna get fed around here, missy."

Mickey laughed and hugged her mother tighter. "Okay, then. But until I quit, I'm going to keep working at the bar. I genuinely like it and the money."

"And what about that boss of yours?" her mother asked, patting her back. "He's a good man?"

"He really is," Mickey said absently.

Rita pulled away from her and gave her a curious smile. "He *really* is?"

Mickey's face burned. "I just meant—"

"Tell the truth, now," her mother interrupted. "Is that man something more to you? Because the way he fretted over you tells me you're not just his employee."

It took her a couple seconds to realize that lying to her mother would be futile. "Diego and I are close."

Her mother nodded. "Close enough to bring him over for a Sunday dinner? Since you're now working at the bar, we're having to change days, you know."

She pulled away and poured herself a glass of water. "Maybe," she said, taking a sip. "I'd have to ask him about it."

Rita scoffed as she went into the fridge and poured herself some more sweet tea. "Well, maybe another guest will help us take down some of this food. You wanna fix a plate and take it to him?"

Her mother was suggesting she feed someone else with this bounty? Mickey watched as her mother went back to cooking. For Rita, the conversation was done, and she'd moved on. For Mickey, a giant weight had been lifted from her shoulders. She finally felt like she could think about the future. "Maybe I'll do that," she said.

When Diego pulled the last pastel out of the boiling water, he burned his fingers and nearly dropped the banana leaf and parchment paper pocket on the floor. "Shit," he hissed, shaking out his hand as he grappled with his tongs. The pastel fell onto the paper towel–covered pan to cool off as he moved on to the next project: frozen buffalo wings.

He'd invited his brother-in-law over for the Cubs and Braves game on TV, telling Ramón, "All you need to bring is yourself." Diego made himself in charge of the snacks. The evening before, when he should have gone to bed, he went to the La Nacional grocery store and shopped for all the things a website said he needed for pasteles. Mickey had said that he might want to try making them again in her comments and he'd taken her advice.

He stayed up and stewed pork until it was soft and tender before going to bed. That morning, he woke up earlier than he should have and assembled them by watching a YouTube video. After fucking up a few, he managed to make some decent pockets and the rhythm eventually came back to him.

He forgot how laborious the effort was, how helpful it was to have a kitchen full of tías to help him. He only bought enough ingredients to help him make a couple dozen instead of the holiday hundred. He also erred on the side of caution and bought ready-made taro and plantain masa. No matter, though. It was just him and Ramón, and if they turned out shitty, there were always buffalo wings.

His doorbell rang, making him pause the wing cooking and tear down his hallway toward the front door. When he threw it open, Ramón lifted a case of beers. "You know I couldn't come empty-handed."

"That's fine," Diego said, letting him through. "I'll put them on ice and serve you something else."

"No work today," Ramón said, heading toward the kitchen. "I'll grab whatever beer you've got. The game is starting in a few minutes."

Diego followed him down the hall. "Are you hungry?"

"Estoy muerto de hambre. What do you have?" Ramón asked, putting the beers straight into the freezer, and looking around the kitchen. "¡Dios mío! Are those tamales?"

"Pasteles," Diego said. "Similar, I guess."

"Ahh, our Puerto Rican cousins," his brother-in-law said, approaching the stove. He picked one up and immediately unwrapped it. Finding it a little too hot and unwieldy, he set it on a plate that Diego quickly retrieved.

"You're gonna need a fork," he said. "They're soft and the achiote oil is a little messy."

Ramón tried a forkful and groaned. "Okay, hermano, muy bien… Who taught you to cook like this?"

Diego's chest puffed a little. "My tías in Chicago. We made them for the holidays when I was a kid."

Ramón gave him an appraising nod. "I thought so. Because I know my sister could never make something like this."

Lucía couldn't cook. In fact, she hated cooking at all. She left that job to Diego, not that he minded. His wife was better suited to mixology, and they both knew it. "Well, Lucía was good at other things."

Ramón nodded as he worked on the rest of his pastel. "I know. One thing about Lucía—she was good at business and troublemaking. I never saw her in the kitchen." Ramón wiped his hands on a paper towel and chuckled. "You know? When she was little, she had this thing where she needed to be the boss of everyone. She used to have this dictator's voice when she talked to her dolls. A real jefe..." His brother-in-law shook his head. "Lucía Maria Rodriguez Silva. We called her Generalissima Silva."

"I didn't know that," Diego said, leaning against his counter. "But that doesn't surprise me."

When he met Lucía, she had definitely taken charge, but in a way that often made him feel like it was his idea. When she dragged him places, it felt like she pulled him out of his shell and made him face the world, but she would be beside him the entire time.

"Oh, yeah, she was a benevolent dictator, I guess. Or what people might call bossy. You mind if I have another?" Ramón asked, pointing to the pan of pasteles.

"Claro," Diego said with a nod. "Help yourself."

"You know, I'm older than her, but she never made it easy to be a big brother. She came out of our mother with demands." Ramón laughed again while he unwrapped another pastel. "I often wonder what she would be like at your age."

He and Lucía were the same age when they met and married. She'd also be forty-two if she were still alive. Diego's heart ached at the thought. "I'm sleeping with Mickey," he said abruptly.

Silence blanketed the kitchen as his brother-in-law quietly chewed. Diego closed his eyes and wondered if blurting out his indiscretions was a good idea. When he took Mickey home on Friday night, he felt as though they were on the same page, sharing the same feelings, building toward something he hadn't felt in ages. Those feelings gave him enough confidence to say something to his dead wife's brother.

"We've been a thing for the last couple weeks." He pushed forward. "What thing, I don't exactly know because I haven't been in a relationship in a while, but I wanted to tell you because...it'll eat me up if I don't."

To his surprise, Ramón laughed at him. The man licked masa from his fingertips and laughed. His reaction confused Diego. Had he said something funny? "Ya lo sabía, hermano," he chuckled. "It wasn't too hard to see."

"You know?" Diego asked.

Ramón dismissed him with a wave of his hand. "The whole bar is talking about it. We took bets on the third day, wondering when your mood would finally change." He shrugged. "That's why I talked to you about dating. I figured you were ready, yeah?"

Diego clutched the edges of his kitchen counter as his heart raced. He tried to remember the details of their talk in Ramón's truck and slowly put the pieces together. "This is okay, then?" he asked sheepishly. "She's my professor, you know?"

Ramón dragged another pastel onto his plate before exiting the kitchen. "The part where she's your professor? Not my business. But the part where she's a member of The Saloon family? I think she's a good fit for it and you." He wandered down the hall and disappeared into the living room. "Remember what I said? She reminds me of Lucía. Maybe not as bossy, though."

Alone in his kitchen, Diego chuckled to himself. There was nothing else that needed to be said to the person who mattered the most. Ramón had already assumed things were heating up before he had. He had permission to be…happy.

He shook out his hands and blew out a sigh of relief. When Diego glanced at the paper pockets drying on his stove, he was amazed that he'd even made an attempt to cook something from his childhood. If Mickey could see what he had accomplished, she would be proud.

It was a curious thought: wanting Mickey to be proud of him. He wanted her approval more than anything else and it struck him as odd and exciting.

27

"I gotta go to the back and sort out a beer shipment with my distributor," Diego said, flinging his rag under the bar. "Can you handle these jackasses while I'm gone?"

He didn't even bother lowering his voice as Mickey poured a Vodka Cranberry for a college student. The bar was full of kids after the Hargrove baseball team's win. He was on edge for most of the evening, just waiting for someone to act a fool.

"I'm fine, Diego." She laughed. "Take care of your business."

"If anyone gives you shit, just holler for Stevie or Jerry," he said as he walked behind her. He laid a reassuring hand on the small of her back. "Don't let these kids walk all over you, Professor."

She glanced over her shoulder. "I think I'll be fine."

He gave her one last heated look that made her stomach dip and then left the bar in her hands. Mickey had clocked enough time behind the bar to feel confident about working alone. Plus, the students didn't bother her as much as they did Diego.

"Hey, Mick," Ollie called, heaving a tray of clean glasses onto the back counter. "You need anything while I'm up here?"

"A little conversation is all. How are you doing these days, Ollie?"

She kneeled down to stack glasses under the bar. "Good news from the home front," she said, raking her fingers through her short purple hair. "Got word from my sister that she's ready to get away from Goshen."

"Oh, wow," Mickey intoned as she opened a beer bottle for a customer. "She's going to need help, right? How does she plan to leave?"

"I've got those friends in Indianapolis," Ollie said, straightening up. "I'm talking to them right now about setting her up in the transition house."

What Ollie described sounded like spy stuff, and it made her a little nervous. An Amish girl on her own for the first time? What if something happened from Goshen to Indianapolis? "How old is your sister?"

"Rebecca is eighteen," Ollie sighed. "But she's only got an eighth-grade education. The last three letters I've gotten from her have been pretty intense, like she's been ready to leave."

Mickey smiled. "There must be a wild streak in the Yoder girls, huh?"

Ollie threw her a cheeky grin. "Yeah, well. I kinda figured she'd follow along… I'm just glad to reunite with at least one of my siblings."

"I know you can't wait to see her," Mickey said, rubbing Ollie's arm.

"I'm gonna drive up to get her next week. I'll get her some new clothes, find her a salon," she chuckled, "and I'll see if I can find her a phone."

"You're a good sister, Ollie. She's lucky to have you in her corner."

She shrugged. "I do what I can."

"Get off of me!" shouted a woman's voice.

Mickey's attention flew to a boiling situation near the back of the bar. A young brunette wrenched her arm away from a young man who towered over her. Mickey glanced at the door where Jerry was by himself, busy carding the steady stream of customers.

Before thinking, Mickey and Ollie ran to the scene, prepared to break up a fight. At first glance, the young man was backing off, but he smacked the drink out of the woman's hand, spraying alcohol on Ollie.

"Okay, okay," Mickey said in her loud authoritative voice. "Let's break it up."

"Fuck you, bitch," the young man said, grabbing at the woman's arm again. Ollie pulled her back just as Mickey put herself between the two.

The beefy-necked kid, who couldn't have been older than twenty-two, now stood over her. His blond hair fell in his red face as he grew angrier. "Look, she's not interested," Mickey said. "You need to let it go."

For the first time, the guy swung his glassy-eyed gaze to Mickey. "Who the fuck asked you?"

Mickey frowned. "I didn't ask you. But now I want you to get the hell out of here, and don't come back." She glanced over his shoulder to find Jerry still occupied. Who even knew where Stevie was.

Blond Guy took a step forward, towering over her. "Make me," he said, eyeing the girl behind her. Ollie had moved her away, closer to the bar, but he wouldn't budge.

Against her better judgment, Mickey took him up on his challenge. She squared her shoulders and used her whole body to shove him back. Since he had already been drinking, he flew backward pretty easily, crashing into an empty table behind him.

The crash alerted Jerry, who pushed through the crowd just

as the young man struggled to stand. When he got to his feet, he shook his head clear and made another attempt to charge toward Mickey. "Jerry, hurry up!" she shouted.

To her amazement, the young man cocked his fist back. But before he could connect with her face, Jerry had grabbed his arm and tackled him to the ground. An arm wrapped around her waist and pulled her away from the fray.

"Goddammit, Mickey!" Diego growled in her ear as he dragged her off.

Before she could say anything in her defense, he pulled her toward the back of the bar, near the jukebox. Ollie was busy comforting the girl. "Let me see to her," she said, pulling out of Diego's tight grasp.

He reluctantly let her go, so he could help Jerry throw the offender out of the bar. "Where the hell is Stevie?" she heard him shout.

"Hey, are you okay?" Mickey asked the woman.

She nodded, brushing her long brown hair out of her face. She was already on the verge of tears as she leaned against Ollie. "I—I don't know," she said in a trembling voice. "He—he bought—he bought me a drink, and when I said I wasn't interested—" she brushed her tears with the back of her hand "—he just freaked out."

Mickey rubbed the girl's arms briskly. "If you weren't interested, that's okay. You're not obligated to anyone who buys you a drink."

Soon, the tiny-but-mighty Irene joined them, wearing a scowl. "Who the hell was that fucker? And where the hell is Stevie? He should have bounced him the minute he went wild."

"Mickey took care of it," Ollie said with a grin. "Did you see him flying?"

"I did," Diego said from behind her.

★★★

When he dispatched the dipshit who started the ruckus, he found the women of his bar surrounding the victim, stroking and coddling her. Diego's chest heaved as images flashed through his mind.

That asshole standing over her, Mickey shoving him backward and him coming back for more. Why in the hell would she put herself in harm's way like that? The guy was actually going to punch her. He'd been on the receiving end of a sloppy punch and couldn't imagine Mickey getting hurt…in *his* bar.

"Why in the fresh-fuck did you think you could take that guy on?" he asked, the volume of his voice climbing with every word.

When Mickey turned to face him, her glare matched his tone. "Excuse me?"

"That guy could have hurt you, Mickey," he said, planting his hands on his hips. "You never get involved in scuffles. That's always the bouncer's job!"

She matched his posture, standing toe to toe with him. "And what if your bouncer is too far away and busy? I was standing right here, and I wasn't about to watch a woman get assaulted."

He shook his head. "He could have hurt you."

"In all the years you've worked here, you've never broken up a fight?"

"I can do that because I'm a man," he snapped.

All four women, including their rescued victim, dropped their jaws in unison. As soon as the words fell from his lips, he realized how he'd fucked up.

"What I mean—it's not just because I'm a man," he said, struggling with his words. "Shit, Mickey, your parents already hate me for letting you work on a hot day. What's it gonna look like when you show up to dinner with a black eye?"

Ollie let out a pained groan. Irene picked up her tray and ran off. The young woman, whom he didn't even know, high-tailed from the scene. Mickey's cheerful face had gone from anger to stony in seconds.

"Let me?" she asked in a voice edged in steel.

"I need to get some glasses," Ollie said as she headed to the kitchen.

"Mickey," he tried.

"I need to get back on the bar," she said. "No one is serving."

When Diego realized no one was behind the bar, he chased her to their workstation. "Mickey, I didn't mean for it to come out like that."

"You *let* me work behind the bar, or did you beg me, Diego?" she asked, pulling a pint for a customer.

"Can I have a Vodka Cran under the Pierce tab?" asked a young man.

He gave the kid a brisk nod and began pouring. "I asked you," he corrected.

"And you *let* me work here, or did Jeanie hire me?" she asked, handing the beer off. "Three dollars."

"I—goddammit—Jeanie hires through me."

She slammed the register shut and returned the change to her customer. The woman shook her head. "Keep it."

"You can fuck me or patronize me, but you don't get to do both," Mickey said, dropping the change in the tip jar. "I won't tolerate it."

"Oh, shit," Irene said at Diego's elbow. She was about to ask for an order, but quickly clamped her mouth shut.

"Mickey, for the love of God," he growled, handing his drink over. "For Pierce, right?"

The kid nodded with widened eyes.

"You cannot talk to me like that out here," he said in what he hoped was a measured voice.

Her eyes flashed with anger. "But you can berate me in front of my colleagues about being a weak woman who can't defend herself or others."

"You know damn well I didn't say that."

"Well, actually," Irene started, "you basically—"

"Can it, Cho!" he snapped.

"You won't have to worry about me talking to you any kind of way," Mickey said, untying her apron strings. "I can just quit now and save you from the verbal abuse."

He watched in disbelief as she whipped her apron off and flung it over her shoulder. "For fuck's sake, Mickey, I'm not letting you quit."

She turned on her heel. "I don't work here for you to *let* me do shit," she said over her shoulder.

"Fuck," he muttered, checking his watch. Two hours before closing time and a full-ass bar. "Fuck."

Had she really just quit?

As if to answer his question, Mickey reappeared from the kitchen with her purse slung over her shoulder. She was cutting a fiery trail toward the door, without even a glance at him.

"Mickey!" he shouted over the music and revelry. "Goddammit, Mickey, get back here!"

When she exited the building, he could barely believe what had transpired in a matter of minutes. Irene was still leaning against the bar, watching the whole thing unfold. "Wow… I really thought she'd stay," she drawled. "But you kinda fucked that up, huh, Boss?"

"What do you want?" he asked, trying his best not to snap.

"Five Slammers."

He closed his eyes and swore under his breath. A familiar wave of nausea rolled over him, reminding him of the night before they hired Mickey. All that was missing was the never-ending chorus of "Don't Stop Believin'" to drive him insane.

Diego held it together, though.

He started pulling five half-pints of Guinness to get them out of the way. The shots, which he'd have to do by himself, would come later. But he kept his head down and got on with it. Because there was no point in crying over spilled beer, or the woman he was falling for as she walked right out of his life.

"Mano, what the hell happened?" Ramón asked, carrying a crate of fresh shot glasses.

Diego almost didn't answer, but he was already in trouble with Ollie and Irene. He might as well take his beating from his brother-in-law. "Mickey quit and I can't talk about it right now."

"Coño, what did you do?"

Diego piled all the finished pints on Irene's tray and started on the shots. "I told her not to get into fistfights and she got mad. If you see your cousin before I do—" The words were barely out of his mouth when he saw Stevie walk past the bar with a plastic cup of water. The young man sipped on it nonchalantly as he strolled through the crowd, making Diego angrier. "Stevie!"

His cousin-in-law stopped abruptly, head whipping in his direction. "Hey, Boss."

Diego poured the rest of his shots before sending Irene on her way. "Is your contact information updated?" he asked Stevie.

The young man's brow furrowed. "Yeah?"

"Good. I'll send your last check there. You're fired."

"What?"

"You weren't on your post, again," Diego hissed, leaning over the bar. "You left Jerry in the middle of a crowded shift, and the women had to break up a fight. Mickey was almost assaulted. I want you gone. I want you out of here *tonight*. The next time you step foot in here, you'll be a customer. Because I am *not* paying a fuckup who keeps ducking out of his job when it pleases him. Got it?"

A surprised Stevie looked between Diego and his cousin who stood nearby in stunned silence. "Are you seriously firing me?"

"Primo," Ramón intervened, "leave."

Stevie's shoulders slumped in resignation as he backed away from the bar. After he disappeared from view, Diego took a breath. It was his first time firing anyone and the adrenaline rolled off him like waves, only to be replaced with the anxiety of Mickey.

"You had to do it," Ramón said. "I don't know where his head is, but you warned him."

Diego nodded, barely listening. He still thought about Mickey and how he'd have to clean up that mess. She'd sounded resolute as she stormed out. Angrier than he'd ever seen her. Thunderclouds had replaced sunshine. He closed his eyes and exhaled hard.

If he couldn't get her back, he was fucked in more ways than one.

28

Mickey had never quit a job before.

Rather, she'd never stormed out of a job. She'd certainly never told her boss off in front of everyone. When she shoved past Stevie, who'd finally turned up, she stood on the sidewalk outside of The Saloon and wondered if she'd made a huge mistake.

No, she told herself as she walked toward her car and drove herself home. The rush of adrenaline from being so confrontational wore off by the time she threw herself onto her bed. In the dark, she asked herself again: *Did I fuck up?*

Diego had insulted her. Simple as that. Instead of congratulating her for standing up to a bully, he fell back on dick-swinging machismo. And then he did exactly what she asked him not to do: throw her fainting incident and illness back in her face like he was her protector. She already had two parents; she didn't need him stepping in to be a third.

Just when she thought she was getting her footing at the bar, Diego confirmed he didn't trust her or her soft hands to work like everyone else. She didn't want special treatment because they were sleeping together, or because she was his instructor. Mickey just wanted to make money.

The next morning, she realized she'd royally fucked up her bag. As she walked to the kitchen for her meds and juice, she did a quick mental calculation of how the rest of the summer's finances would go. The last two weeks' tips were incredibly helpful for her frugal lifestyle, but it wouldn't last until her next temporary Hargrove contract.

When she considered the alternatives, her stomach dropped. Mickey didn't want to work for her brother or Mayor Keaton. Both would require training that she didn't have time for—and good lord, the boredom would kill her.

She padded back to her bedroom to find her phone. She'd received a few text notifications, from Irene, Ollie and even Jeanie, all of which read, please don't quit, or something to that effect. It was Jeanie's text that squeezed her heart.

I heard what happened and I chewed him out. I'll cover your shift tonight if you don't feel like coming in. And if you want to return to the floor with Irene, that's also cool.

Jeanie was still trying to find a home health-care worker for her mother. She didn't have time to worry about Mickey's fight with Diego.

She sighed and pressed the call button for Jeanie, who answered after only two rings.

"Hey, girl." Jeanie's voice was warm but concerned. "Are you okay?"

"Hey, Jeanie, I think so..." Mickey answered cautiously. "You talked to Diego?"

"If you wanna call it talking," she chuckled. "He'd probably call it a one-sided attack on his pride. But yeah, I got a version of the events from him after I talked to Irene."

"Yeah?" Mickey asked, sitting on her bed. "How bad did it sound?"

"If you're wondering if Irene told me about you and Diego, you'd be right." Before Mickey could defend herself, Jeanie continued, "But I could have guessed by the way he was acting last week. He's smitten, Mick."

"Be that as it may—"

"I know, he's old-fashioned and hypocritical about shit like that. I've broken up my fair share of Saloon fights in the past. Even though he yelled at me about it, he was thankful I took out the trash."

That made Mickey pause.

"If it makes you feel better, he yelled at Ramón for doing what his cousin Stevie was supposed to do. Of course, he fired Stevie last night, which was a long time comin'. Shit, I don't know, Diego just likes to bark." Jeanie laughed. "I've just learned to tune him out."

Mickey sighed. "But it's different with me, isn't it? I'm not imagining that he handles me with kid gloves, right?"

"No, you're probably right," Jeanie admitted. "And if you could stand to work behind the bar with him for the last two weeks, you're a lot stronger than I thought. Whatever you said to him before you left, he probably deserved it."

"Maybe he did," Mickey said. "But maybe he didn't deserve the way I said it. I could have pulled him aside."

"Maybe, but sometimes Diego responds better to blunt force."

Mickey pursed her lips as she stared out her window. "I hate to say it, but maybe I shot my mouth off too fast. I don't know if I should have quit like that."

"Girl, I get it, but you're welcome to come back anytime. Whether or not he wants to admit it, he needs you—swinging fists and all."

The word *need* snagged in her mind. How did Diego need her exactly? "I'm not really in a hurry to find another job…" she murmured.

"It's really up to you," Jeanie said. "You don't have to work the bar tonight. I can jump in."

"What about your mom?"

"She's trying to get rid of me," Jeanie said. "So, I can pick up some slack. Just know that The Saloon loves you."

Jeanie had worked so hard to reassure her, to calm her down, that it was difficult to decide what to do. She needed time to think about it. "Let me call you back in a couple hours. I just want to reconsider some things."

"Sure." As Mickey was about to hang up, Jeanie quickly added, "But, Mickey, you both need to eventually talk about your relationship because Diego really cares about you. Give him shit about the job, but also let him know about…how you feel." She heaved a sigh. "I think—hell, the bar thinks—you're good for him."

Mickey squeezed her eyes shut. "I'll think about it and get back to you."

"Okay then, we'll talk later."

"Alright," she said, hanging up. Mickey flopped onto her back and stared at the ceiling. "Fuck."

She was probably going back to work tonight, and she would do it for Jeanie's sake. Mickey liked her team, and even though she was angry with Diego, she liked him, too. But instead of listening to secondhand accounts of his contrition, she'd rather hear it from *him*. Until then, she'd get behind the bar, but she wasn't about to talk to him.

She needed to get out of her apartment, possibly out of her head, and hang out with Cleo. It had been a minute since the two had properly caught up, not since the bachelorette party. Back when Mickey gleefully disregarded her best friend's advice.

But even as Cleo Green opened her apartment door, she didn't wear a smug expression. Nor did she say I told you so. She simply hugged Mickey and poured her a coffee. "What are you working on today?" she asked, returning to her command center, a mega desk with three computer monitors.

"I thought it was your day off," Mickey said, spreading her own work materials out on the kitchen table.

"I don't have to go to the office, but there are some campaign things I'd like to take care of while Keaton isn't in my face."

"Fair." Mickey nodded. "Well, considering last night's clusterfuck, I'm looking for gainful employment for the fall."

Cleo glanced up from her screen. "Oh, really? You think the fight went that bad?"

"I'm preparing for a contingency plan."

"You know I'm all about backup plans for my backups," Cleo said with a grin. "Besides, Diego's not going to fire you. Not after the way you probably put it on him."

After her conversation with Jeanie, Mickey wasn't worried about that. The Saloon wanted her to stay but she didn't know if it was a good idea to be so close to Diego. She sighed. "I know you're not saying the obvious, but you were right."

"I know that," her friend said, returning to her computer screen. "But you were a cute couple while it lasted… I'm sure the sex was great?"

"More than great. That man fucks like it's his number one priority."

"Mmm-hmm… I could tell when he was flirting with you at the bachelorette party," Cleo chuckled. "By the way, Beth absolutely loved it. She's telling everybody and their momma about it."

Mickey stopped scrolling through her résumé. "Really?"

"Oh, yeah. Even though you did most of the work, I feel like a fucking hero. You know what?" She tapped a pencil to her lips. "That's what you should be doing."

Before Cleo could get the words out, the wheels in Mickey's head were already turning. "You're right," she murmured, opening her internet browser. She quickly googled "wedding planners + Columbus, GA" and looked through the results. Nelly's Nuptials was at the top, boasting high ratings and a lovely website. She looked at their small team of wedding professionals and wondered if they needed help. She jotted down their contact information and sat back. "What do you think about Mickey, the Wedding Planner?"

"I think it sounds perfect for you. What skills would you bring to the table?" Cleo asked in her press conference voice.

"I'm highly organized. I'm very good at managing my time and others. I have a lot of creative ideas that apparently make brides feel special. And I can handle large groups of people, keep them on task. I've got a good teacher's voice."

"And you're an extrovert who loves a good party."

"I pump up the crowd," Mickey said with more confidence.

"You're the perfect hype-woman."

"You really think I could do something like this?"

Cleo swiveled in her office chair to face her. "Bitch, you can do anything."

If she could work at a place like The Saloon, perhaps her friend was right. Though, the prospect of no longer working there bothered her. Even if she and Diego were in the middle of a falling out, she still loved the rest of her colleagues, her friends. She felt a part of their weird little family and didn't want to give that up.

"What's on your mind?" Cleo asked.

Mickey tried to relax the frown that had scrunched her

eyebrows. "I just realized that I don't have the same attachment to Hargrove as I do The Saloon… When I think about giving up the classroom, I'm not quite as sad. What do you think that means?"

"You're dedicated to both jobs but it sounds like only one is offering some semblance of loyalty. Hargrove would drop you in a minute if they had to reconsider their budget. Universities are like any other large corporation—they're mostly worried about their bottom line. At least at The Saloon you know you're needed in a more meaningful way."

"Exactly," Mickey breathed. "I'm completely expendable at school. Lara is a nice lady, but she knows there's plenty of other desperate adjuncts out there."

"Willing to create courses out of thin air for pennies on the dollar," Cleo added. "Girl, that place is scamming you."

She knew that much. Now it was just a matter of cutting the tether that bound her. "Okay then, I'm going to start looking for something else. Something worthy of my time."

"Perfect! Now what are you going to do with Diego?"

Mickey sighed. "Do we have to figure that out right now?"

Cleo laughed as she walked to the kitchen for another coffee. "You act like you didn't spend our last Sunday Funday making me prep for a party I didn't feel like attending. Trust me, Mick, once you come up with a plan for Diego, you'll feel better."

Mickey was doubtful.

Although she didn't know how she'd approach him, she *was* certain that they needed to stop whatever it was they were doing. No more sex, no more distractions. Just teach him, grade him and keep things as they should have been: professional.

29

Diego showed up early as usual and quickly retreated to his office to escape the glares of his employees. No one would tell him if Mickey would arrive for her shift tonight, but Jeanie's absence told him there was hope.

Even Ramón ducked in and out of the kitchen without so much as a friendly nod. Diego was on the outside looking in on his own business. Everyone was officially mad at him, even the Newest Girl, Gina. After all, Mickey was her professor before he was the girl's boss.

Goddammit, what was he thinking? No telling what this was doing to his grade... No, she said she could separate messiness from grading. And if Diego were honest with himself, his standing with Mickey was more important than any grade he could earn in her class. She could fail him, drop him from her course, get him expelled, and he'd still crawl back to her on his knees, looking for forgiveness.

Except that wasn't entirely true.

While he didn't care about his grade, he did care that she'd overstepped her bounds as a bartender. There was no reason for her to jump in the middle of a dangerous situation and he didn't regret telling her that. Maybe he should have pulled her aside and told her he was concerned for her safety, but he hadn't. He admitted, to her face, that her safety was paramount. She just didn't hear it the way he'd needed her to.

After he fired Stevie, he closed down the bar in silence. Well, almost… Jeanie called him while he counted both registers and chewed him out over Mickey. The punishment hadn't ended with her that night. Everyone from Ramón to Gina's quiet judgment told him—quite loudly—he'd fucked up. But no one knew what Mickey meant to him. And he wasn't ready to admit it out loud.

After hiding for a while, he heard Mickey through his office door. She greeted her coworkers and settled into a conversation with Ollie in the kitchen. He lifted his eyes to the ceiling and crossed himself. She came to work…

And she was cutting garnish. A task that Mickey hated to do, but she was probably doing it to avoid being in the same space as him. He'd eventually have to leave his office and work alongside her. And when he did, he wouldn't know how he'd react to her latest sundress or her perfume. Diego finally left the safety of his office and faced his punishment.

When he walked to the front of the house, he met up with his brother-in-law, who shot him a glare. "Apologize."

"And then what?" he asked, watching Ramón supply him with clean glasses.

"And then, maybe, she'll want to keep working here," Ramón said in a huff as he stacked the last of his glasses. He grabbed his empty crate and carried it away without another word. Irene and Gina came to the front of the house to take care of the stragglers who would soon close out their tabs.

One of them was the crime writer Mickey had chatted with last week. Terry, Kerry or something. Diego couldn't remember. She hunched over her laptop, only to look up when

Gina asked her about another beer. The woman nodded and held up one finger, signifying one more before closing out. Diego reached under the bar for the fridge and retrieved a Bud Light for Gina.

He kept glancing back toward the kitchen, though.

He wondered when Mickey was going to appear and what she might say to him. Better yet, what was he going to say? Was an apology good enough for her? The alternative should have scared him straight. Without her in his life, he was probably destined to be alone for the rest of his days. He scoffed to himself. *Okay, perhaps a little too dramatic...* But did he really want to lose her over one silly disagreement?

"Can I have a Bud Light for Tara?" Gina asked.

"Sure," he said, pushing the bottle toward her.

She took it without a thank-you. Jesus, he really was in the doghouse with everyone. When Mickey finally appeared, she carried three tubs of citrus garnish with her. She wore another pretty sundress, a key lime green number he hadn't seen before. She'd styled her hair in a ponytail with a few curls framing her face. As usual, she looked magical and spritely, entirely too polished to work at The Saloon.

"We should be all set," she said in a polite voice as she sat the tubs side by side on the bar.

"Would you like to have a quick office meeting?" he asked abruptly.

Mickey moved around him without looking up. She swept one curl behind her ear and began wiping down bottles he'd already cleaned. "No, thank you," she said lightly.

"I cleaned those," he said.

She paused with a bottle of gin in her grasp. "Then why do they still feel sticky?"

Diego pressed his lips into a thin line and breathed through his nose. So, this was how they'd work. "Suit yourself."

She continued her mission in silence. He watched her clean each bottle with his arms crossed over his chest. "You're sure you don't want to talk in my office?" he asked, breaking through the quiet.

Mickey turned around and flashed him what looked to be the fakest smile she could muster. And while the smile creased her cute dimples, it never reached her eyes. "I don't think we should have any more office meetings until you and I figure out how to keep out of trouble."

It never felt good to have his words flung back at him, but Diego knew he probably deserved it. "Fountain City tomorrow, then?"

"I don't think I'll be there," she said.

He sighed. "This is where we are?"

"I'm only here because I need the money," she said in a low voice, avoiding attention from Irene, who stood nearby. "And *that* need can't be confused with anything else right now."

She fidgeted with the strings of her apron as she cut her gaze away from him. Her confession squeezed his heart. He'd put her in a vulnerable position: needing money to survive the summer…yet he'd fucked it up by sleeping with her. The power imbalance didn't make him feel so bad when he was kissing and caressing her. Now, he felt like an ass.

"I'm sorry, Mickey," he said in a volume matching hers. "I shouldn't have been Mr. Macho last night." He stood beside her while they watched the floor. He tried to give her distance as she straightened cocktail napkins and stirrers, but once he caught her coconut scent…he fell back into her orbit. She didn't move away, though, so that was something. "I shouldn't have made you feel small."

Mickey's head dropped as she fiddled with the stirrers. When she didn't answer him, Diego ran a hand over his mouth. He didn't know what else to say. He wished she would look at him, speak to him, make him feel like less of a jerk.

"I don't want to lose you," he added.

She lifted her head, but didn't quite meet his eyes. Her gaze fastened onto his mouth instead. "You don't want to lose an employee?" she asked.

He rolled his eyes. "No, but you know what I meant."

Her eyes darted to his. "Well, I don't want to quit..." She licked her lips. "I like working here."

Diego's heart hammered in his chest as he looked around the bar. Every customer was taken care of. It was the slowest they'd ever been at seven o'clock. He and Mickey, standing together at this moment, felt significant. Like they were on the precipice of something. "I might have an idea," he said, inching his hand to her side. His pinkie lightly grazed hers, but she didn't move away.

"What?" Mickey whispered.

"We start over," he said, pulling away. "But this time, we take a break until your class is over and I'm no longer your student."

She scoffed. "Like Cleo said..."

"What do you mean?"

Mickey shook her head. "Oh, nothing. My friend warned me this was a bad idea. I didn't listen," she said, smirking.

"I didn't listen to my gut, either."

"Two weeks?"

He nodded. "We'll come back to the subject of me making sweet tender love to you," he whispered in her ear.

Her eyes flashed with a mix of shock and amusement. "Excuse me?"

"I'm just being a dick," Diego murmured. "Would you like that?"

A grin slid over her face. "Your dick?"

"A two-week break," he said with a chuckle. Seeing her smile was a huge relief. "And again, I'm sorry, Mick."

She nodded.

The writer, Tara Keller, interrupted them by stopping at the bar on her way out. "Hey, lady," she said, setting her empty bottle before them. "I thought about what you said, about the writing, and I've joined the Columbus Crime Writers' group."

Mickey made a little squeaking noise. "That's awesome news, Tara!" She leaned closer and gave a sly grin. "Oh, how I wish I could see all of y'alls internet search histories."

Tara mocked zipping her lips and throwing away the key. "I'm not telling. Anyway, I told myself if I really want to do this, I better start hanging out with like-minded people. I've only been to one workshop, but I like the other authors."

"Other *authors*, you say?"

Tara chuckled. "Yeah, that's what I said. I'll see you guys around," she said, heading to the door.

"Wait a minute now, that doesn't mean we're going to lose your business to the Crime Writers, are we?" Diego called.

"I still need a beer or two," Tara replied with a wave.

Mickey turned to him. "I think we should shake on it."

He was perfectly fine with shaking her hand, so long as he could touch her one last time. "If I need help with this upcoming research paper, I will email you like the rest of your students."

"That sounds good," she agreed, taking his hand. "I always answer my emails promptly."

As he shook her hand, he tried to stop his thumb from rubbing her over the soft delicate skin of her wrist. Just a few shakes and he'd let her go. Not forever, just for now. They needed to rethink how to approach one another, and he needed to prove himself to her all over again. What's more, he found himself *wanting* to.

He eventually let her hand go but missed the warmth and comfort it gave him. Two weeks of proving that he wasn't an ill-tempered, grumpy asshole who doesn't respect her as a bartender was something he looked forward to.

30

Two fucking weeks?

Why had she agreed to this?

Four days into their agreement, she'd forgiven Diego and things around the bar had gone back to normal…except Mickey was horny.

She didn't know when it had started, but she was fully aware of it every goddamn minute that Friday night. The place was hopping after people realized Karaoke Fridays were here to stay. Patrick was fairly busy with a long queue of customers. It was hot inside The Saloon and seeing Diego's skin shine with perspiration did something to her.

She almost wished that Jeanie were working this shift, but she had taken Diego up on his offer to help Todd during the day shift. She'd found a nurse for her mother and welcomed a less rowdy schedule at the bar. Mickey was glad for her but could barely tear her eyes away from Diego as he pulled his shirttail up to wipe his face. She glanced at his abs and rolled her eyes. She wondered if he'd done that shit on purpose.

"Mickey, get me six Lemon Drops," he called out.

She sprang into action with her shaker and jigger. "On it,"

she called back as another patron took to the stage. A man in his sixties swayed back and forth as he warbled "Wild Horses" by The Rolling Stones off-key.

She snatched six shot glasses and carried them to his side of the bar, right on top of Gina's tray, while Diego pulled pints.

"Here's your vodka," he said, reaching around her, setting the bottle beside her.

"Thank you," she said, focusing on her task. She mixed all of her ingredients in the shaker and added ice before shaking. As soon as she made the loud ruckus, Diego's attention zeroed in on her. His eyes held an unmistakable heat as they latched on to her breasts. Mickey's face warmed under his gaze, but she continued to shake. She wanted her drink to be properly mixed, but she also wanted to show Diego what he was missing.

Only when beer sloshed over his pint glass did he return to his task.

Mickey poured her shots in record time, proud of how quickly she had learned the craft. Now whenever Diego needed help with cocktails, he could use her skills instead of putting her on beer duty.

When there was a break in the chaos, he politely talked shop with her. They discussed his research paper, the taps in the basement or if they were good on scotch inventory. Diego was true to his word: nice and professional. She nodded along, watching the landscape of the bar while she listened, trying her best not to stare at his mouth.

"Are you going to sing tonight?" he asked, pulling her from her thoughts.

Mickey shrugged. "I don't have a partner this week," she faltered. She didn't really need Cleo to get up on a stage and make a fool of herself. She had her repertoire of pop songs on hand.

"I get it," he said, flipping his white rag over his shoulder. "You don't sing until the boss sings."

"I didn't mean—"

"No, I should probably sing something before I tease my people, huh?" he asked with a smirk. They watched a woman stumble onto the stage to sing Alanis Morissette's "You Oughta Know." It was messy, but she was passionate. "You're due for a break, Mickey."

"So are you," she said easily. Either one of them could leave the bar, so long as she got relief from looking at his sweaty body. "I'll hold down the fort while you're gone," she offered.

Diego shrugged and slipped his towel off his shoulder. "If you say so, Mickey. But when I get back, you need to take a rest."

Before she could speak, he stood in front of her and grasped her by the shoulders. The heat of his large hands permeated her T-shirt and warmed her chest. He didn't have to do this, hold her in place and tell her to rest. She almost objected to his familiarity, but leaned into his touch instead. "I will," she said softly.

"I want you to rest, Mickey," he said, meeting her halfway and whispering in her ear. The tiny vibrations against her face traveled to her breasts, causing her nipples to stiffen. She froze under his gaze and could only nod.

"I will."

Diego patted her shoulder before releasing her. "Good. I'll be back in fifteen."

When he left, Mickey let out a shuddering breath and immediately took care of another customer. Could anyone tell that her cheeks were hot? Was she blushing? She brushed a curl out of her face as she popped open a bottle of Corona and set it on the bar. The man she served wanted to start a tab, and she complied absently.

"Diego is on deck!" Patrick said over the general noise of the bar. At the register, Mickey's head snapped toward the stage. Her boss was up there, mic in hand, ready for his song.

"He's singing," Irene said in awe as she laid her tray down.

Since she didn't ask for an order, Mickey didn't press. Together, they watched Diego stare at the television monitors above him as he clutched a microphone with both hands. When he yelled out the first line of Steve Perry's "Oh Sherrie," Mickey let out a choked laugh.

Good lord, he was right.

Diego could not carry a note, but he tried. Something about his effort made her heart bloom and her panties wet. As Mickey squeezed her thighs together, Diego performed to a willing crowd who filled in the words he skipped. Why was this so damn attractive?

Midway through the song, he pivoted and pointed directly at the bar, addressing Mickey. She froze on the spot, uncertain that anyone could see what he did. She was stuck in place, watching him sing to her, his hooded eyes planted on her. She glanced around, only to find Irene glancing back. Irene's expression suggested that she understood what was going on. "He's singing to you," she squealed.

Mickey shook her head. "No, he's not."

But Diego *was* singing to her. Mickey stood, transfixed, unable to move to the next task. She felt as though she needed to see his strange, warbled performance through. He couldn't hit any of the notes that Steve Perry perfected because his voice was so deep, but he tried.

He was trying.

She couldn't get that out of her mind. In the same way he described trying out things with his late wife… Mickey cleared her throat and asked Irene what she needed.

"Two Guinnesses," Irene said, unable to take her eyes off

Diego. Mickey forced herself to move from her spot and get back to work. She pulled the pints as Diego had trained her, but her gaze flitted back to him every so often, listening to him sing his heart out.

31

"Thank you for coming in, Mickey," Dr. Byron Curtis said as he washed his hands in the nearby sink.

She hopped down from the examination table and grabbed her purse. "Yeah, well, my prescription is going to expire soon, so..."

Mickey's doctor, who had treated her since she was a young adult, leaned against the counter and chuckled. "I know, I know, kiddo. But I gotta keep an eye on how you're doing," he said, drying his hands. When he turned to face her, a bright smile lit his deep ebony face, making the wrinkles near his eyes crease. "We can't get complacent about these meds, you know? What works today, might not work tomorrow."

She sighed. It wasn't Dr. Curtis's fault that seeing him was so damn expensive. She should have been grateful that he was a competent doctor. After seeing a couple general practitioners, he was the only one who got her diagnosis correct and treated her with dignity. "I get it."

He tilted his head to the side to regard her. "I know the pills can add up, but I tried to stick with the generic."

Mickey nodded but stayed quiet.

Dr. Curtis crossed his slender brown arms over his chest. "Your health is good. T3 and T4 levels looked fine in your last blood test. I like where your cholesterol and weight are. Blood pressure is a little higher than I'd want, but we'll work on that. Feeling stressed about anything?"

At the risk of treating him like her therapist, she admitted what nagged her. "Work," she said with a sigh. "I'm trying to figure out what employment looks like in the next few months."

He nodded. "Sure. You still at the university?"

Mickey's face went hot. "I have a class there, but I'm also working at The Saloon?"

Dr. Curtis raised a brow. "Well, now..."

"I have things to think about," she admitted.

Dr. Curtis opened the door for her, allowing her to walk to the front desk. "Yes, ma'am, I'll bet you do. Just make sure you're taking care of yourself, wherever you're working. I don't want to hear about skipped dosages again," he said in a stern voice.

"Won't happen again, Dr. Curtis," Mickey said, still feeling embarrassed that she'd had to tell him about the Blues Festival incident.

"All right now, kiddo. You say hello to your daddy for me."

"Will do," Mickey said as she walked past the front desk. She didn't have to pay after her visits, which was a blessing. She could hold on to her money for a little while longer while she saved. Surely, when the bill arrived, she'd be better prepared for the amount.

Mickey dug around her purse for her keys as she let herself through the exit, her mind on the next task ahead of her. It all came crashing down around her when she ran up against a wall of muscles. "Excuse—"

"Mickey," Diego grunted as he stepped back.

She hadn't expected to literally run into Diego Acosta right after a doctor's visit. "Hey," she breathed. "I'm sorry about that... What are you doing here?"

He cracked a smile and adjusted the White Sox baseball cap on his head. She'd never seen him in a hat before and thought he was just as cute. He looked around the strip mall and pointed at the Piggly Wiggly down the way. "I'm getting groceries." He glanced at the building she'd just exited. "What are you up to?"

"Doctor's appointment," she said, twisting her hands behind her back.

Diego nodded. "You feeling all—" He stopped himself. He wore a conflicted expression as his eyes quickly scanned her body.

"Everything's fine," she said quickly. "Clean bill of health." They stepped aside for a young mother and her stroller. Mickey brushed against Diego's arm, and she suddenly remembered what it felt like to be close to him. She took a deep breath of warm humid air and waited for the butterflies in her stomach to settle.

One week left.

One last assignment and then she'd have to sort out what it meant to work with her boss/student. Last week's karaoke performance hadn't helped her butterflies, either. Every time she looked at him, she heard him belting out "You shoulda been gone" and had to stop herself from laughing.

"What's that smile for?" he asked from beneath the brim of his cap.

Mickey shook her head. "Nothing, nothing."

"Would you like to go grocery shopping with me?" he asked.

"I—um..." She looked at the Piggly Wiggly and thought about the list of things she needed to get done that day. Getting her own groceries was on that list. "Sure." It couldn't hurt—this wasn't a date; it was just food. "So long as it's only shopping."

As if he read her mind, he rolled his eyes. "It's not a date," he murmured, letting her lead the way. "Nothing sexy happens at the Piggly Wiggly."

Mickey gave a nervous laugh as they entered the produce area. "No, of course not."

Okay, now…this is not a big deal.

Mickey licked her lips and averted her eyes from Diego, who tested the firmness of cantaloupe melons, balancing two at a time in his large hands. *Nothing sexy happens in the Piggly Wiggly, my ass.* "What are you planning to make?" she asked in a light voice.

Diego set one of the melons back. "How do you know if these are ripe? I can never remember."

Mickey sighed inwardly as she approached him. "Well…that one is probably okay. It's, um, more tan than this one." She gestured to the discarded melon. "You should give it a sniff, too."

He held it to his nose and inhaled. "What am I smelling?"

Mickey took a step closer and pressed her face to the other side of the melon. Only the cantaloupe separated them as they quietly sniffed. "It's sweet, a little musky," she said. "This smells right."

"That's it?" he asked, gazing down at her.

"You should check the stem, too," she said, taking the melon from him and rolling it over in her hands. "If this bit is a little puckered, you're good to go."

"Oh, yeah?"

"Just run your fingers over it. Feel it."

Mickey realized her mistake when Diego brushed his fingers along the small nubbin where a stem used to be. His movements were achingly familiar, making her nipples stiffen beneath her T-shirt. Once she understood her response to his gentle caress, she shoved the cantaloupe to his chest. "It's a good one," she said, louder than she meant.

His eyebrows went to work again, scrutinizing her every move. Or, at least, that's what it felt like when she quickly retreated to her shopping cart. "To answer your question, I don't know what I plan to make. I just wanted something to fill the fridge. Sometimes I forget to go shopping."

They moved on from the melon fruit and made a stop at the vegetable bins. "Maybe you get a little busy with the bar?" she asked while picking through the onions. When she found the ones she wanted, Mickey reached for the roll of plastic bags.

"I've got it," Diego said, tearing off a bag for her. He puckered his lips and blew softly at the edges, before rubbing them together. Mickey could barely tear her eyes away. As he shook the bag open, he took the onions from her hands and bagged them without explanation. "And there's no maybe about it," he added. "I never figured out how to manage my free time and the bar. But with school, I think I need to work on it. It's time to cook at home more often."

"What kinds of things would you like to make?" Mickey asked, moving on to the garlic. Diego ripped another bag for her, ready for her selection. The butterflies intensified with every little movement he made. There shouldn't have been anything seductive about grocery shopping, yet here she was, heart pounding and knees wobbling.

"No, no, you've had the chance to read about my food habits and history," he tsked. "Tell me about you."

Mickey dropped her garlic into his waiting bag. "What do you want to know?" she asked cautiously.

Diego flashed her an arresting smile that scrambled her brain for a few seconds. "What's your earliest food memory?"

Mickey blinked as she pushed her cart forward. She should have written down a shopping list. With his handsome face distracting her, she'd never get everything she needed. "You're playing teacher today?"

He pushed his cart alongside her and shrugged his shoulders. "I'm curious."

While she searched her memory for something, Diego stopped to toss a bag of chips into his cart. "Are those any good?" she asked.

"Chicharrones? Yeah, Lucía used to eat them with hot sauce."

Mickey paused. "You know what? I never think about getting pork rinds."

Before she could ask, Diego tossed a bag into her cart. "Now you can," he said.

"Well—"

"And get Frank's RedHot."

Mickey grimaced. "Really? I've got a bottle of Yucateco at home that will do just fine."

Diego peered at her with a bemused expression.

"What?" she asked.

He shook his head. "Nothing. That was her favorite sauce, too. I didn't get into it," he said, pushing forward. "Too spicy for me."

Mickey grinned. "She had incredible taste," she said. Teasing him felt like safe territory.

"Food memory?" he reminded her.

"Easter dinner when I was seven."

"Describe it to me."

Mickey leaned on her forearms as they strolled through the store. Piggly Wiggly was awfully quiet in the middle of the day, making it a perfect time to leisurely shop. "That was when my grandmother was still alive. My daddy's mother.

Her name was Pearl, and she made me this beautiful dress for Easter." Mickey chuckled when she pulled a carton of almond milk from the fridge. "It was white and satin with a pink sash across my belly. And, of course, I wore white patent-leather shoes and umbrella socks."

"This is more fashion than food," Diego said.

"I'm getting there." They stopped at the meat counter, where Diego grabbed some ground beef and found a couple packs of chicken breasts. "We had to go to church first, which was boring. But after, I got to do the Easter egg hunt with all the kids."

"Lots of candy?"

"Oh, my god, so much. It was almost as fun as Halloween. My parents always got my brother and me the largest Easter baskets. You know, the kind with toys in them?"

"I'm familiar," he said with a smile.

Mickey was so engrossed in her memory that she was almost able to ignore how handsome he looked. Pushing his cart, wearing his standard T-shirt (burnt orange today) and navy blue shorts. "Anyway, it was my mom's turn to host Easter dinner, so we had all the family come to our house. I had so many cousins to play with until dinner. I just remember running around, rolling in the grass, climbing trees..." She drifted off as she recalled a simpler time in her life. No bills, no illness, just the safety of her parents.

"And dinner?" Diego asked, pulling her from her trance.

"Oh, there was so much. We had honey-baked ham, fried chicken, turnip greens, macaroni and cheese... I know I'm forgetting a lot, but I don't think the food was all that important."

"It was the family," he said.

She nodded silently.

"And you miss it."

Mickey took a deep shuddering breath, caught off guard

by how emotional she was about to become in the bread aisle. "I do," she whispered. "A lot changed when I got older." She busied herself by pretending to be picky about loaves. "When I got sick, my parents didn't have time to worry about Easter dinners. We'd try to make it to my Aunt Janel's house when I was feeling up to it."

Tears swam in her eyes as she finally picked up a loaf of sliced potato bread. Mickey kept her back to him as she tossed it in her cart. But when he grabbed a pack of hamburger buns, he stopped short. "Are you okay?" he asked in a low voice.

Mickey dashed her arm across her eyes and sniffed. "Oh, I'm fine."

His heavy palm rested on her shoulder, near her neck. "Would you like a hug?"

She looked up at him, half alarmed by and half grateful for the offer. After a quick glance around the empty aisle, she bit her lip and shook her head. "We'd better not," she said.

A serious expression crossed Diego's face as his heavy brow furrowed. "I don't like to make women cry at Piggly Wiggly."

Mickey laughed abruptly and her shoulders relaxed under his hand. "Fine, then… A professional hug?"

He rolled his eyes as he drew her against him. "Shut up, Professor, and let me hug you."

When he embraced her, the heart-pounding fear that crept around every corner seemed to disappear. His arms were like a shield, protecting her from anxiety and reminding her she was safe. Mickey breathed against his chest, smelling warm cologne, soap and his sweat. She could have stood there for ages, drying her wet face against his shirt, but she remembered where they were. "Thank you," she said, pulling away.

Diego went back to his cart. "Of course. As many times as you've listened to me, I don't mind it at all."

They lightened the mood as they continued shopping, chattering about foodstuff they liked or found disgusting. Time almost got away from them when they finally arrived at the checkout.

"I've got to get this stuff home and get ready for tonight," Mickey said, glancing at her phone.

Diego took his bag from the cashier and followed Mickey out the front door. "Can I walk you to your car?"

"Sure."

They left the store and walked through the parking lot. When she found her car, Diego helped her with her groceries before slamming the trunk closed. "I'll see you tonight?" he asked, leaning on her car.

"Where else would I be?"

He shrugged, trying to look nonchalant. "Just confirming you know your schedule."

Mickey scoffed as she got in the driver's side. "I know my schedule, Boss. Do you know your due dates?"

Diego leaned over her window, blocking out the sun with his body. "I'm almost done with my paper, Professor. You'll get it in time."

"I'd better. I'll see you tonight, Diego."

He backed away as she turned over the engine. "I'll see you, Mick." He looked as though he wanted to say something else but thought better of it. As she backed away, he watched her for a moment, hands in his pockets, standing beside his own basket. Mickey waved. He smiled.

Whatever they had shared in the Piggly Wiggly pulled at her heart as she left the shopping center. It made her think toward the future.

One more week…

32

Grades were up!

And on a Sunday, no less. Diego's palms itched as he opened his grade portal. He drew in a shuddered breath and waited for the Final Research Assignment to show up. He wrote about Hurricane Maria's impact on the Puerto Rican restaurant industry. While he was interested in writing about the topic, he felt a little shaky about executing it.

His nerves were on edge, not just because of the grade, but also his class was finally over. Sunday evening marked the end of their polite and platonic work relationship. They hadn't had a private moment since grocery shopping together. When he got to hug her tightly and listen to her Easter story.

As she'd pulled out of that parking lot, he wanted to stop her, tell her this whole two-week hiatus was silly. But he knew better. It was for the best that they kept things neutral. He just hadn't realized how full she made his life until he had to put space between them. All he wanted was to wrap her up in his arms and never let her go again.

Diego shook his hands vigorously as he let out a harsh

breath. Once he steadied himself, he clicked on "Final Research Assignment."

B-

Had he read it correctly?

Diego ran his hand over his jaw and blinked at the grade. He'd earned himself a B-minus on a six-page paper. He hadn't written six pages of anything in several years, and now…

He let out a loud victory shout and punched the air. "B-minus! B-minus! B-fuckin'-minus!" He ended his chant with laughter. "Oh, my god…"

He opened his document, where he found her comments, and read over them quickly. She needed him to elaborate on a few claims he made, she said the thesis statement could have been clearer and some of his citations needed fixing. But overall, the ideas were there, and they were solid enough to warrant a B-minus.

Diego shook with excitement, wondering whom he could tell. It was just one class out of god knew how many, but this was the first step. In the fall, he'd get his bar schedule straight and take classes on campus. He felt confident enough to start the semester with two, maybe three courses. His excitement made him leave his desk chair and pace his office. He shook out his hands and rolled his neck.

He wanted to call Mickey so badly.

He needed to hear her breathless voice in his ear.

"Fuck it," he muttered as he grabbed his phone. After their pause, calling her wouldn't be against the rules. He wanted to thank her for an excellent class, anyway. As he listened to his phone ring, he walked downstairs and through his living room.

"Hey," she breathed in a surprised tone.

"Hey—hi, how are you? How's it going?" he asked. He

squeezed his eyes and silently cursed himself for sounding so nervous. "What are you up to?"

"Oh, I'm fine," she said. There were clattering noises in the background. "Shit," she muttered. "I'm just trying to make a chicken curry and it's going poorly."

"Indian or Thai?" he asked, as if it mattered. He didn't know how to cook either.

"Indian," she said. "I was about to get started, but this chicken I bought is off. I'm smelling it right now." She sniffed. "This isn't good."

Diego bit back a smile. "Do you need some help?"

"Maybe," she sighed. "I really had a taste for this curry. I read the recipes and bought all the ingredients today."

He pursed his lips and thought about his next words. "Would you like for me to swing by Publix on the way to your apartment? I can do that."

She scoffed. "What?"

"What do you say, Mickey?" he asked, getting bolder. "Would you like to talk about what comes next while I help you make chicken curry?"

The pause on the line had him holding his breath. Diego knew he was being forward as fuck, but the need to see her overrode any good sense he had before calling.

"Bring a red wine with the two pounds of chicken breasts," she finally replied. "I'll pay you back."

He almost told her not to worry about it. "Sounds good," he said instead. "I'll see you in thirty minutes."

"Alright, then. Bye, Diego."

"Bye, Mickey."

He hung up and let out another victory whoop. Before leaving the house, he changed his shirt, brushed his teeth and ran a comb through his hair.

"Chicken breast and red wine," he chanted. "Chicken breast and red wine."

Good lord, he was excited to see Mickey.

Mickey hated chopping garnish at the bar, so it made sense chopping mise en place for a curry was a nightmare. But she made a habit of cooking something new at the end of each class she taught. It gave her an opportunity to wash her hands of the course and move on to something else. The trouble with Punjabi chicken curry was that it still needed a ton of chopped ginger.

And now Diego was coming to her house.

Instead of questioning if it was a good idea, she jumped at the opportunity to see him outside of work. At the bar, he was cordial; he didn't hound her about her drinks. He just let her be. And it was nice not to be watched closely for fuck-ups or treated with kid gloves. She just worked like a normal person, and guess what? Mickey was damned good at her job.

An authoritative knock came from her door, causing her to jump. She laid her knife down and rushed through her kitchen. When Mickey threw open her door, Diego held up a bottle of wine and a bag of groceries. He wore a dark gray T-shirt, jeans and a smile.

"There was a sale on chicken breasts, so you might wanna put one of these in the freezer."

Mickey let him through. "Thank you," she said, smoothing down her rumpled T-shirt and fluffing up her sweaty curls. She didn't think to change into something cuter while she was busy chopping garlic and ginger.

"You've got a whole situation going on in here," he murmured from the kitchen. "Where's your corkscrew?"

She closed the door behind him. "I'll get it." In her small

galley kitchen, he looked almost too big to navigate it. "Can I put you to work?" she asked.

"You can do whatever you want to me," he said, leaning against her counter.

She handed him the corkscrew. "So, our pause is definitely up, huh?"

A devilish grin slid over his face as he looked her up and down. Her skin heated under his close observation, but she stood her ground and continued to meet his gaze.

"We have things to talk about, Mickey."

He had to know how she felt when he caressed her name with his lips. It was small, and possibly insignificant to someone else, but it made her heart beat faster. "Let's talk while we chop," she said, handing him her knife. She went into the dishwasher to retrieve her own, and when she looked up, his expression made her laugh. "What?"

Diego frowned at the knife in his hands. "I don't do enough garnish at work?"

"I've been doing it for the last week," she chuckled. "I need at least ten cloves of garlic. I'll help you."

He heaved a sigh. "Can I at least pour us some wine?"

"I would love some. Glasses are right above you." While she peeled the cloves and disposed of the waste, he poured wine and set one glass beside her. "Thank you."

"Of course, honey," he said before taking a large gulp.

"Honey?" She passed him a handful of garlic cloves.

"I'm trying to sweet-talk you," he said in a low voice. "Being in the kitchen, helping a woman cook, warrants a honey or two, yeah?"

Mickey tried to ignore the deep rumbling coming from his chest and focused on her knife work. She would not cut her finger because of his voice. "Just chop."

He grunted and began working. “What kind of Indian curry is this?”

“Punjabi chicken.”

“Sounds spicy,” he said.

“I’ve got red chilies for you to work on next,” she said, pointing her knife at a pile of ingredients.

“So, how do we start this talk, Mickey?”

She pressed her lips together and sliced the garlic with a careful hand. “I hadn’t thought about it,” she replied honestly. She thought more about his body, having him back in her home, but not what they would *discuss*. She was just trying to keep her hands to herself.

“I could help us along,” he offered, his voice dipping another octave.

She sliced another clove. “Fine.”

“Have I behaved myself for the past few weeks?”

Mickey nodded. “You have.”

“And you’ve forgiven me?”

“I have.”

Diego made quick work of slicing his garlic and began chopping. Mickey was still on the slicing stage. “Do you miss my touch yet?”

She paused, sucking in a deep breath. She willed her hand not to shake as she worked.

He leaned over and whispered, “Do you feel the same ache I feel?”

Mickey refused to answer his question. “You can dump your garlic in that bowl,” she said.

“I lie awake at night and wonder if you think about me, Mickey. I wonder if you miss my hands on your body,” he continued, laying down his knife. “Do you need me to touch you?”

Goddammit, she’d never finish the curry at this rate.

She set her knife on the counter and looked up at him. "What are you doing?"

"I'm trying to talk to you," he said, moving around her, backing her against the kitchen sink. She let him, wanting to see where this led. "Now…do you miss my hands on your body, Mickey?"

She nodded.

He used his arms to cage her against the counter and leaned over her. Good god, Mickey missed the heat of his body pressed against her. She leaned back to look him in the eye. He bit his lip and gazed at her with darkened eyes. "I miss your taste. I dream of running my tongue over your clit until your thighs shake around my ears." He licked the lip he bit and continued, "You taste so good, I could drink you nightly. I wanna get drunk off you, Mickey."

Heat climbed up her neck and burned her face as she listened to his words. Her own words were stuck in her throat.

"I wanna taste you again," he whispered. "I want you to ride my face until you collapse. And then I want to fill your tight wet pussy until I spill myself in you. What do you think about that, Mickey?"

"Yes," she said in a shaky voice.

"To which part?" he asked. "Me licking you clean or me fucking you one long stroke at a time?"

"Yes," Mickey repeated. Her mind went to mush at the mention of licking.

Diego pressed his lower body against her. His jeans rubbed against her bare thighs; the hot friction made her breath shallow and set her skin on fire with desire. "So does this conclude our talk, Mickey?"

She slowly nodded her head.

"Do you want me to take you to your bedroom, Mickey?"

She swallowed as she held herself up against the counter. "No."

Diego raised a brow. "No?"

"I wanna take *you* to my bedroom," Mickey said, taking him by the collar and pulling him in for a kiss.

His mouth came crashing down on her. He let out a surprised grunt as she nipped at his bottom lip. It felt full in her mouth, so goddamn suckable. Diego immediately wrapped his arms around her waist and ground his hips against her soft belly. "Fuck, Mickey..." he moaned into her mouth.

"Yes, but in the bedroom," she whispered.

She walked him—no—dragged him through the kitchen, down the hallway, until they bumped into a side table and knocked several knickknacks on the floor. "Let me get that," Diego rasped, releasing her lips.

"Leave it." Mickey pulled him in for another kiss, boldly drinking her fill until she gasped for breath. Once inside her bedroom, she glanced at her unmade bed and cringed. No matter, they would mess it up momentarily.

Diego took her hands and pulled her to the foot of her bed as he sat. She stood before him, watching him expectantly. With a swift yank, he pulled her shorts down to her ankles, leaving her bottomless. As Diego peered under her baggy shirt, his wicked grin grew wider. "Mickey Chambers, did you answer the door without panties?"

Gruff Diego knew how to push her erotic buttons, but Mickey quickly found herself liking Naughty Diego with his playful smile. "My apartment, my rules," she said with a shrug. "Sometimes I don't wear panties."

His large hands covered the backs of her thighs, dragging her onto his lap. As she settled onto his sturdy legs, her thighs spread scandalously, threatening to leave a damp spot on his jeans. “A girl can get into a lot of trouble answering the door to a man—” he squeezed her ass cheeks “—this indecent.”

She chuckled as she sat atop him. From this angle, she took time to admire his handsome smile, his salt-and-pepper hair swept away from his forehead. His long black lashes lowered as he stared back. His nostrils flared every time she shifted her hips, so she did it again. “I like a little trouble,” she murmured.

When his tongue swiped across his bottom lip, she mimicked him involuntarily. “Well, if you insist on being indecent, go ahead and take *everything* off.”

She complied easily. As soon as she shucked her shirt and bra to the floor, Mickey bared her breasts to him and asked, “How’s that?”

His eyes flitted to her tits and his smile went ear to ear. “Perfection,” he said, letting his hands rub up and down her back. “I missed you very much,” he admitted, meeting her gaze again.

His sentimentality caught her off guard. A vulnerable Diego was rare, but when she got glimpses of him, she wanted to hold on tighter. “I missed you, too,” she confessed.

“I jerked off thinking about you,” he said with a dark chuckle, blush spotting his tanned cheeks. “But I also missed holding you and talking to you.”

Hearing his words made her heart thump like a little hummingbird on a sugar high. Instead of being cautious, she pressed him further. “I care about you a lot, Diego,” she said.

He answered her by leaning forward and gently kissing her lips, then her cheek and finally the spot between her jaw and earlobe. “I care about you, too,” he whispered in her ear. “And I hope you’ll allow me to care for you from now on.”

When he pulled back, he nervously licked his lips, reached behind his neck and pulled his shirt over his head. He tossed it somewhere behind her. While holding a muscular arm around her waist, he drew her closer and fanned his fingers across her breasts.

"Not in a possessive way," he added. "Just normal, like a boyfriend."

She nodded vigorously. "I'd like that," she said, trying to sound calmer than she felt. "Starting now."

He squeezed her breast until his fingers slid to the tip and tweaked her nipple. Mickey couldn't help the moan that pushed past her lips as her eyes fell shut. "I'm trying to talk to you," he teased. "And you just want my dick, don't you?"

She was too engrossed in the way he rolled and pinched her sensitive nipple to give him a witty answer. "Yes," Mickey whimpered.

Diego leaned back until he lay on the bed. "In good time, honey. But first, you need to do something for me," he said, beckoning her with his forefinger.

She thought back to what he'd mentioned in her kitchen and immediately blushed. "Were you serious?"

"You know I don't have a sense of humor," he said in a dry voice, but amusement lit his eyes. "Get up here and let me eat you like you need me to."

She couldn't deny she needed his mouth against her. She'd been panting for it for the last two weeks. As she inched her way up his torso, Mickey asked, "You're sure I'm not, you know…too heavy?"

Diego frowned as she made her way to his chest. "You think this is my first day or something? I'm not gonna tell you twice, Mickey."

She playfully slapped his chest. "I see the asshole is back," she chuckled as she hovered over his face. But as soon as his tongue flicked against her wet sensitive folds, her laughter died in her throat. "Oh!" she squeaked.

Diego's tongue dragged a slow languorous course from

her opening to her clit and back until Mickey's thighs trembled from the intense pleasure. He'd only just started… As he noisily licked her, slowly and then rapidly, she heard a zipping sound from behind her. Over her shoulder, she watched as Diego pulled his hardened dick from his jeans and stroked himself.

Mickey quickly faced her headboard. If she saw any more, she'd come too quickly, and she wanted to put his mouth to work. Not just his mouth, the scruff on his chin and his nose worked together to rub her in all the right places. She rocked her hips against his face, chasing the feeling that unfurled deep within her belly and made her breath come in short pants.

"Oh, god, Diego," she gasped as his tongue slid between her lips and hit her clit. Her arms buckled as another jolt hit her womb. He replied by sucking her clit between his lips and humming against her pussy. The sudden vibration sent a wave of heat through her body and more dampness between her thighs. Soon, she wouldn't be able to tell what were her juices and what was Diego. The thought was near enough to make her climb out of her own skin with desire. "Oh, oh, right there," she breathed.

He'd released his own dick to take hold of her thighs, which were on either side of his ears. As he held her hips down in an iron-tight grasp, Diego groaned rhythmically against her pussy, keeping time with her rocking hips.

His moans, his tight hold on her thighs, his entire face pleasuring her…it was all too overwhelming on Mickey's senses. She came with a full body-clenching orgasm that lifted her feet from the bed and bowed her back. She moaned as she jerked from the shuddering wave that hit her.

Not that Diego was intent on quitting soon. He continued licking as though her thighs were cutting off his air supply. Mickey was boneless, but each swipe of his tongue against her too-sensitive flesh made her twitch. Regretfully, she had to leave his face. Mickey moaned as she crawled forward and collapsed at the head of the bed.

"Christ," she breathed.

Diego chuckled as he shrugged out of his jeans, his belt buckle clattering as he went. "You said you liked trouble."

She peeked at him through her fingers, unable to bite back her grin. "You promised me something else, didn't you?"

Completely naked, and fully aroused, Diego climbed up the bed for her. "I did. Now why don't you spread those beautiful thighs and let me give it to you."

Mickey giggled in anticipation but did what he said. She wasn't about to be told twice.

33

Full bar on a Monday night.

One bouncer.

Two servers.

Two bartenders.

Two barbacks.

Diego felt blessed to work with a full crew and the woman he loved behind the bar. Of course, he hadn't told Mickey he loved her. He'd come mighty close last night after they'd made love.

It was when they reluctantly returned to the kitchen for more curry-making. She put him on chili-slicing detail and demanded he cut the pieces diagonally. Mickey wore this no-nonsense face as she tried to boss him around, but needed to purse her lips to keep from smiling. He stared deep into her large brown eyes and almost said the words *I love you, Mickey.* But he kissed her instead.

He didn't want to scare her off in her own home. She'd only agreed to be his "girlfriend" last night, which felt strange to hear at his age. He liked what it meant, but wanted to call her something more serious, like his partner, or his equal. The sun to his moon sounded better than the paltry title of "girlfriend."

"Diego?" Mickey asked, breathing through his rumination.

His eyes focused on her face. "What's up?"

Mickey's face broke out in a wide grin, creasing her dimples. He wanted to kiss them both, but knew he had to pay attention to the bar. "I have something for you." She sneaked a glance around the bar, looking for customers who needed service. "It's a gift..."

Diego furrowed his brow, trying to remember what he could have done to deserve one. If it was the dicking down she got last night, he wanted her to know the pleasure was all his. His eyes went to her hands, which were stuffed inside her apron pocket. "What is it?"

She quickly pulled out a slender rectangle covered in gold wrapping paper and handed it to him. "You should open it."

It felt like a book. Diego slid his fingers over the smooth paper, feeling for a seam to rip. He carefully peeled back the gold, revealing the words *Lucía's Liquors*, and his heart tightened. He glanced up to see Mickey staring at him with soft eyes. "What..."

"I just wanted to keep a piece of her alive for you, for the bar," she murmured. "I hope that's okay."

Okay? Diego didn't know what to say as he freed the small paperback from its wrapper. He marveled over the cover, the red lettering, the bright photography featuring a Bloody Maria, and let out a halted breath. The book was called *Lucía's Liquors: The Saloon Selection*. The author was Lucía Acosta. His wife.

"Does it look okay?" Mickey asked, standing beside him as he flipped through the pages. "When you let me practice with her recipes, I started making the drinks at home. I took pictures and put them together. I just got it back from the print shop today."

He barely heard her as he glanced through the book. It was fun, whimsical and stylish, just like Lucía. It was perfect. Diego finally looked up, his vision blurred with tears. "It's beautiful."

Mickey beamed. "I'm so glad you like it! I only had one printed, so if you want more, just let me know."

He nodded absently. "This is…" He tried to speak, but emotion forced him to turn from the bar and wipe his eyes instead. Her hand rested on his back, rubbing a small circle of warmth he could feel through his shirt.

"You don't have to start making the drinks here," she said in a soft voice. "But I didn't want them to disappear from your life, either."

He stared at the book, nodding still. When the shock eventually wore off, Diego straightened up and thought about the small surprise he had picked up for Mickey and her new colleagues. It paled in comparison to this.

This book, no more than thirty-something pages, was a tribute to a woman he'd never forget. But it was also a prized gift from a woman who refused to let him forget. Mickey didn't feel threatened or uncomfortable about this loss; she embraced it because it was a part of him.

"Thank you," he finally said. "I can't even begin to tell you…"

"You're welcome," she said, offering him a sweet smile. "I don't want to be a dick right now, but I feel like I should tell you—there's no crying in bartending."

He let out a surprised laugh and quickly wiped his face. "You're right," he said. "I know."

"It's almost one, can I ring the bell and make the last call?" she asked, gesturing to the clock.

"By all means," he said, ready to end the shift so he could

take her home and throw her down into his bed. His hands trembled at the thought of undressing her and just…holding her close to his body as they both drifted off to sleep.

She climbed onto the step stool and rang the bell. "Last call," she shouted as she turned the jukebox off. She got the usual grumbles but also the noise of chairs scraping the floor filled the air, anyway. Irene and Gina rushed around with their receipts, ready to close out tabs. Diego turned the lights up and took care of those who were closest to the bar.

They now used Mickey's method of keeping open tabs behind the bar, which turned out to be neater and more efficient. According to her little system, he quickly discovered they only had five tabs between the two of them. Diego had yet to admit her changes to the bar gave it new life. He should really thank her for more things.

Karaoke night was a success, and he'd already gotten another request for a bachelorette party. Maybe the wedding season would bring all the single ladies to The Saloon. If he was lucky, his bar would start looking unattractive to the younger clientele.

After a good thirty minutes, the bar had cleared out and Jerry stacked chairs. While the servers counted their money and Ramón mopped the floor, Diego quietly sneaked off to his office, where he placed Lucía's book of cocktail recipes on his desk. In the silence of his messy office, he bowed his head and closed his eyes.

"I don't know if you had any hand in bringing her into my life, Lucía," he whispered. "If you did, then I thank you for looking after me. I think I may have found love again."

He listened to the busy chatter of his employees in the front and opened his eyes. They quietly celebrated the end of their shift in their own way. Irene was giving Ollie guff, while Jerry cracked jokes with Ramón. Gina, sitting at the bar, soaked up the scene with a quiet smile and her usual bottle of Corona.

And Mickey…

She'd most likely be humming some tune while counting her drawer. Probably pouring someone their end-of-shift drink. Maybe she was pouring herself a gin and soda… Whatever Mickey was up to, she did it as a solid member of The Saloon family. Just the way Diego wanted it.

He pressed his palm to the book one last time before rushing to the kitchen to retrieve something he'd purchased for the new employees. He had hoped they would appreciate the gesture. Especially his girlfriend.

Just as Mickey finished counting her drawer, the jukebox came on and blared the Backstreet Boys' "I Want It That Way." She slammed the cash register shut and turned toward the kitchen.

Diego stood next to the jukebox holding a large tray of cupcakes. The rest of the crew stopped what they were doing to give him their attention. "What's going on?" Jerry called out.

"I want to congratulate our newest employees," he said, hoisting his cupcakes in the air. "They've lasted longer than the usual three weeks and I think that calls for a celebration."

Mickey glanced at Gina and Ollie, who grinned with a mixture of surprise and amusement. "Are you kidding?" she laughed. "That's a thing?"

"It's a thing now," Diego said, placing the cupcakes on the bar. "This is a celebration for Irene, too. She's trained enough servers to own this place, and I appreciate her work, too."

Irene laughed outright. "Thank you! I have definitely paid my dues. Thanks for the raise, by the way."

Mickey's body flooded with warmth as she looked between Diego and his cupcake gift. She certainly hadn't expected him to get as emotional as he had when she gave him the book gift. But she was relieved. She had wanted to say something last night, but figured a surprise would make more of an impact. She almost cried while witnessing his shock, but managed to hold it together with a joke.

She stared at Diego passing around cupcakes to his employees and grinned. He looked so handsome, dressed in his T-shirt and jeans, his dark hair flopping over his broad forehead. She wanted to kiss him so badly…but remembered how they hadn't announced anything to the others.

Fuck that noise.

Mickey marched over to where he stood, took him by the face and planted a kiss right on his lips. Silence fell over the bar as Diego's body tensed against hers. It took a little coaxing, but his arms eventually wrapped around her waist and he pulled her close. Before their kiss deepened to something more sultry, she pulled her face away and stared into his eyes.

Diego raised a brow as he smiled down at her. "What was that for?" he asked with halted breath.

"For being you."

Someone cleared their throat, pulling her attention to the rest of the bar. "Damn, girl, it's just cupcakes," Ollie joked.

Mickey blushed, and was about to pull herself out of Diego's grasp, but he held on tighter. "Uh, we're dating," she said through nervous laughter.

Irene rolled her eyes. "I called it," she said, raising her hand.

"Finally." Ramón laughed. "Finally they say something." He walked up to them and pulled his brother-in-law's face for a kiss on his cheek. "You two…" He clapped Diego's back roughly.

"And I love him," Mickey blurted out. Her face burned as she said the words, they needed to leave her mouth and enter the air. She just hadn't expected to say them in front of the entire Saloon family.

Everyone's reaction was a mixture of shock and "duh." Jerry's eyes widened, Ollie's jaw dropped, Irene and Gina squealed, and Ramón shook his head in amusement.

Diego's reaction was the last thing she saw. When her gaze went back to his face, her heart thundered in her chest. What would he say? What would he do? His hold around her waist never loosened, but she was still frightened by what might happen.

His eyes flitted from her eyes to her mouth before speaking. It felt like the longest five seconds of her life. "And I love her, too," he said in a gravelly voice as he stroked her back with his thumb.

Mickey's knees buckled under his declaration. "Yeah?"

"Of course," he said fiercely.

To her surprise, Ramón wrapped them both in a bear hug. "Finally," he whispered in Diego's ear.

Mickey didn't know what he meant, but she was thankful for his approval. The brother of Lucía Acosta gave his blessing.

When he released them, he gave a deep belly laugh. "I'm glad you're done sneaking around."

Diego nodded. "Me, too."

Mickey couldn't stop grinning. The immense joy she felt could only be increased with a cupcake. She grabbed one and kissed Diego on the cheek. "Me, too, Boss."

Epilogue

A year later…

After her Literature 200 course, Mickey all but ran down the hall, straight to her shared office space. A Tupperware container of pasteles awaited her and she wanted to enjoy her meal before getting to her next job. In the spring, she had given her résumé to Nelly's Nuptials, Columbus's premiere wedding planning company, and was hired by Nelly herself. Since then, Mickey had coordinated one July wedding and was in the middle of planning an October wedding.

It felt so good to tell her English chair that she only wanted one class. Teaching her excited students still brought her joy, but wedding planning really brought out Mickey's passion for parties. And she had just the sunny personality for it. She figured if she could handle a bar fight at The Saloon, a bridal meltdown was a cakewalk.

As she unlocked the door and let herself in, she breathed a sigh of relief. She had the space to herself with the other adjuncts, Matt and Jared, off for the day. With no office hours planned, Mickey would use her forty-five minutes to kick her feet up, nibble on Diego's delicious lunch and watch YouTube videos. But as soon as she settled behind her desk, she heard a soft knock at the door.

"I'm busy," she called out, not caring if it was a student or her department chair.

"Too busy for your boyfriend?"

Mickey's gaze flew to the door. Diego leaned against the doorjamb with a smile tugging at his lips and a wicked gleam in his dark eyes. Today's T-shirt was black and just as tight as his others, and his dark jeans hugged his thighs and ass just how she liked. Mickey didn't think she'd ever tire of staring at his body.

Even after a year of making love to him, he stole her breath every time he entered a room. "Hey there."

"You have the office to yourself?" he asked, closing the door behind him.

When she heard the small click of him locking it, she licked her lips. "I'm by myself on Tuesdays and Thursdays," she breathed.

Diego walked—no, prowled—to her desk, pulling his satchel from his shoulder, lowering it to the floor. "I'm gonna make a note of that," he said. "I'll be back on Thursday, too."

Mickey scoffed as she leaned back in her chair. "Please tell me that you have your own class schedule to follow, Mr. Acosta."

His smile widened as he sat on the corner of her desk. It tickled him to no end when she regarded him as a student. Even at forty-three, with one year of school under his belt, Diego still needed to know he belonged on Hargrove's campus. "I do," he admitted. "I've got Ceramics 101 in an hour. My last class for the day."

She tried not to squeal when she heard him say ceramics. After his first on-campus semester, Diego changed his major from Business Management to History, but he still managed to sneak a couple art classes in. "I don't know how I feel about you in a class full of young women working with a potter's wheel," she said, scrunching her nose. "They might get Patrick Swayze thoughts."

He chuckled as he pulled her chin up for a quick peck on the lips. "First of all," he murmured as he brushed his lips against hers, "you're the only young lady I have eyes for... Second, I doubt any of the kids in that class have even seen *Ghost*."

Mickey sat up straight to kiss his mouth firmly, giving his bottom lip a tiny nip for extra measure. His tongue swept over and tangled with hers, almost making her forget they were in her office, on campus.

Diego seemed to remember as he pulled away and ran his fingers along her jaw. "Although, I do like this little bit of jealousy," he said, smirking in amusement. "It's very cute on you."

Mickey untangled herself from his hands to dig through her bag for her lunch. "By the way, my dad wants to know if you're available this Sunday for digging something up in the backyard."

"Can I have the specifics?" he asked, moving to a free chair beside her.

She shook her head as she sprinkled hot sauce on her pastel. "I think it's plant-based digging," she said, licking her fingers. "When Dad starts talking about around-the-house projects, I kinda zone out."

"We're going to be there for dinner," Diego said. "Might as well show up early so I can help. It's probably those pecan trees he talked about last week. Your mother didn't want him lifting them by himself."

Her eyes darted to him while he mused aloud. Diego hadn't noticed how close he'd gotten to her family, but Mickey had. He'd been nervous about meeting her parents for the first Sunday dinner, but after about three visits, he quickly made himself a part of the Chambers Clan. And now he was conspiring with her mother to keep her father from overexerting himself. "Mmm-hmm, that's probably it," she said, biting back her grin.

Diego hadn't interrupted her lunch to talk to her about ceramics or her father's tinkering. But the thought of revealing his true intent was quickly making him lose his nerve.

No, no. It was time, and he was more than ready to take this next step. They were already living together, after he asked Mickey to not renew her lease on that tiny apartment on McLean Avenue. She denied him a few times, but finally relented when he convinced her he was ready to share his large empty house with another woman.

The ring in his pocket felt heavy.

Diego had wanted to give it to her as soon as her bright smile filled the doorway, but he still hadn't found the right words to say. She was now a wedding planner who'd probably heard a million cute stories about romantic proposals. He had stiff competition, but they were far too busy for hot-air balloons. Since taking up a new career, Mickey had dropped her teaching load and only worked at the bar a couple nights a week. Diego had committed to attending school part-time, but was working his way to a full course load.

"So, how's your literature class going?" he asked, tucking his hand under his thigh to steady its nervous tremble.

Mickey forked at her lunch as she opened a notebook on her desk. "Oh, it's just a regular survey course and I'm working straight from the textbook..."

Diego half listened to his girlfriend rattle off details about her class, but he mostly focused on how lovely this moment was. How gorgeous she was. The way she relaxed beside him, one leg tucked under the other, her light pink skirt spread over her thighs. The string of pearls hanging from her neck, resting just above her pale yellow cardigan.

As he rested his chin on his fist and stared at the shining curls tucked behind the delicate shell of her ear, he thought about how close they'd gotten over the last year. Mickey brought so much to his bar—his life—he didn't know how he'd be able to repay her.

She brought ideas like Trivia Night and Karaoke Night to The Saloon, which as her friend Cleo predicted led to a sharp drop in young college patrons. His girlfriend was also clever enough to bring her teaching skills to work. Once a month, she hosted a short class for suburban mothers who wanted to learn how to make Gaucho Juice and Bloody Marias. Simply put, everything Mickey touched was a success. Diego loosened the reins and stepped out of her way.

More importantly, she brought love to his life outside of the bar. After getting close to her family, he decided to stop avoiding his own family in Chicago. He pushed aside his guilt and pride, and rebuilt connections he'd been too ashamed to face after his mother's death. And then there was his education… While he slaved over his homework and sat through exams, she had been there to encourage him every step of the way.

Mickey brought warmth to his home.

It excited him to know that she'd be in his bed after a long night at the bar. That he could crawl in beside her warm, soft body and nuzzle her neck. Kiss her back to sleep, and wake up next to her.

"I doubt they'll be excited about Raymond Carver but I'll try to make it as fun as I can," Mickey finished with a chuckle. "Ugh…that's probably asking too much from *Cathedral*, right?"

Diego frowned. "Huh?"

She rolled her eyes. "Themes, short stories? Are you listening?"

He sat up straighter and felt around his back pocket. "I'm not," he admitted. "I was thinking about something else. Now before you get annoyed about that, I have something to ask you."

Mickey wiped her mouth and hands on a napkin before pushing away her pastel. "What's wrong?"

"Nothing," he said quickly. And for the first time in many years, it felt like the truth. "Everything feels right every time I look into your eyes, Mickey." Her expression softened as she smiled. When she opened her mouth to speak, he cut her off. "I'm sorry, but I have to get this out before you say anything."

He pushed his chair in front of her and clutched both of her hands. Mickey's expression volleyed between confused and amused, but her eyes never left him as he leaned close to her. "I love you…so much. And I hope you love me." She nodded. "Okay, then," he said, sliding from the chair onto one knee.

Her eyes widened and her fingers tightened around him. "What are you doing?" she asked in a hushed voice.

Diego reached into his back pocket for the small velvet box he'd been hiding for three months. With the help of Jeanie and Irene, he'd purchased Mickey's engagement ring soon after the anniversary of her first day at The Saloon. Since then, he'd thought of a million different ways of asking her, but none of them felt right. When he held the small box at her knees, he took a deep breath.

"Mickey, will you let me love you for the rest of my life? Will you continue being the sun to my moon?" he asked, opening the box. "Will you marry me?"

Tears sprang to Mickey's eyes as she glanced from his face to the ring. Her knees trembled beneath his hands as she drew a shuddered breath. "Diego…"

He certainly hoped her tears were happy ones. He'd even

settle for shocked tears if it meant she said yes. But the longer her answer hung in the air, the more nervous he got. "I'll keep cutting the garnish," he added as a strained joke.

Mickey released a watery sob as she took him by the face and pulled him closer. He followed her to his feet, standing over her with the ring between them. "Of course," she whispered, hugging him tightly. "Of course I'll marry you."

With her crushed against his chest, wetting his shirt with her tears, Diego almost doubled over with dizzying relief. She said yes. He was barely aware of the ring in his hands as she wrapped her arms around his neck and kissed him deeply. The force of her passionate kiss almost knocked him against her desk, but he regained his footing and returned her love with the same fervor.

"You'll let me put it on?" he asked when she finally released his mouth.

She panted through her laughter, looking down at the forgotten ring. "Yes," she breathed. "Oh, my god, yes please."

He fumbled with the box, reopening it, pulling the ring from its snug little nest. It was a perfect fit on her finger. Diego had stolen a ring from her jewelry box when he went shopping with the women. But watching it slide up and lock on her finger still excited him. "Perfect," he murmured. "Do you like it?"

"I love it, and I love you." She extended her hand, preening at the sparkles. "I don't know how you can expect me to finish eating, then take this to work. I'm gonna have to start planning my own wedding!"

He pulled back to stare at his beautiful fiancée. "Just call it a back-to-school gift," he said with a grin.

Mickey laughed at him, flashing both adorable dimples, effectively turning his heart into a puddle of goo. "If I don't get this out of my system, my clients are going to think I'm a lunatic."

"Nonsense. You're still capable of talking to them about centerpieces or whatever."

"Today is seating arrangements," Mickey said as she playfully slapped at his chest.

"That, too." Diego wrapped his arms around her and pulled her close. "I love you, Professor."

This time, Mickey didn't correct him. She just smiled as she sank against him. "I love you, too, Boss."

★★★★★

Acknowledgments

I have to start by thanking my incredible husband, Noah. You've helped me understand how the university system works and, more importantly, how not to lose myself in it. Because of your unwavering support, inside and outside of the classroom, I'm able to write what's most meaningful to me. Thank you, my love.

To my family: Ronnie, Carolyn, Kristi, Janel and Mary Beth. Thank you for continually supporting my writing. Whenever I sit down to work, you're with me, cheering me on with your enthusiasm and encouragement. I love you all.

To my mother, Mary Lee Reid: thank you for giving me my name. I want to take the time to write your name and keep it alive for posterity. Every person deserves to be known. You were known.

I want to thank my writing friends, who have kept me going from afar. Every time I log on for a Zoom call to laugh, cry and write with you, I feel your warmth. You keep me included in the writing community with your love, friendship and tweets. Sandra, Phil, Stefanie, Alicia, Cassandra, Denise, Taj: you're all beautiful people.

To the beta readers of this novel: thank you Ariana, Regina, Sandra and Stefanie for helping me get this story into shape. I appreciate your time and expertise.

To my editor, Errin Toma: thank you for believing in this book. When people in publishing say things like "It only takes one opportunity," I believe it. You were mine. Your excitement for Mickey and Diego meant a lot to me. I can't wait to see what else we can do.

To my agent, Saritza Hernandez: when I took "the call" with you in 2018, I knew instantly that you were the person who could best represent me and my career. In this rapidly changing industry, you have helped clients like me exist and be seen.

Lastly, I need to thank the bars that have helped me write this book.

Scruffy Murphy's: thank you for being the first and last pub I'd work at. The hard floors, spilled drinks and rowdy customers wore me down but gave me character (and helped me create characters). It was rough work, but I couldn't imagine doing it without my motley crew. Also, thank you for training me when I was the Newest Girl, Stormy.

Neligan's Bar in Dingle, Ireland: thanks, lads, for sharing a pint with me while I edited and titled this novel.